CW00521930

Introduction.

Lucas A Payne was a well-educated Engl   who had
served six years in the British army fighting the war in Bosnia.
After leaving the army he became a prison counsellor and
married his wife Haylee who was a schoolteacher. Lucas was
tired of seeing all of Britain's problems ending up in front of him
on a daily basis. The prison service couldn't keep all staff and
inmates safe which had been made worse by far too many long
serving prison officers leaving the service for good.

Lucas had been happily married and reaching the top of his
profession for over 20 years when two life changing events
happened. This made him think hard on what he would do for
the rest of his life.

One of Lucas strengths was his ability to organise and with a
private database of some of the country's top criminals he was
going to make the powers that be sit up and take notice. Lucas
had always been neutral when it came to national political
parties, and he always voted for the person he felt would do the
job to their best ability and not follow a single party. Over the
years he had seen good and bad laws passed by both the Labour
and the Conservative parties and even when a party had the
majority of MPs in parliament, they still didn't make the serious
changes to the way the country was being run. The rich
continued to get richer and the poor poorer and important
matters such as the NHS, education and protection of the public
never gets any better. During the book Lucas picks out several
of the continuing problems that face Britain today and hopefully
offer a way to resolve many of the problems, so that we can all
put the "Great" back in Britain once again.

***

Chapter 1. About Lucas Payne

I'm glad you are joining me on the journey I've arranged for a few friends and people I've met during the past twenty years. Let me start by telling you a little about myself, but if you bear with me, I'll keep details of the heist I've arranged until later in the book, but it's well worth waiting for.

My name is Lucas A Payne, and I've been described as a typical English gentleman by most people I have come to know. I'm 53 years young and have been told by many ladies that I'm quite good-looking and having had free access to a gym for most of my adult life, I have kept myself in good shape.

I grew up in a town called Stony Stratford which is now part of the new city of Milton Keynes. The only thing I can remember about Stony Stratford is the phrase 'a load of cock and bull', which is often said if someone is stretching the truth or telling a white lie (the word 'politician' springs to mind). The history behind the saying relates to the two public houses (pubs), which were staging posts for the stagecoaches that stopped for a short or overnight stay as this was on the old A5 trunk road (Watling Street) that ran from Canterbury via London, St. Albans and on to Holyhead in north Wales. The route was serviced by various stagecoach companies, with some stopping at the Cock Hotel and others at the Bull Hotel, which is about 200 yards further down the Watling Street. This was long before emails, telephones, radio, and TV, so the news was spread nationwide via these main routes. If a stagecoach stopped at the Cock Hotel with a message that the Queen was unwell with a nasty bout of flu, staff would pass the message on to their friends who worked at the Bull Hotel, but the message would now be that the Queen was dead. Hence the saying, 'what a load of cock and bull'.

I wouldn't say I liked school that much. I was always left out of things, ending up playing the cymbal in the so-called school orchestra, and being the last kid to be picked for a team. I think this was down to being the older brother of a "mentally retarded spastic." That's the title cruel kids gave him, and their parents weren't much better. Nobody understood what autism was about, and to have an autistic/spastic brother never did me any favours. It didn't worry me as I knew my multi-handicapped brother was more substantial and braver than my classmates. If the King had given bravery medals to ordinary people, my brother would be first in line as he fought harder than any man, I knew just to stay alive. As I moved up to senior school, I managed to be free of my brother, and made a few friends, and we had some great times together. The one big thing that bugged me was that my friends had better clothes and went on family holidays and loved to brag about places they had visited and the fun they'd had. I never had any of these luxuries, as going away with an autistic child wasn't possible. Being severely autistic meant they couldn't tolerate changes and would self-harm and be very vocal letting everyone know of his displeasure.

In 1982 I left school after obtaining 6 GCSE grades, A* to C, including English and Maths, and 2 A-levels. I was never particularly good at written coursework, and I'm sure I learnt a lot more since leaving school than I did in the 11 years I spent there. My childhood was anything but typical as most of it was spent being an unpaid carer for my multi-handicapped brother and my extremely sick mother. My father couldn't cope with my brother being disabled and left when I was six, so I have little respect for him, and few happy childhood memories. Although I loved my disabled sibling with all my heart, I knew the only way I would obtain freedom and a life of my own was to go for a place at university and ensure it wasn't anywhere close to home.

In the end, I took a place at Nottingham University studying Nursing (Mental Health), and at the end of the three-year course, I ended up with a BSc Hons (Bachelor of Science). I loved the city of Nottingham, which is based in the middle of England and famous for the legend of Robin Hood, a heroic outlaw in English folklore who, according to legend, was a highly skilled archer and swordsman. Traditionally dressed in Lincoln green, he is often portrayed as "robbing from the rich and giving to the poor" along with his band of Merry Men. Robin Hood became a popular folk figure in the late-medieval period and continues to be widely represented in literature, films, and in television. With 1% of the United Kingdom owning more property and money than the remaining 99%, you could say that we could do with the return of Robin Hood, but this time he would be for real. I did a lot of online research before making the University of Nottingham my first choice. I also visited the city several times and asked several students what they thought about the university and the city itself. They said the Students' Union offered various societies, organisations, student groups, community projects and campaigns to join. There were scores of activities and events for students at the university: associations, clubs, student-run groups and more. Asking about the nightlife, I was informed by many female students that there are cafes, bars, clubs, art and performance, common rooms, and associations. The social life here, I was told, is vibrant, diverse, and abundant, but it isn't for everyone. One student said that she didn't like the nightlife (or the drugs and booze) that many students went for. Still, she did become a volunteer, as the university offers plenty of volunteering opportunities for all students.

I didn't get involved in the hectic nightlife mainly because I had never been to a nightclub or disco in my life and was a relatively private person. While at university, I saw the results of drinking and drugs, with many students being asked to leave. However, I made a lovely group of friends who were also into volunteering and helping others. A few students did both and only joined the various volunteering bodies so that it would look good on their CVs. There was also plenty to see and do in Nottingham. There was Trent Bridge for cricket lovers, Nottingham Forest for football fans and an ice-Skating rink where Nottingham ice-dancing legends Jayne Torvill and Christopher Dean will live on forever. Towards the end of the second year at university, several career workshops were arranged with many of the country's top employers attending, trying to tempt students to join once they had achieved their BSc. If I got my BSc, it looked like the world was my oyster, but I needed to think about what I wanted to do for the rest of my life. I could have chosen a career in the NHS, but I didn't want to work in an environment that I alone couldn't change, and I would probably need a psychiatrist's help after banging my head against a brick wall. I had seen and witnessed the nearly non-existent support made available by the cash-starved NHS to anyone (such as my mother) with mental health problems.

Having a multi-handicapped sibling who turned out to be severely autistic meant that childhood memories of donkey rides and building sandcastles on a lovely sandy beach were never possible. I should have hated my brother for everything he prevented me from doing, but I didn't, but don't ask me why, as I couldn't answer. Love is the most potent medicine, yet you can't get a prescription from the NHS. If any social worker or NHS psychiatrist had asked me what I wanted or even bothered to check up on how I - the primary carer was doing, then perhaps they could have given a bit of love back in the way of respite care for my brother, or even arranged a few activities for all the school children who like me were unpaid carers. If my mum had been given more help at the start, perhaps she wouldn't have ended up being so depressed and living off various pills daily. I hate to think about the cost of those pills during my mother's lifetime. I bet it would be far more than the respite care or extra help she didn't receive.

I had already grasped most of what I would need to achieve a BA at the end of my three years at uni. I could have gone straight into a job in my local community, but the salary didn't offer that much of a pull, and I decided that a career in the army would suit me better. I passed my entrance exam with flying colours and, after 13 weeks, was posted to a barracks at Catterick Garrison, which is in North Yorkshire, and was the British Army's largest training establishment in the United Kingdom. Unlike many of my comrades, I soon settled in and didn't get homesick, probably due to not having many happy memories of my home life. Surprisingly, as soon as I left home, the local social services put into place a care package for my disabled brother as they soon recognised that, without me, the home couldn't function; it makes you wonder how many other teenage carers there are in the UK that become unpaid carers and, like me, missed out on everyday life.

In my fifth year of service, my battalion and I were sent to Bosnia, the stories I could tell of my time there would fill another book, but I tried to block out what happened as some of it was too terrible to remember. The widespread media coverage of the atrocities by Serbian paramilitary and military forces against Bosnian women and children drew international condemnation of the Serbian troops. Our role was to move in after many conflicts and bring normality back to the region. The worst part for me and many of my comrades was dealing with the devastation of young children being raped and the systematic genocide of their parents just because they were of a different religion. I had only signed up initially for three years but had extended it to six years and was asked if I wanted to develop it further, but I had decided that six years was long enough. The horrors we all witnessed in Bosnia broke many of my comrades, who were discharged on medical grounds.

I had never heard of PTSD before joining the army, but having witnessed post-traumatic stress disorder first-hand, I knew I wanted to use my BSc to help those suffering from it. I contacted the charity MIND about two months before my leaving date and set up an interview with the charity to see if they could use my services. As it turned out, I never did attend the interview.

Within days of my returning home as a hero, my mother told me about a local young man named Geoff Harding, who had also served in Bosnia but had been discharged a year earlier and had PTSD. To cut a long story short, he hadn't coped well and couldn't settle back into mainstream life and ended up sleeping on the streets and got in trouble with the law over several issues, including robbery and GBH. My mother told me that the GBH had been the straw that broke the camel's back, and he had been imprisoned for three years. I contacted the young man's family for permission to visit him in prison. They felt that it could help him to talk to someone who had witnessed what he had been through. It only took eight days for my visiting permit to arrive, and I went to see him. Seeing Geoffrey's state shocked me, which nearly brought me to tears. I had seen photos of him at his parents' home, but he was a fraction of his size when they were taken. I asked him what treatment he was receiving for his PTSD, and he said that he was waiting to see a counsellor, but it was a long wait as they were short-staffed. In the meantime, he had been prescribed some strong anti-depressants, but they didn't look like they were doing any good whatsoever. One of the most common side effects of anti-depressants was that they suppressed the need to eat, and it looked as if the medication he was on was making matters worse and not better.

On the drive back, I knew then that I would become a prison counsellor and help people like Geoff Harding. When I returned home, I logged on to my laptop and learned how to work for the prison service. As I held a BSc Hons, I could take the National Offender Management Service graduate programme, which, when qualified, paid a lot more than the standard prison officer rate. It involved six weeks of training at the national training centre in Rugby, a lovely market town in Warwickshire, England, and home of the beloved game of Rugby Union. The six-week course taught you how to use handcuffs, and taught primary control, restraint techniques, and how to carry out searches. Most of the first five weeks were spent in the classroom, which became rather dull, but on the sixth week you were shadowing an officer in prison for your first posting. You would then take on the role yourself. During the next eighteen months, I gained more experience and responsibility and progressed from prison officer to supervisor officer level - the first step on the ladder. After a further eighteen months, I was sent to another prison to take up the role of custodial manager, with a group of staff to manage. After a few months, they decided that I could handle the middle-management governor-grade role as an operational manager. After a rapid 30 months of my life, I was now qualified and could take on more training in my chosen field to reduce re-offending. I could have taken on more management roles, but this would involve moving around the country, but I wanted to stay close enough to keep an eye on what was happening to my brother and mother. The HM Prison Service - runs 110 of the 123 prisons in England and Wales, with the others being privately managed. As I didn't want to be posted anywhere in the UK, I opted to apply at my chosen prison to take on the role of a Prison Counsellor. The big drawback was that you can't be a prison counsellor, and a prison officer as a counsellor should seem to be neutral to the prisoner and not be part of the "system". By luck, my chosen place of work was a male-only prison that catered for category B & C inmates. As the role of prison counsellor was still being defined during my early years, I found myself a guinea pig developing a way forward. Thankfully, I had a great governor in Jack Smithers, who thought it a good idea, and anything that helped to stop prisoners from requesting a meeting with the governor was okay in his book. I soon realised that delivering counselling in prisons was highly challenging for me, both ethically and personally.

Daily, I had the environment to wrestle with diverse and complex issues, including security, confidentiality and, perhaps most significantly of all, how to develop a therapeutic relationship to promote psychological growth in an environment that mitigates against such processes. Things may be complicated further by prisoners' unique backgrounds and the offence. For example, a counsellor may work with an offender who was sexually abused but sentenced to custodial care for attacking his perpetrator. One of the biggest problems I faced involved confidentiality. For example, an inmate may tell a therapist he wishes to escape; what does the therapist do with this information? Or, in the case of record-keeping, who keeps the records? Where should they be saved? Whom can they be shared with? This requires agreement with the counselee on what can and cannot be shared. Ultimately, I agreed with the Governor to do what I thought was best and knock on his door if I needed help. As my workload expanded with all the caps I wore, I kept a copy of all files on my computer at home. This enabled me to check on where I was with certain inmates so that I would have meetings planned for the next day. This one decision would prove extremely helpful later.

***

Chapter 2

As I had a free run across all the prison wings, I soon got to know most of the staff and built a rapport with them. After being in my prison of choice for just over two years, I was asked by a few staff members if I would take the vacant role of becoming the prison's shop steward for the Prison Officers Association, which is the largest union in the United Kingdom representing Uniformed Prison Grades and staff. This is an unpaid role and can take up a lot of your time, but I could see their reason for asking me to take on the role, so I spoke to Jack Smithers, the governor, to hear his point of view. He couldn't forbid me to accept, but I had always been honest with him and helpful to him and thought it only right to ask. He said that I was a likeable chap but also levelheaded, so it shouldn't be a problem. With the Governor's blessing, I accepted the stewardship.

Much of my work as a shop steward was mundane, and members' demands were nearly always the same from year to year. Members wanted better financial rewards and protection from violent prisoners. Towards the end of my time as a shop steward, the government planned to increase the retirement age to 68 for all officers. Protests were made, along with a rally and lobbying of Parliament. So large were the numbers that the police closed Whitehall so that POA members could proudly march behind a piper past Downing Street and Parliament. The government is still sticking to the new 68 years, but the union wants the retirement age to be the same as for police officers, which is 60. While a Conservative government exists, I fear the period will remain at 68.

If you were working class, that meant you were second class, and you had to follow their rules or end up breaking the law. Like all public service providers, we were told that we had to participate in the government's austerity measures, and faced a pay cap of 1% yearly. This meant that with the inflation rate being more than 1%, everyone would be paid less in real terms than the previous year. London's bankers and financial leeches, who caused the crash in 2007/8, faced no such cap and paid themselves massive bonuses, even though their bank continued to make a loss. A lot was said by the government of the day about the austerity measures that it needed to put in place. Still, all that happened was that people experiencing poverty continued to get poorer, and the government continued to borrow more money to balance the books.

Prison officers wanted the same retirement age granted to police officers who can retire at 60. I pointed out that under Section 8 of the Prison Act 1952, while acting as such, prison officers have all the powers, authority, protection, and privileges of a police constable. Prison officers can intervene in "999" situations in prisons and take proactive steps to prevent a crime, such as arresting members of the public who attempt to smuggle illicit items into prisons, such as drugs and mobile phones. Police officers, under new pension arrangements, will have the right to retire at 60, and we wanted the same option.

One of the members' biggest gripes was assaults on staff. After many years of promises from both Labour and Conservative governments, the level of assaults remains unacceptably high, with over 3,000 assaults on staff yearly. There were 33,803 prisoner attacks in the year to the end of September 2018— 20% up on the previous year. Use weapons during assaults is increasing, with almost 200 reported yearly. There needs to be more lockdowns and searches made, but to do that there needs to be more prison officers to control the aftermath violence which always comes after a lockdown.

As a body, the POA constantly calls on the government, Ministry of Justice and National Offender Management Service to produce detailed, evidence-based reports to support their stance on reducing prison violence. As of now, their demands have been ignored. For many years, large volumes have been written about the virtues or otherwise of private sector companies being called upon by the British government to operate our prisons (and many other leading services such as the NHS). The problem I can see with this is that these private companies are run for the profit of their shareholders, not prisoners' well-being. The POA has been consistent in its approach to this issue: removing a person's liberty is a matter for the state; it is then the role of the state and not private enterprise to oversee that loss of freedom.

The concept of privatisation of prisons was imported from the United States of America. This system is now starting to feel and experience the difficulties of allowing private profit to outweigh social duty. Successive competition programs have moved public sector prisons into private ownership, and most new jails are being outsourced to the private sector. It is unknown what the final cost will be to the British taxpayer. The image of the private security sector in 2012 and 2013 took a severe hit following the problems surrounding the London Olympics and the government's decision to investigate the work and charging by some private sector companies. Evidence of 'inconsistent management' into Government Contracts outsources to the private sector demonstrates the need for public ownership. Some of these areas include the Judiciary and Home Office, but it has been well-publicised that privatising other public services involves considerable hidden costs to the taxpayer.

Poor pay was one of the biggest concerns mentioned at every meeting. In 2001 the salary and remuneration of POA members working in public sector prisons in England, Wales and Northern Ireland had their pay levels considered by the Prison Service Pay Review Body. The PSPRB was set up under Section 128 of the Criminal Justice and Public Order Act 1994 as a compensatory mechanism for removing the right to take industrial action under Section 127. This process has continued annually despite the POA seeking legal redress, alternative methods, and an application to the International Labour Organisation (ILO) because the process is neither fair nor just. One of the members' questions I must try to answer is this: With the government introducing the 1% pay cap on public service staff, it has done away with the Prison Service Pay Review Body as they can no longer set an appropriate wage level. Members IMO rightly state that if the government can legally stop the PSPRB from doing its job, the benefit of removing the right to take industrial action under Section 127 of that Act should also be classed as null and void. The government can't have its cake as well as eat it.

***

Chapter 3. Haylee, the Love of My Life.

During one of my home leaves while in the army, I met Haylee, and there was an instant liking between us; however, Haylee didn't want a serious relationship with someone who had a dangerous job as I had back then. After a few dates and my return to the army, we decided to be good friends, and she said she would write to me during my time overseas, but we both knew that the candle had been lit and only God could blow it out.

Within months of my leaving the army, we were always together, and decided to get married in 1991. Haylee was a couple of years younger than me, and we met by chance just over 26 years ago when we were introduced by a friend at a local fund-raising function to do with the village school where Haylee worked. The infant school needed urgent repairs that the county couldn't afford, so it was up to teachers and parents to do what they could. We all pay our council and country taxes, but that isn't enough to provide the future generation with a decent school.

I never really went for teachers, having been put off them at school. It took them two years to realise that I was dyslexic, and it took a lot of hard work to regain those lost years. My dad always joked that he had wanted to be a schoolteacher but thought he should get a full-time job instead of part-time. He always said teachers had too many holidays, especially during the summer. He loved telling his childhood story; he went to Kent every summer with his family to pick fruit and hops. Those years were some of the happiest he could remember. He always liked to point out to any teacher he met that the long holidays were introduced so the kids could help bring in the harvest. Now it's all done by massive combines, and kids would become lost if they went anywhere near a field.

Once I had met Haylee, I was hooked. They say you only get one chance to find your true soulmate, and I knew this was my chance. We mostly liked the same things apart from my previous job as a soldier in the British army. Haylee hated anything to do with war, probably due to losing her favourite uncle in the British Navy during the Falklands conflict in 1982 when a right old argy-bargy was going on thousands of miles from the UK. He was a sailor on the HMS Sheffield, hit by an Exocet air-launched anti-ship missile from a Super Etendard aircraft belonging to the Argentine Navy on 4 May 1982 and foundered on 10 May 1982. Her uncle was killed instantly by a direct hit, so he didn't know much about it. According to her aunt, it was six days before the ship finally sank, but not before 19 brave sailors had died. She said, 'It was on the news every day, but in those days, you couldn't click on the record button to save things,' and she wished she had been able to. She said that she went on to learn a lot about the HMS Sheffield and had a completed folder with photos and love letters from her uncle. She once told us that she had found out that the ship was built at the Vickers in Barrow-in-Furness in 1970. During its construction, an explosion killed two dockyard workers. It damaged a section of the hull, which was replaced by a section from an identical ship, Hercules, being built for the Argentine Navy. She joked that Argentina was only trying to regain what they felt was theirs by right. Having heard about Haylee's reasons, you could see why she hated anything about the war, so we never raised that subject again.

As Haylee was a schoolteacher, she said she 'had enough kids during the day and never really wanted a family.' At first, we never discussed the matter, but after five years, relatives kept asking the same question. When are you going to have a baby together? For the next few years, we kept coming back with the same old answer, that we would when the time was right, but that never stopped them from popping the question every time we met up. Ultimately, we decided to change our story and say that we couldn't have children and would not try IVF or adoption. In the end, they stopped asking. Haylee loved teaching, and according to the children's parents she was good at her job, and the kids thought she was the bee's knees. She was offered a promotion several times, but she didn't want it, nor did she need the extra salary as I was working full time as a prison counsellor, and, with both of us earning a reasonable amount, we didn't want the additional paperwork that comes with promotion.

As we both loved walking, we decided to get a dog to extend our family. We discussed the idea for several years and debated whether to buy a pedigree puppy or go for a rescue dog. We both liked the rescue idea and went to our local pet rescue centre to discuss rehoming. They asked about our line of work, and when we told them that we both worked full-time, their interest level hit rock bottom. Haylee explained that her workplace was a few minutes' walk from home, so she could 'come home at lunchtime and leave the dog in the garden for an empty'. My wife also mentioned that she was home at around 4p.m. every school day, so it shouldn't be that bad. The rescue centre said that they would have to do a home check to see if the garden was secure, and we arranged for them to come and visit on a date that we knew we would both be able to attend. The lady who did the home check was pleased with what she saw, and she said that the centre would write to us in a week with their decision. We spoke about what type of dog we should get. Haylee like small compact dogs like the Norwich terrier, but I have always wanted to own a large dog and loved the look of Rottweilers and German Shepherds. We were accepted by the rescue centre and invited to come for a chat and talk about the suitability of certain breeds.

We decided to wait a few months to take a holiday at the beginning of the summer school holidays, and then we could have a few weeks at home so that the new dog could settle in. Well, that was what we planned to do, but there are always dogs around the prison, including sniffer dogs who can detect drugs and larger dogs for security. One of the dog handlers, Jake, had become a close friend of mine over the years, and obviously he was delighted to hear that we were going to rescue. I met Jake one day at the prison, and he had this beautiful German shepherd dog with him that looked stunning. I went up to say hello, and the dog jumped up and wanted to kiss me. I said, 'That was nice,' and my friend said, 'It wasn't.' He said he had been trying to get the dog to look more threatening but was losing the battle. I asked my friend, 'What would happen to the dog if he didn't make the grade?' He said, 'It would be put down as they never liked offering trained dogs to rescue centres as you never know where they will end up.'

I told him I would buy him, and I'm sure the dog could understand as he jumped up and licked my face. I said, 'I will have to speak with Haylee about it, but I can't see a problem.' When I got home, Haylee had dinner ready, and she opened a bottle of red wine which went well with the rib-eye steaks. I told Haylee about the wonderful GSD I had seen at work, but as it wasn't aggressive looking, it would be put to sleep in a few days as the dog didn't make the grade. She said that that was awful and asked why the dog couldn't be put up for re-homing at a rescue centre. I explained that the prison service never did that as they could never be sure how the dog would cope with children and other animals. Haylee looked sad and said, 'That's wrong. We could give the dog a home.' I smiled at her and said, 'I will speak with Jake in the morning and ask the question.'

We finished dinner, and Haylee switched on her laptop and started to read about the breed. She asked what colour the dog was, and I told her it had a lovely tan/gold colour on parts of his head and neck, but the rest was black apart from some tan colouring on his back legs. She picked up the laptop, and we both moved to the table to see some pictures on Google Images. Haylee asked me to show her the colouring, and I pointed to one image and said that he could be the dog, but that his hindquarters didn't slope like that. Haylee said the dog was a black and tan, and the picture was of a champion dog that had won more championship shows than any other GSD last year. She said she didn't like the sloping rear end as it didn't look like the dog could last an hour herding sheep, let alone days in the field. Haylee also said that sooner or later it would cause health problems in the breed, and wondered when the kennel club would do something about it. She also said that she never understood why a breeder would want to produce puppies that would end up with a health problem. They're supposed to love their animals, but many were only interested in winning a small trophy or a rosette, and that the animal's well-being came a poor second. She kept reading and said that the new sloping rear was the latest fashion, but she noted that many people were stating that the dog wasn't fit for purpose and therefore shouldn't have become a champion. She showed me a picture of Ramacon Swashbuckler, a GSD who had become Cruft's best-in-show winner in 1971 and another photo of the best-in-show winner in 1965 named Fenton of Kentwood. Both dogs had a non-sloping rear and looked like they could run all day.

Haylee read that many puppies were prone to hip dysplasia, so they would have to check that out. I saw Jake at work the next day and asked if we could come over on Saturday to meet the dog. We set a time, and I phoned Haylee with the good news. Haylee was so excited that she reminded me of a child waiting for Santa to arrive on Christmas Eve. When she met the dog, it was love at first sight, and we said that we would love to offer him a loving forever home. We arranged to collect our new family member the following Saturday as this would give us time to get everything he needed. We asked about his hip score, and he showed us it was fine. He had been neutered, and his vaccinations were up to date. We asked about his diet and were given a sheet explaining what and when he was fed, but we were told that we would have to change to tinned meat as he cooked his tripe as he needed a lot of it. We called in Pets at Home on the way back, and Haylee was like a little girl let loose in a toy shop. We decided to call him Robin as Haylee's dad had been a great lover of Robin Hood. We had some great holidays with Robin, and he went everywhere with us. We visited every corner of the UK and met some wonderful people and fellow dog lovers.

Move forward a few years, and everything was going nicely, but Robin kept jumping up and sniffing at Haylee's breast. He had never done this before, and we thought it strange and promised to ask Jake if this was a common trait with GSDs. Before I could ask Jake, Haylee noticed a small lump in her right breast. Her GP sent her for a mammogram, and the nurse could feel the tiniest lump on her inner right breast. After an ultrasound and biopsy, we were told that it was cancer. We were shell-shocked, but we tried convincing each other that everything would be fine as treatment was much better these days and new drugs were being developed regularly.

After a short discussion, we chose the bilateral mastectomy with an immediate reconstruction route. Surgery determined no node involvement, early stage but triple positive. My wife's initial diagnostics showed she had a form of breast cancer known as HER2 positive. After talking with two oncologists, we did the dreaded chemo for extra insurance. As an additional protection, she would be given the Trastuzumab drug, available on the NHS. Haylee finished her last Taxol six months after diagnosis and had Herceptin for a year. It was a terrible time for both of us as the chemo was very tough. She took sick leave, and I took time off work to become her full-time career. Robin stayed by her side and wouldn't leave her. We realised that Robin had warned her that something was wrong, and Haylee had said that she had read that many dogs could smell cancer on a person and that much work was being done to test more types of cancer and other life-threatening problems. Haylee spent a lot of her time on her laptop finding out more about dogs detecting cancer, and she found lots of charities working with various owners whose dogs were detecting various illnesses and making their owners aware of any problems, such as knowing when the owner was about to have a fit. She said that most were charities and relied on donations to continue their research. She found it difficult to understand why the government sent millions of pounds overseas yearly instead of investing the money in these charities' research programs.

About six months after the chemo ended, Robin looked ill, so we took him to our local vet, who took a blood test and gave Robin an injection of steroids to see if that would help. A few days later, we were called back and told that Robin's kidneys were packing up, and that the vet could do little else. We asked him if Robin was in pain, and the vet said that he was, but we could give him painkillers to help, but there was nothing he could do to fix the kidney problem. He was honest with us and said that the only thing we could do was to put him to sleep so that he was no longer in pain. The vet said to go away and think about it and let him know our decision. We went home, and both cried in each other's arms, and Robin came up to give us both a big cuddle. We decided that the best thing would be to put him to sleep so that he was no longer in pain, and I decided to call the vet the following day and make the appointment. He said, 'It's the right choice, and shows how much we love Robin.' I stayed with him while he passed over the rainbow bridge, and we asked for him to be cremated and his ashes to be returned. We planted a rose bush in the garden and sprinkled his ashes around it. The rose bush grew, and its flowers were of a bright golden tan colour, just like Robin.

After the first year and a few months of grieving for our beloved Robin, things started to look a bit brighter, and we both went back to work thinking we had survived the earthquake. It wasn't until we went back to see her consultant that we realised things weren't as rosy as we thought. He wanted to run more tests and told us 'not to worry as they are just standard tests.' However, a few days later, we received a call from the consultants' secretary asking us both to return. The 'both' word kept us awake at night as, if things had been normal, they would have just requested Haylee to attend. Ten painfully long days later, we arrived at the hospital, dreading to hear what, by now, just had to be bad news. As usual, we had difficulty finding somewhere to park but eventually noticed a space and paid a fortune for the pleasure. As our appointment was extra to his regular load, we had been stuck on the end of his patient list, and we knew from previous experience that he would be running late. I started to worry that the two-hour parking slot we had paid for would not be enough.

Thankfully, the waiting area had a small café run by the British Red Cross. We were too nervous to eat or drink anything, but I hoped the lady would give us some change for the meter. She knew what I wanted even before I asked but was very pleasant. We briefly chatted, and she told me that parking was an ongoing problem that kept getting worse. I joked with her that she was lucky as she probably got free parking, being a volunteer. I must admit that very few things shock me anymore, but I was taken aback when she told me she had to pay just like the nurses and doctors. The lovely lady said they struggled to get volunteers to run the small café as people couldn't afford to pay for the parking. This was shocking news to me, it was wrong. How low can the NHS get? It's funny how things like this stick in your mind when you're faced with the possibility of a tragedy.

We finally got in to see the consultant, and you could tell by the look on his face that he wasn't going to tell us we had won the lottery. What came next took us to a new low. He explained that the initial treatment had worked well, but when they ran the check-up test a few weeks ago, they found a growth in the scar tissue. We assumed this would mean more chemo followed by more surgery, but he said he was not optimistic about the outcome as cancer could have spread to other body parts. We would have to decide if going through the chemo route again was worth it, as he couldn't see it extending Haylee's life expectancy.

We sat in sheer disbelief, and eventually got back the strength to ask him if there was another drug or anything else that would help. Even if it gave us a few more months together, we would try anything, including herbal or witchcraft. He said that a new drug was out, called Kadcyla, but it wasn't available on the NHS as Nice hadn't approved it. He noted that Kadcyla could treat HER2-positive breast cancer that has spread to other body parts (metastatic breast cancer) after prior treatment with trastuzumab (Herceptin®) and a taxane. He explained further that Kadcyla is made to find HER2-positive cells and attach itself to them. It tells the cells to stop growing and the body's immune system to destroy them. Kadcyla also goes inside the cell to keep fighting from the inside. Kadcyla releases the chemotherapy inside the cell. The chemotherapy works inside the cell, causing it to die. It sounded ideal, but without it being available on the NHS, there was no way we could afford it. If it were to save Haylee's life, we would sell the house and start fundraising to help meet the cost, but Haylee said that she would not let me take that route to have a few extra months or a few years with me. I had never cried in public before, but I couldn't keep it in. Our consultant said, 'Go away and think about the route we wanted to take.'

We went away and, after a thousand million tears later, came up with the only option left open to us: to try to find a way to get the government to step in and make this wonder drug available to all who needed it. The small amount of research I did online showed that the NHS spent more than £1bn on drugs developed from publically funded research in 2016. One campaigning group, Global Justice Now, stated that in many cases the UK taxpayer effectively pays twice for medicines: first through investing in R&D, then by paying high prices for the resulting medicine once ownership has been transferred to a private company. It stated, 'Drug companies are generating huge private profits from public funds.' The internet told me that there are around 45,000 new breast cancer diagnoses annually in England. After digging deeper, I felt furious, and if I had met the Secretary of State for Health, Jeremy Hunt MP, I would probably have ripped his throat out with my bare hands, and ended up in a real mess.

A husband is there to protect his wife, and I couldn't do a thing to help. I did the usual stuff like having a meeting with my local MP, but all he promised was to raise the matter with the Secretary of State and gave me a load of bullshit about why the NHS couldn't buy every drug out there. My local MP had taken over the role from his father, who in turn had taken over from his father. I was living in a part of the UK where the voters go through the motions every few years, which wastes time and money. It is one of the safest conservative seats in the country, and if they were to place a blue rosette on the backside of a cow, the yokels would vote for it. I even wrote to the then Prime Minister but got a standard reply. I then decided to write to the Secretary of State and copy the letter to all the national press I could think of in the vain hope that they may print it and embarrass the Government into doing something about the chronic situation.

Dear Secretary of State,

My wife is dying from breast cancer. She has a form known as HER2 positive. We have been told there is a drug called Kadcyla, produced in the USA by the Genentech group, which is part of the massive Roche Group, and that it could give my wife a few more years of life. We were, however, told that the drug isn't available on the NHS as it's too expensive and that the wrongly named organisation called NICE have not approved its use. Without this new drug, my wife will die many decades before her time. I urge you to get tough with these drug companies to make the price they charge more reasonable and affordable to the NHS. I know that you will say that your civil servants would have already tried that route and have a point that it costs drug companies a fortune to develop the drug, and they want a return on their investment. Therefore, I hope you won't mind me suggesting a way around the problem which would hopefully postpone my wife's death and bring hope to thousands of people living with cancer in the UK.

This is what needs to be done. Both you and the Prime Minister call the CEO of the drug company Roche to an urgent meeting at Downing Street, and inform them that you wish to speak with them face-to-face about many of the drugs they supply to the NHS. Before this meeting, you need to get your civil servants to produce a list of medications, other medical equipment, and supplies that the NHS purchases yearly from Roche. They should also find an alternative supplier for the main common drugs from another NHS supplier. At the meeting, you present the facts to the CEO, stating that you want these new drugs supplied at a reasonable price. It would be best if you also inform the CEO that you want an answer by 16:00 hours tomorrow as you have called a meeting of the national and international press where we will announce either that we have come to an undisclosed agreement with Roche to supply these wonder drugs at an affordable price, or that the NHS will give notice to the Roche group that the NHS will no longer use their services. The PM should inform the CEO that he has requested that Roche shares be suspended on all stock markets until 17:00 GMT tomorrow due to some important news that will be made public then. This move is implemented so that there is no insider trading, especially if certain people want to sell their shares at the current high rate.

Of course, if you decide that you can't meet our demand, we will tell the press that Roche has lost one of its biggest customers worldwide. I hate to think about your share price if you decide to take that route.
We look forward to hearing from you soon.

Unfortunately, none of the nationals printed the letter, and the minister never even replied as he was too busy fighting the Junior Doctors, forcing new contracts upon them. It was also probably down to the fact that large international companies donate vast sums of money to the Conservative Party so that they can finance the cost of the next general election. Sadly, my wife passed away a few weeks later, and I swore then that I would make those responsible pay for their in-action. One thing was for sure: they won't be getting an invite to my gathering in Bedford, but, hopefully, they will pull their fingers out and man up for the job they were elected to do.

***

Chapter 4. Lucas Returns to Work.

After my wife's funeral, attended by many of her friends from the county's education establishments, and hundreds of prison officers who had come to support me, I decided I wouldn't sit around and mope and watch daytime TV. There is only so much TV you can take after hearing about another shooting in an American school and another famine in Africa (both could be less traumatic if their governments faced their continuing nightmare). I feel sorry for the USA as many innocent children are slaughtered yearly, and nobody does sod-all about it. The gun lobby in the Senate must love having blood on their hands, as they are still living in the good old days when Wyatt Earp would come along and sort out the bad boys. They stick to the same old tune that it's the right of every American to own a gun. This may have been OK years ago, but didn't they realise that children are now brought up playing violent computer games and that many more Americans are now hooked on drugs? So, my message to them is, if you want to continue playing Russian roulette with children's lives, please place a media ban on this matter, as I get sick of hearing about it on the TV news. I was welcomed back by many officers, who offered their condolences, and even the inmates had heard of my loss and kindly sent their most profound sympathy card around the wings, which over 100 inmates signed.

One thing that had been kept away from me during my wife's illness was that my old friend, Governor Jack Smithers, had had a heart attack and had thankfully survived, but had been forced to retire early. I was summoned to the new governor's office on my second day back, and we immediately hated each other. Jack Smithers had made the post of governor after rising through the ranks, and he was one of the lads, although he knew when to draw the line. A fast-track officer had replaced him, called Marcus Hunt, who was more interested in seeing his name on the door than in spending time on the shop floor. He didn't even bother to offer his condolences. I was told in no uncertain terms that he didn't like me 'being the shop steward for the Prison Officers Association and a prison counsellor'.

The Prison Officers Association had been fighting the management for the right to strike for years and wasn't loved by the establishment. I told him, 'I have been a counsellor for many years, and my work has been recognised by HMP service and is believed to be one of the best in the land.' He said they would be employing outside counsellors, and my post would no longer exist. I informed him that 'regarding the POA, it's up to the officers to select whom they want to represent them and not the management.' He started to go red in the face, and went even redder when I told him, 'I will take any dismissal to the POA and the courts.' I left before I strangled the bastard.

Two days passed, and I heard no more about it, but was again called to the governor's office. When I entered, there were two other staff members I didn't recognise, but they probably came from the same rent-a-suit shop that the new governor came from. I was told to sit down, and that a prisoner had reported that the mobile phone he had been found with had been supplied by me. I was shocked and asked who had made such an allegation, but I was told it was confidential. I said it was untrue and that the Prison Officers Association would fight my case. He said he didn't care what I did, but I had a choice. I looked at him blankly, and he said I could either take early retirement with a full pension or face the music. He also said that he would give me until noon tomorrow to give him an answer. I left early that day, went home, and had a long chat with Haylee (who of course wasn't there) and a large bottle of whisky. My mind kept saying fight the bastard, yet Haylee said take retirement and start to live again. Haylee won the battle.

The following day, I arranged to see four inmates for counselling, and I told them that this would be our last session, and the reason why. They were angry, not at me, but at the establishment. All of them said that they knew I would never do such a thing and that some inmate would be getting a few years off his sentence for helping solve the new governor's problem. They all asked who it was that had accused me, and I said that they wouldn't say. I shook their hand and wished them all the best. As soon as I knew the new governor's name, I ran a check on him to see where he had come from. Finding out was more difficult than I had first thought, as the establishment (quite rightly) didn't want prisoners getting hold of any data regarding staff. In the end, I called an old friend who told me that 'Marcus Hunt has risen through the ranks, working at the "Private" prisons.' Just so you understand what I'm rabbiting on about, the UK has two types of prisons. There are 14 privately managed prisons in England and Wales, shared between three companies. Five are in the hands of G4S; four are operated by the French firm Sodexo and the other five are under the control of outsourcing company Serco. Private institutions comprise around 15% of the country's prisons, with the rest managed by the National Offender Management Service (NOMS). State-run prisons' end goal is to house prisoners to rehabilitate them and, at the same time, remove them from the streets. A private prison, on the other hand, is run by a corporation. That corporation aims to profit from anything they deal in. I'll let you decide which option is best.

Liz Truss, the then Justice Secretary, said G4S would have to pay for the special Tornado units sent into HMP Birmingham during the 2018 riots. There have been a series of other fines, further souring public opinion against a company already scowled upon for its failure to provide enough security staff for the 2012 London Olympics, resulting in army reinforcements being parachuted in. As another example, an electronic tagging scandal that engulfed both Serco and G4S in 2013 led to the abandonment of plans to privatise three prisons in South Yorkshire, for which Serco was the leading bidder. My friend could tell me that Marcus Hunt had been working at the privately run HM Prison Northumberland, a Category C men's prison operated by the private prison firm Sodexo Justice

Services under contract with Her Majesty's Prison Service. It is rumoured that he couldn't handle it at HMP Northumberland, one of Britain's biggest jails. It had descended into chaos, with failing alarms, prisoners calling the shots and a troubling drug problem sweeping its corridors. He had jumped ship before it sank as he didn't want to go down with it as the captain.

At five minutes to twelve, I was about to meet the new governor and accept his offer, but there was a commotion from A Wing, and it got out that someone had been knifed and had died. As I walked down to the dead man's cell, a couple of inmates whispered to me that he wouldn't be 'making up any stories any longer'. I was a few minutes late for my meeting but explained to the new governor and his two look-a-like cronies that 'his little trick hadn't worked and had cost an inmate his life'. I told him he may have gotten away by pulling tricks at Northumberland (a nursery category C prison), but he won't get away with it at a category B prison. I went on and told him that with the death of his source, he had no evidence now, but to his surprise, I told him I was taking early retirement as I didn't want to work under an amateur like him. He would have to learn that actions in a small, closed community had consequences, and I didn't want to be part of his dirty work. I told him every inmate and warden knows about his dirty work, but he must work and live with that. I also told him I would retire on my terms within four to six weeks.' He was speechless as I left, and I couldn't have been prouder about how I had handled the nasty piece of shit. I worked on it for five weeks, which gave me time to back up all the files I held at home and see them on my current list of inmates receiving counselling. I was also able to hand over the work I had done as a shop steward for the POA to another warden, and I wished him well.

After leaving the prison, I heard that the inmates had nearly rioted once they learned that I had been forced out. Still, sad as I was to go, I knew I was now a free man to make those pay for my wife's early death, and for HMP service treating me like crap, after giving the prison service nearly 25 years of my life. I knew then that this was the start of the Bedford Heist, where I could show the world that the average working man wouldn't let them get away with treating the masses like dog dirt.

A few other factors helped me decide to get my own back on the useless civil servants running our beloved country. These were to do with how the austerity measures hit only the working class, and how the rich were getting richer, and the working men and women were getting poorer. I will get on to the exciting part of my story soon. Still, I wanted to let you know that it just wasn't the way the NHS failed to help my beloved wife, nor was it to do solely about the way Her Majesty's Prison Service treated me, but being a counsellor, I did meet many interesting people. It's also their stories that have left me in no doubt about organising the Bedford Heist. Along with their sad stories, there was also the problem with prison overhaul, which keeps raising its ugly head every few years, and the UK's austerity measures that only affected the working classes.

***

Chapter 5. Prisons Overhaul.

Just before I was forced to take early retirement from a job I loved and was good at, there had been much talk about prison overhaul and reforms. This is nothing new, as there has always been a lot of discussion and suggestions on how to fix the service, but very little ever got put into practice. Before stepping down as Prime Minister (after the Brexit vote), David Cameron said that the 'failure' of the current system is 'scandalous.' He stated that six 'reform prisons' will be created in England and Wales as part of a government pilot scheme to tackle high levels of violence and re-offending. Prison governors will have autonomy over their operations and budgets, while graduate teachers will be recruited for jails. Mr Cameron stated that 'current levels of prison violence, drug-taking and self-harm should shame us all', with a typical week seeing incidents of self-harm, at least one suicide and a rising number of assaults on staff.

As of June 2019, the prison population in England and Wales was 82,710, it was 8,205 in Scotland and 1,487 in Northern Ireland. The cost per prisoner or prison place? In 2017/18, the average direct cost per prison place was £26,274 in England and Wales, £35,293 in Scotland, and £55,304 in Northern Ireland.

In his speech, the then prime minister announced that prison governors would control how they run their prisons, which he said would empower staff, drive up standards and cut reoffending. Mr Cameron said, 'We need prisons. Some people - including rapists, murderers, child abusers, gang leaders - belong in them. For me, punishment—deprivation of liberty—is not a dirty word, but he also added: 'I also strongly believe that we must offer chances to change; that for those trying hard to turn themselves around, we should offer hope; that in a compassionate country, we should help those who've made mistakes to find their way back onto the right path.' He said that prisoners should be seen as potential assets to be harnessed, and the failure of our system today is scandalous. He also highlighted figures showing that 46% of all prisoners re-offend within a year of release and said that the cycle of reoffending costs up to £13bn a year. Being on the sharp end of any reforms, I can only agree with what the then PM stated but forgive me for being pessimistic as I have heard it all before, and we are still waiting, as we are in a heck of a mess.

A couple of years before I was forced to leave, there was a riot at HMP Bedford, which saw prison officers from across the country brought into control hundreds of inmates who had taken over two wings. Scores of prisoners reportedly flooded the prison's gangways in a chaotic scene. Police and specially trained officers (whom I had helped train) were called to the Category B prison amid reports of loud bangs or explosions coming from inside. The Prison Officers Association (POA) said that about 230 inmates got out of their cells, seized keys, broke into medicine stores, and started small fires. The Prison Service explained on the BBC that the situation was controlled after an operation that lasted more than six hours. Nobody was seriously hurt, but I had warned the prison service that this would probably happen, but again I may as well have been talking to a brick wall. In a recent report on HMP Bedford, I mentioned that inmates claimed it was easier to get hold of drugs than clothes or bedding. The inmate numbers had risen so fast that items such as clothes and bedding had not kept pace with the intake of prisoners. I had read in a report on Bedford Prison published in September 2017 that almost twice the number of prisoners said it was 'easy' to access drugs compared to a previous inspection in February 2014. The number saying, they had developed a drug problem while in prison increased from 4% to 14%. The prison system is due to urgent changes, not just words.

In November 2016, the then Justice Secretary Liz Truss unveiled a White Paper detailing £1.3bn investment in new prisons over the next five years, and plans for 2,100 extra officers, drug tests, and more autonomy for governors. Let's see what happens.

Update: October 2023.

As with most of the Tory Party promises very few ever materialise. In fact, only 206 places were created in the last four years. So, in February 2022 the Conservative government announced that an unprecedented expansion and refurbishment programme will create more than 4,000 new prison places across the country, the Deputy Prime Minister Dominic Raab announced.

These new places are part of the government's £4 billion investment to create 20,000 modern and innovative prison places, ensuring the right conditions are in place to truly rehabilitate prisoners. This will give prisoners the education, skills and addiction support they need to live crime-free lives on release, helping to cut crime and protect the public.

IMO they should have put Liz Truss in prison as this would have stopped her becoming Prime Minister in 2022 where her Right-Wing Conservative cabinet sent shockwaves through the financial world and sent inflation and interest rates to a new level. This affected mortgage rates which will mean that the working Men & Women will have to pay more at a time when budgets are already squeezed due to the cost-of-living crisis.

Update Plus: October 2023.

On the 12th of October 2023 The Guardian newspaper reported that Judges have been told to delay the sentencing of convicted criminals currently on bail – including rapists and burglars – because prisons are full, the Guardian understands.

The guidance reportedly came from the senior presiding judge for England and Wales, Lord Justice Edis, on a private call with senior crown court judges.

On 6 September 2023, former British Army soldier Daniel Abed Khalife, who was on remand awaiting trial on terrorism charges, escaped from HM Prison Wandsworth in London. This escape triggered a nationwide police search and delays at major transport hubs. Khalife is believed to have escaped by strapping himself to the bottom of a food delivery lorry while working in the prison's kitchen. After three days on the run, he was captured by the Metropolitan Police in Northolt, London.

I'm sorry to say that our prisons are no longer "Fit for Purpose" and drastic action needs to be taken if we are to keep citizens safe.

***

Chapter 6. Why I Changed from Gamekeeper to Poacher.

My life outlook had changed with two shattering blows in less than six months. I didn't give a dam about myself, and I wanted someone to pay for the early death of my wife, and for someone to pay for the way Her Majesty's Prison Service had treated me after I had given it over twenty years of my life. The prison service didn't realise that I had a database of hundreds of criminals, and, as I was good at organising things. I would use these two things to both gain revenge and hopefully put the 'Great' back in front of Britain again.

Before I get to the heist I have planned, I want to share with you some things that happened while I was a prison counsellor, all of which will highlight what is wrong with this country as most of its failures end up at the prison gate. These sad stories also helped me decide to jump ship.

The prison system itself isn't working, and the following chapters will show you some of the problems that occur regularly and need fixing fast. Subjects covered are rape in prison, drugs in British prisons, bullying, IPP, austerity, Brexit, coronavirus, racism, non-dom status, greedy companies, and the UK PAYE system. Once I have highlighted these sad story's (and use some of the inmates mentioned) the novel will proceed to the actual heist which brings the market town of Bedford to its knees.

***

Chapter 7. Rape in Prison.

Warning: This chapter includes sexual content so you may wish to move straight to chapter 8.

Sexual abuse in Britain's penal system is a significant problem for both the victim and prison staff, as many victims are too scared to speak out. Transgender and gay prisoners are at higher risk of sexual assault than heterosexual inmates. All the officers can do is keep an eye and ear open and, if possible, relocate the victims to a safer prison section.

I'll never forget the day when all hell was let loose when the screams of a prisoner echoed around the west wing. During the so-called open-door stage of the day, prisoners were returned to their wing, but instead of locking all the cell doors, they were left open so that inmates could chat and play together securely locked in their prison wing. This meant that prisoners could visit other inmates' cells to play cards, swap books and even trade in what merchandise they had, usually drugs. Prison officers could then relax with very few problems. That was until this day. A scream came from the west wing's hardman Sean Bailey who shared a cell with another inmate. When I arrived at his cell, I saw a lot of blood on the floor, especially on his bunk. Someone had gotten hold of a knife, and unable to take abuse or a beating from the hardman any longer, took action. What surprised me was that the blood came from an open wound on Sean's penis. It looked as if he were about to bugger another inmate, who had retaliated and cut off the tip of his pride and joy. Our main priority was to call for an ambulance and try to stop the bleeding before Sean bled out. I had the unpleasant task of tying a tourniquet to Sean's penis, which may have saved his life. Before sending Sean on his way, the paramedic asked if anyone had found the tip of Sean's penis, as sometimes the surgeon can stitch things back on. We searched high and low but couldn't see it, which seemed strange. Ultimately, we gave up, and Sean was on his way to the hospital with a correctional officer handcuffed to him.

As soon as he was gone, I instructed all prisoners to return to their cells as there would be a lock-in and a full inspection of all cells and inmates. Sean's cellmate was Tom Grace, a skinny man in his mid-forties, and he was questioned first in my office whilst his cell was thoroughly searched and cleaned up. I asked Tom what he had seen, but I might as well have asked the brick wall. He said that he was elsewhere on the wing when he heard the scream, but I knew this was a lie as Tom was always nearby to do Sean's wishes. I even assumed he wiped Sean's bum after using the in-cell toilet. Tom was timid and wouldn't fart without first asking Sean's permission. He was playing dumb, as Sean hadn't told him what to say. Once Sean's cell had been checked and no sign of any unwanted body parts had been found, we started questioning everyone on the wing.

It didn't take long to find the culprit as, two cells down, Timmy Willis resided with James Wells, and Timmy had a tiny speck of blood on his right ear that he had missed when cleaning himself up. Timmy, who was twenty-three, had long blonde hair that he kept tied back in a ponytail. He also had sea-blue eyes and a pale pink complexion. I asked Timmy how he had a speck of blood on his right ear. He returned quickly with, 'I cut myself shaving.' That was not a good answer, as only electric razors were allowed for obvious reasons. He continued to play dumb, and, after a while, I went behind him and lifted his ponytail. He started to panic and asked me what I was doing. I said, 'I was just checking because I was once told that if you lift a pony's tail, all you will see is its arsehole.' He didn't laugh, and I told him to 'stop being an arsehole and tell me what happened', so I could deal with it before it went upstairs to the governor and several years were added to his current sentence. He looked at me, and could see that I wasn't messing about, and he just sat there and started to cry and cry. I let him get on with it for several minutes and then sat back after informing him that I was all ears. After serving 18 months for drug offences, Timmy started rambling about how he couldn't take it anymore. I asked him if he wanted a cup of tea or would he prefer coffee. He said, 'I would die for a lovely Costa cappuccino, but a cup of tea or coffee will do.'

Once Timmy was settled, I asked him to start from the beginning. What he told me was pretty shocking, and after 20 years in the service, I thought I had heard and seen it all. He said it started just days after his arrival, and, due to his looks, most thought he was gay, but they were wrong. He had nothing against gays, what someone does behind closed doors is their business.

'It took less than a week for Sean Bailey to claim me as his, and no one could touch or even look at me in the wrong way. I thought that I had landed on my two feet and found myself a fairy godmother who would look after me here. However, two days later, during the open-door session, I was told to report to Sean as he wanted me. My cellmate giggled when he heard the part about "wanting me", and I didn't click on it then. A few minutes after arriving in Sean's cell, he told his mate to guard the door as he wanted some time to get to know me better. I thought he just wanted to talk, but how could I be so thick, or should it be naïve to think that? It took only seconds to realise that he was going to bugger me, and it would be pointless to try and fight back as he was much stronger than me. I just closed my eyes and tried to think of friendly holidays I had enjoyed, but the pain was too much, and I passed out. His cellmate threw water over my face and told me to dress and get back to my cell and not tell anyone what had happened, or it would be unwelcome news for me. He drew a finger across his throat, ensuring I got the message loud and clear. I went back to my cell and cried like a baby.'

Timmy said, 'The abuse went on for several weeks, and in the end, I did tell a warden, but I was told not to be silly and accept it as part of my sentence.' I asked Timmy why he hadn't asked to see me, and he said, 'I had but was told that you were on leave, looking after a sick family member.' So, Timmy went on, as he wanted to tell his side of the story before he lost his nerve. He said it had been going on for some time, but he wasn't used as much as he had been when it all started. 'When I was called to his cell today, I decided I wouldn't be used any longer. I knew I couldn't fight him off and that telling a warden was pointless, so I came up with the only thing I could do.' As usual, Sean was waiting for me, and told his cellmate to stand guard outside the door. As soon as he had left, I told Sean that the last time we had sex, he hurt me and had caused a rip in the walls of my anus. Could he please spare me for a few more days? He said no, as he had been looking forward to this for some time and was all worked up. I said I could give him a blow job instead, but I knew he didn't like BJs as much as he liked anal sex. I said I was good at giving BJs, and he would like it. If he didn't, then he could have me as usual. He said that he was willing to give it a go, and he dropped his trousers and presented me with his already hard cock, which stank to high heaven. I got on my knees, started to lick up from his balls to his helmet, and paid particular attention to the part below his helmet. He began to moan and told me to 'get it inside my mouth', but I had better not scratch his meat with my teeth, or I would be in big trouble. I did as I was ordered, and he started to enjoy it, but he pushed in too hard, trying to get it down my throat. I have had oral sex before with a few girlfriends, so I knew what a man liked, but I never tried to get it all in but had come in their mouths on several occasions. Some liked the taste, but others didn't, so I only tried it on again with the ones I knew didn't mind the taste. There were plenty of other ways to satisfy both partners' needs. Well, I didn't like it down my throat and decided to carry out my plan and face the consequences as it couldn't be any worse than what was going on here with everyone's blessing. On the outward stroke, I stopped just as the helmet of his massive 9-inch cock reached my teeth. Then all hell was let loose, and Sean started to scream as I bit into the helmet of his penis. I moved my head from side to side, giving my teeth a saw-like action, and as Sean pushed on my head, trying to dislodge me, it gave me the extra leverage to bite through his meat with the helmet firmly in my mouth. I turned and spat it out into the cell toilet and flushed. I then ran out and headed for my cell, just as all the prisoners from the other cells were poking their heads around their cell doors, trying to see what had gone on.'

After telling me his side of the story, Jimmy asked me 'what will happen next'. I told him it would depend on the outcome with Sean because he had lost a lot of blood, and if he died, then there was no way I could cover that up. I told Jimmy to return to his cell and say nothing to anyone, and we will sit back and wait to see what develops. A few days passed, and the good news was that Sean made it, but he will never be the same again. Without the helmet of his pride and joy, they could do little. They installed a small tube into the urinary meatus, but using his penis for anything apart from peeing will be impossible. Some would say that he got what he deserved after what he had done to his fellow prisoners. I did visit him as soon as he was well enough to be interviewed, as I needed to get his side of the story to send a full report to the governor. He said the same as Jimmy but said that 'Jimmy has fallen in love with me and wanted to show his love by giving me a blow job.'

I told Sean that he had just said what I expected him to say, but I made it noticeably clear that his story about Jimmy being the instigator of the sexual happenings was a load of bullshit. He ranted and raved about how he was going to sue the prison and Jimmy, but I soon brought him back to earth with a bang when I told him that fifteen other prisoners had made a complaint since the accident, and all were willing to testify in court that he had raped them. I said that we could play this two ways; firstly, he could try and sue, but with Jimmy and fifteen others willing to go public, he stood little chance of winning. By trying to sue HMP, he would give the tabloids a cheap and funny story. The second option would be to say nothing, and I would get him transferred to another prison. He couldn't return to us as the other inmates would finish him off together. He soon decided that a transfer would be best.

When I returned to my office in the prison, I visited Timmy with the good news, and he was pleased. I also told him that he would have to submit to various blood tests to check that he was clear of HIV, as Sean's blood could have given Timmy HIV. He wasn't pleased to hear that, but I told him it was unlikely but worth getting checked out. I had placed Timmy on our drug rehabilitation course, and he had done well.

***

Chapter 8. Drugs in British Prisons.

As with the outside world, drugs are a mammoth problem for the prison service. You would think that an establishment surrounded by high walls and secure gates wouldn't have a drug problem, but I can tell you that you would be wrong. An analysis of data by Think Tank Reform shows that one in seven prisoners are becoming addicted to illicit substances whilst in prison, with the figure increasing from 6% to 15% between 2014 and 2019. This was when so-called 'legal highs' such as Spice were freely available and was challenging for prison officers to detect. Three of these facts cause me the most significant concern. They are: Firstly, two-thirds of women and almost 40% of men in prison report committing offences to get money to buy drugs. Secondly, reconviction rates are more than double for prisoners who reported using drugs in the four weeks before custody compared with prisoners who had never used drugs. And thirdly, half of the prisoners reporting an alcohol problem also reported a drug problem, with an extra 44% cent saying they also had an emotional or mental health issue.

I want to mention my three main concerns, as the lack of action from consecutive governments in tackling these problems was one of the reasons, I decided to leave the job I loved doing, which resulted in the Bedford Heist being set up. Many inmates would openly tell you that drugs are more accessible to obtain than soap was in prison. The Reform report pointed to the example of HMP Nottingham, a category B prison with high violence and drug use levels. The institution received a body scanner after being given the most severe warning from the prison's inspectorate, while HMP Bedford, which received the same warning, did not.

The research by Reform also found prisons in poor condition, being overcrowded, and struggling to retain experienced staff. The report argued that using short-term prison sentences was counterintuitive and contributed to overcrowding in the prison population. Analysis of official figures showed that the use of community sentences for minor offences had decreased by 52% since 2010, despite evidence that they are more effective and around a ninth of the annual cost of prisons. The think tank recommended that the Ministry of Justice consider banning or reducing short custodial sentences.

Treatment programmes and drug testing have not eradicated drugs in prison and probably never will. Prescription drugs and heroin, which clears the body quickly, are favoured to get around random mandatory drug tests. Drug addicts are given heroin substitutes such as methadone and Subutex, a brand of opioid buprenorphine, and these can be traded. I remember an inmate telling me that the dosage supplied of methadone was too low, and he had to buy other drugs to satisfy his habit.

Drugs enter prisons in a variety of ways. Offenders released on temporary licences smuggle in contraband, as do some staff. Visitors conceal drugs wrapped in cling film in body orifices (known as "plugging" or "crutching") or in babies' nappies, then slip them to prisoners in cups of tea or crisp packets. Drugs are thrown over prison walls, concealed in tennis balls or dead pigeons. Some arrive by post as not all letters are scanned. The prison drug market does not run on cash. Small sales are generally paid for with tobacco or other items from the canteen, bought with prisoners' limited earnings or with money sent from outside. Drugs tend to sell in prison for about ten times the street price. Large transactions are usually coordinated externally. Technology makes that easier. Mobile banking apps mean convicted dealers can manage payments made outside the prison before doling out drugs. Satellite maps on smartphones facilitate placing a package over the walls. Prisoners are not supposed to have mobile phones, but these are also smuggled in. The flow of drugs could undoubtedly be reduced. Visits could take place in partitioned rooms. Intimate searches could be performed on all visitors. Prisoners could spend more time locked up in their cells and kept out of exercise yards. Windows could always be locked and barred. In my opinion it would be better to reform the laws on drugs and manage their distribution. That would eliminate the violence and debt associated with the trade and reduce the cost of sending people to prison.

My third observation deals with the fact that over half of prisoners reporting an alcohol problem also reported a drug problem, with an extra 44% saying they also had an emotional or mental health issue. Alcoholism is a significant problem both inside and outside of prison. A survey by the Inspectorate of Prisons in 2012 found that 60% of those entering prison with an alcohol problem left custody with their addiction not addressed. Drugs have always been a problem and will continue as the police are underfunded and understaffed. All parties in Westminster have tried to tackle the problem, but the problem is getting worse.

The drug problem—both inside prisons and outside, needs an all-party group to take a serious look at this growing problem and consider following the system in Portugal, where in 2001 the country decriminalised the usage of drugs for personal use, and now hardly anyone dies from a drug overdose. The country has three overdose deaths per million citizens, compared to the EU average of 17.3. Weed, cocaine, heroin, you name it— Portugal decided to treat possession and use of small quantities of these drugs as a public health issue, not a criminal one. The drugs were still illegal, of course. But now, getting caught with them meant a small fine and maybe a referral to a drug treatment program—not jail time and a criminal record.

In my opinion, if an addict could legally buy weed for £2, the drug pushers would go out of business, and the gang mentality and knife crime would be drastically reduced. The quality of the weed would be better than the illegal type, and it can be grown in the UK. From my time as a prison counsellor, I have seen the problem caused by drugs, drinking, gambling, and other addictions getting worse. I believe any addiction should be treated as a mental health problem, and addicts should be forced to attend and follow an addition correction course. If they don't, the police can request that the addict be sectioned, like the sanction used on severe mental health sufferers. No section of the community should be forgotten, and groups such as people without housing and ex-military should be treated with dignity under the new addiction laws. If this were to happen, we wouldn't need to spend millions on building new prisons, as half of our current stock would be vacant.

Update: September 2023.
I'm pleased to report that the usage of drugs in UK prisons has slightly reduced according to a report by the UK Gov. This report can be seen at https://data.justice.gov.uk/prisons *There are plans in the government White Paper—proposals for future laws—including assessing every new inmate for drug addiction upon arrival. Ministers say the "stringent targets" will hold prison governors to account. More can be seen on this at* https://www.bbc.co.uk/news/uk-59557786

***

Chapter 9. Bullying.

Sean Williams is 25 years and single from Bletchley, which is now part of the new city of Milton Keynes. Sean was a good-looking young man and could be a double of the pop singer Ed Sheeran. He was just under 6 feet, and like his look-a-like Ed, he also had wavy ginger hair. Sean was serving four years for GBH and had many problems adjusting to prison life when he arrived. I had moved him three times since his arrival 18 months ago as being a 'pretty boy' he was always picked upon by older and heavier inmates. With more and more inmates ending up on my list, I had only briefly spoken to Sean in his first year, but I had a duty to try and understand what led him to my door and try and find an exit route for him so that he didn't come back.

As with all the inmates, I asked Sean 'what had led to him being sent to prison for GBH.' He said that 'it all started when he was a young child. He was the only son of a single mother and grew up on the Pond's estate in Bletchley.' I had heard of the estate before, so I knew he would have had a tough time growing up. The estate was originally built to house some families who were being relocated from the overcrowded estates in east London before being swamped by the new city of Milton Keynes. You were sent to the Ponds estate if hell was full. Problem families from around the Bletchley area who had been evicted from other more excellent estates ended up on the Ponds estate, and it had become a dumping ground for problem families. It had a high proportion of single-parent families, with over 66 per cent living off benefits. Sean said that 'he was bullied horrifically throughout 5th and sixth grade. I got bullied because I had terrible anxiety attacks, and I also had nervous tics. The boy sitting beside me in math class noticed and asked me about it, but I ignored him. A while later, one of my best friends and I walked out of our class and saw another one of our classmates who was almost in tears. I asked him why he was sad, and it took a lot of asking before he told me that he was being bullied and couldn't stand it any longer. I asked him if he told a teacher about it, but he said he had, but all the teacher said that I was to ignore it as every school had bullies and there was little anyone could do about it. In school, we stuck together, but it was the journey home that the bullying really got bad.

They would wait with their friends and catch you in one of the narrow streets on the estate, and as there were about 8 of them, I had to take it. The bullying continued, and to console me, my mum got me a kitten who became my best friend. I could talk to it every night in my bedroom, and surprisingly, it just sat on my bed and listened. One night in December, I was walking home from school, and again the bullies were waiting for me, but this time they had hold of my kitten and were making it cry out in pain. I went berserk but didn't stand a chance as they outnumbered me 8 to 1. They held me down after hitting and kicking me, and their gang leader told me that I shouldn't have tried to hit them as they saw it as a sign of disrespect, and I would have to pay the price. Before I could realise what was happening, the leader they called Freddy had a knife in his right hand, and he held my kitten dangling from its rear legs in his other hand. As I screamed at him to let my kitten go, he just looked at me and laughed while he slit my best friend's throat. He threw the kitten over a hedge leading down to the railway embankment. I knew there was nothing I could do, and after telling my mum what had happened, she said that we would move out, and I ended up living with my mother's relatives in Norfolk.'

He told me he attended the Smithton High School in Hunstanton, Norfolk, and it was like living in a different country. I soon made friends and had a new way of life. With a great beach that stretched for miles when the tide was out, I spent most summers swimming and having fun with all my new friends. I did well at my new school and was a star pupil, with all my exam results being B+ or above. I then went to University and passed out with a degree in Mathematics. With good results, I could apply for a wide range of jobs and decided to join Barclays Bank, which offered me a position in Cromer, where I became deputy branch manager.

When I was 22, my mother died from breast cancer, and I was very lonely. When we moved to Norfolk, I had relatives we stayed with for about four months before renting a private house. A year after moving to my new home, my uncle and his family returned to Newport Pagnell, a small town on the northern edge of the new Milton Keynes city. I visited them a few times, and Newport Pagnell retained much of its original charm and was different from the pond's estate in Bletchley. With my mother now gone, I wanted to move to Newport Pagnell so that I had at least some relatives to whom I owed so much. I asked the regional manager at Barclays if any posts were becoming available around the Newport Pagnell area – but not in Bletchley and he said he would look and get back to me. As luck would have it, they had a deputy manager position available in Olney - famous for its pancake race on Shrove Tuesday, which had been run since 1445. It was also known for its renowned Cowper and Newton Museum, which celebrates the unique literary heritage of two men, and the place where the hymn 'Amazing Grace' was written. I accepted straight away.'

My uncle said, 'I could stay with them until I found a flat, as Olney was only 7 miles north of Newport Pagnell. He said that he knew the small market town of Olney well, as he had a good friend who lived there as a teenager. He said that his friend Richard Soul was a great mate as his dad owned the local private coach company, and he got his first car after passing his driving test when he was just turned 17. He said that after they had been to the pictures in Newport Pagnell, he was driving us home, and we got stopped by a young police officer. He could see that Richard was rather young, and I bet he didn't think he had passed his test. He stopped us and asked Richard if he had his driving license with him, but he said he had left it at home. You could see the half smile on the young copper's face thinking that he had heard that one before, so he asked him for his name and date of birth. He said R Soul, and he wasn't given time to state his date of birth as the copper pulled him out of the car and pushed him to the ground and handcuffed him. After he had done that, the young copper's sergeant got out of the police car wondering what the hell was going on, and he looked at my mate in handcuffs and said hello Richard, how's your father keeping? He asked the young copper what the problem was, and he said that he had asked the young man for his name and date of birth, and then he swore at him. The sergeant asked what swear word he used, and the young copper whispered arsehole. The Sergeant nearly fell over laughing, and when he got control back, he told the young copper to un-cuff Richard and let him go on his way. The younger cop did as he was told, and as we were driving away, I looked back and could see the young coppers face turning to a bright shade of red.' My aunty said, 'It must have been the hundredth time he had told that little story, but it always made her chuckle.'

Sean said 'everything was going great until he was out with his girlfriend in the Dolphin pub in Newport Pagnell celebrating his 23rd birthday, when he bumps into Freddy, his all-time worse enemy. Freddy didn't recognise me until I followed him into the gent's toilet in the pub. I had changed from a young teenager to a respectful young man, but when I said hello to Freddy, he still didn't recognise me.' He said, 'Who the fuck are you' and I said, 'I'm your worst nightmare. For years you had been my worst nightmare, but things changed over the years – well, for some of us, it does, as you still look like the ugly bully that killed my kitten and made every kid's life hell on the Pond estate. He tried to push past me, but I was now bigger and stronger than before, and I just pushed him back. As I did, he slipped up on the wet toilet floor and banged the back of his head on one of the urinals. Blood was everywhere, and some must have slashed onto my boot after I kicked him when he was out cold on the toilet floor. I said that kick was from my little kitten, you bastard. He didn't move, so I grabbed my girlfriend and walked her home. She knew something was wrong, and I couldn't lie to her, so I told her everything.' She said, 'We must call for an ambulance, or he could lay there for a long time and die.' 'I tried to tell her not to, but she has always been brighter than me, and she did the right thing. Old Freddy thankfully survived and, when he regained consciousness, told the police that I had beaten him up, and he gave them my name. The rest is history. Old Freddy tried to get compensation, but the case had gained so much publicity in the Milton Keynes Citizen that over 50 locals came forward and said that Freddy and his gang had also bullied them. He decided to drop the case. I'm sorry for what I did, but it was an accident, but my biggest crime was not calling an ambulance the minute it happened. The judge said that if I had done so, the charge of GBH would never have reached the court. He said he was sympathetic to my story, but as I had pleaded guilty to the charge, he could only pass the smallest sentence for GBH, which was four years.

Sean said that he was glad that the national press and several magazines had picked up the case as it might just send a message out to all bullies that roles change, and they could quickly be bullied themselves. Sean also said that the bank would keep his job open as they had read about the cause of the accident and noted that many good people spoke up for him in court, and my work record was outstanding.' I'm glad I had a chance to listen to Sean's story, and it was rare to have an inmate that wasn't an addict, and as his job would be waiting for him when he was released, no training was needed.

However, he offered to speak to any inmate who needed mathematical education and explain what banks did and how they helped others with loans and mortgages. I took Sean up on his offer, and he helped a lot of fellow inmates who never grasped simple maths whilst at school. I couldn't help considering why society allows estates like the Ponds to get so bad. Surely it would be better to restrict entry to such estates to one road only. This would be controlled like a gated estate and have a security system with more CCTV's covering every angle. If someone wanted to enter the estate, they would need to seek permission and state where they were going. They wouldn't be allowed entry if they didn't have an answer. If they lied just to get access, security would track them via the CCTV, and if they were seen to be dealing, they would be arrested when trying to leave. I checked on Sean after his release, and he had returned to his old job, and his girlfriend had waited for him, and they were now planning their wedding. I declined an invitation to the wedding as I had a heist to arrange, but I didn't mention that to Sean.

Update September 2023.
I came across this fix to end bullying in schools as no child should be bullied and the excuse of "it's part of growing up" should be a thing of the past.

Julie-Annes Law.
Children have always been bullied in schools but a seven-year-old girl who lived in Spalding came up with a way to stop bullies in her school. Julie-Annes mother was a school governor, and this helped her to set up her anti-bullying campaign in her school.

Each school year should be given a form so they could nominate the pupil they want to become that years Anti-Bullying Prefect. The headteacher will then let the pupils know who had gained the most votes.

If any child was being bullied, then they should tell the Anti-Bullying Prefect who would then take it up with the headteacher on a weekly basis.
The pupil(s) who was doing the bullying would be dealt with by the headteacher. A letter would be posted to the bullies' parents informing the parent that if the pupil did not mend their ways, then they would be expelled for 7 days and if the bullying continued then they would be permanently expelled.
The headteacher would make all pupils aware that any bullying of the named Anti-Bullying prefect would be treated very severely and could end up with permanent expulsion of the bully.

***

Chapter 10. Prison and IPP.

During my many years working in the prison service, I have seen many cases where the inmate has been treated harshly, and many given sentences well below the level to fit their crime. Still, there was one group of prisoners that I felt sorry for: those placed on the IPP system instead of being given a set prison term to serve. IPP, which is short for Indeterminate sentence for Public Protection (IPP), is a complicated system, and for you to understand how IPP came to sit on our statute books, you'll need to read the short history behind IPP. Still, briefly, this is the history behind this crackpot idea. In 1997, Tony Blair led his Labour Party to a landslide victory. While in opposition, Labour had talked about putting the prison system to rights. In 1993, when Blair was shadow home secretary, he said: 'The purpose of any justice system should not just be to punish and deter, but also to rehabilitate, for the good of society as well as the criminal.' Once in power, though, Labour changed its tune. As shadow home secretary, Blair had promised to be 'tough on crime, tough on the underlying causes of crime'—but, in my opinion, as prime minister, he stayed true only to the first part of that pledge.

Thousands of new laws were introduced, which increased the prison population by 20,000. The Labour government seemed intent on slapping every kid on a deprived estate with Anti-Social Behaviour Orders (ASBOs). But in my book, the worst offence came with the introduction in 2005 of Indeterminate sentences for Public Protection (IPPs), a scheme dreamed up by David Blunkett. The idea was that high-risk criminals, mainly convicted of violent or sexual offences, would be given a tariff instead of a fixed-term sentence. They could only be released at the end of that tariff if the Parole Board was satisfied that they could be managed safely in the community. If not, they stayed in jail. However, the judiciary went beyond the stated remit of IPPs. Between 2005 and 2012, when the sentence was abolished, 8,711 prisoners were given IPPs. Most of those had tariffs of four years or less, which showed that the offences were off the scale of seriousness for which IPPs were supposedly brought in.

The plight of James Ward, who has served 11 years in jail after initially being sentenced with an IPP to a minimum of ten months for arson in 2006, is just the latest case to be highlighted—he is now due to be released shortly. As of November 2019, years after IPPs were abolished, 2,223 people are serving IPP sentences, and a further 1,206 serving an IPP sentence are back in prison, having been recalled while on licence. Despite its abolition in 2012, 93% serving an IPP sentence are still in prison, having passed their tariff expiry date. This is not because the Parole Board considers them a threat (though some may well be) but because the system cannot cope with the logistics of putting these prisoners through the required release process. Before satisfying the Parole Board, IPP prisoners must complete an offending behaviour course, but many are still waiting to participate in such classes. Not all prisons run the required methods, and prisoners can wait months or years for transfer to a jail that does. The Prisoners' Advice Service, which helps many in this situation, told me that some of their IPP clients experience cognitive difficulties, making it challenging to complete the behaviour course.

The chair of the Parole Board, Nick Hardwick, was appointed in March 2016. He was deeply concerned about the IPP situation and has made progress since he took charge, hearing more cases in less time. 2017 has seen more IPP prisoners released than any year since they came into being. However, he said the situation is still unacceptable and cites the high level of suicide and self-harm among those caught up in this shameful legal limbo. Unfortunately, in 2018, Nick Hardwick resigned as judges overturned a decision to release the rapist John Worboys from jail. One lady that writes about the prison system is Polly Toynbee, a British journalist and writer who has been a columnist for *The Guardian* newspaper since 1998. Polly, whose real name is Mary Louisa Toynbee, wrote an article, 'Tough on Crime', which created the prison crisis. 'It's time for justice to be rational.' The article stated that Tony Blair liked 'eye-catching' anti-crime announcements, and Labour made over 3,500 new criminal offences in 50 criminal justice bills. In an issue of *Inside Time*, the national newspaper for prisoners and detainees, Nick Hardwick, proposed that the rules of this cruel game should be changed. He says that for those with a tariff of two years or fewer, the onus should be on the state to prove they are likely to commit another offence rather than on the prisoner to show that they are not. Hardwick, the former chief inspector of prisons, is a good and humane man whom I am loathed to disagree with—but I do on this. Change the rules, but let the state prove danger in all these cases. The state created this lousy logjam and should use its executive power to free those undeservedly trapped.

During my time as a prison counsellor, several IPP inmates were on my list, but there was little I could do for these inmates as I had no release date to work with. With over 3,000 IPP prisoners still behind bars, the system not only makes our prisons overcrowded but costs the state over £1.35 billion yearly to keep them locked up. It's about time the government listened to people such as Polly Toynbee and organisations such as the Howard League and set up a plan to tackle problems such as IPP, drug addiction and alcoholism. If they did this, we wouldn't need to spend billions of pounds (money we don't have) on building new prisons, and save on prison staff's salary and pension costs, as just a few changes could make a big difference. In my opinion, it would be worth testing new rules for prisoners with an addiction. If they had not been clean of their addiction for six months, they shouldn't be released, as figures show that they have a higher chance of reoffending if not 100% clean.

Update September 2023.

In an article by Jessica Murray in the Guardian on Feb 9, 2023, she reported that the UK government rejects call to resentence prisoners detained indefinitely. She went on to state that almost 3,000 people were still behind bars in England and Wales under 'imprisonment for public protection' scheme abolished in 2012. Sir Bob Neill, a Conservative MP and chair of the justice committee, said the government had "missed an opportunity to right a wrong that has left nearly 3,000 people behind". This sorry state of affairs needs fixing but for some unknown reason the justice secretary, Dominic Raab, needs to fine an answer instead of wasting millions every year of taxpayers money. Jessica's article can be read by going to https://www.theguardian.com/society/2023/feb/09/uk-government-rejects-call-resentence-prisoners-detained-indefinitely

***

Chapter 11. Muslim Inmates and Illegal Immigrants.

We have all faiths and nationalities in prison, and we try to assist in all beliefs with prayer times, diet, et cetera, but many prisoners do try to go too far. I will never forget Mohammed Alfresi, who originated from Saudi Arabia. He pushed and pushed, trying to change the way we ran things. He was serving a five-year sentence for fraud as he was caught trying to pass himself off as a Saudi Prince, and not paying his hotel bill in some of the top London hotels. I had had my fill with his constant moaning, and I told him, 'If you don't like our system, the UK has just agreed to a prisoner exchange with Saudi Arabia, and if you wish, I could place you first on the exchange list.'

It took him only a nano-second to say no, as he knew you wouldn't wish for your worst enemy to be a prisoner in a Saudi jail. I clarified where I stood and told him he should stop moaning about how bad it was for Muslims in the U.K. I told him that if I visited Saudi Arabia (the home of Islam), I couldn't pray in a church as churches were not allowed, yet he had a choice of nearly 400 mosques in the UK. If I wanted to take a Bible into the home of Islam, it would be binned at the airport. Yet, he could read, buy, or borrow a copy of the Quran anywhere in the U.K. Once out of prison, he could visit any city in the UK, yet as a non-muslin, I would be barred from many cities in his ideal land. I told him that it doesn't matter what church, mosque, or synagogue you worship in, as we all worship one God. The faith that worries me the most is atheism, as atheists only worship themselves. I finished by saying that if I heard any more whinging from him, I would prioritise adding him to the exchange prisoner list. I have never heard another thing from him since.

Catering for ethnic minorities is a continuing struggle as we cater to all religions and their diets. At the end of March 2018, just under half of the prison population was of the Christian faith (48%)—a decrease of just over ten percentage points compared to June 2002. The proportion of Muslim prisoners, however, has increased from 8% in 2002 to 16% in 2018. The ratio of prisoners without religion in 2019, 30%, decreased slightly from 31.5% in 2002.

Also, at the end of March 2019, just over 9,000 foreign nationals were within the prison population. Foreign nationals came from 161 different countries. Of that, 9,000 from Europe accounted for the most significant proportion of the prison population, 43% from European Economic Area (EEA) and 11% from non-EEA European countries. Those from Africa (18%) and Asia (12%) contributed the second and third most significant proportion respectively.

Diet is also a significant challenge as we must cater for all religions. Prisoners are given a minimum of five choices for dinner each night under new guidelines. Inmates can choose their dinner from menus, which are varied frequently so that there is a different range of options for every day in each month. Every menu must contain at least one hot, cold, vegetarian, dairy-free and halal option, while the menu must meet prisoners' 'cultural, nutritional and diversity needs. It's the Halal option which worries me most. I have dealt with a few former butchers that have passed my door, and some of them wanted to be assured that they were not being fed 'Halal' meat as they were firmly against how the animals are slaughtered. 85% of animals are slaughtered humanely in the UK by stunning (electric shock to the brain) the animal first before killing the animal. Halal slaughter means no stunning; the animal's throat is slit while the animal is still conscious. According to the butcher, without stunning, all the muscles (the meat we eat) tighten up due to the shock, and you end up with very tough meat. Fred Griffin, one such butcher and a Sunday preacher, said that the Bible, Genesis 1:26, states, "God said, Let us make man in our image, after our likeness. And let them have dominion over the fish of the sea and the birds of the heavens, over the livestock and all the earth and every creeping thing that creeps on the earth." Fred also quoted Proverbs 27:23. "God requires the merciful treatment and humane care of these creatures of His." Fred was adamant that slitting an animal's throat was anything but merciful. He also informed me that all animals and birds slaughtered in Denmark had to be stung first.

While working in prison, I was constantly being challenged by one religion or another. A work friend of mine had an uncle who worked in the Middle East, and he always followed what was happening in the region. I also took an interest, and we would discuss matters such as the Iran war, the Jewish settlement in the West Bank and so on. Even though my work friend is no longer with us, I still take an interest in anything Middle East. One story about the Middle East that linked my work friends' interest in the area and my interest in anything to do with prison was a story I had read in *The Independent* newspaper. It concerned the UK, which had always had a strong relationship with Saudi Arabia. Still, it was reported in the paper that the British government lost over a million pounds on a Ministry of Justice commercial venture that was due to run the Saudi Arabian prison system, an investigation by the National Audit Office, the Government's spending watchdog, found that Just Solutions International (JSI) had costs £2.1 million and generated an income of £1 million during its short existence. JSI, the trading face of the Ministry of Justice, was set up by civil servants in 2012 to bid for commercial contracts abroad using UK state expertise. In the autumn of 2015, Michael Gove, the then newly appointed Conservative Justice Secretary, wound up the venture and pulled out of contracts in countries with poor human rights records, such as Saudi Arabia and Oman. To me, it beggars' belief that some non-elected civil servants could devise such a stupid scheme that cost the British taxpayer over a million pounds to provide services to a country that publically executes prisoners on a Friday morning. It does make me wonder who precisely is running the country. I thought it was the elected parliament, but the more I dig, I keep finding that the non-elected civil servants are steering the ship.

I strongly feel that Religious Education (RE) in schools should cover all the main religions and that all faiths should be taught in the same classroom with no opt-outs allowed. If this were the case, then children would leave school with an understanding of what different religions believe in and how all religions should accept and understand others.

If a non-UK person appears in court for any offence and is found guilty, they and their family should be deported from the UK. You will get people who state that this would be against their human rights and the 1951 Refugee Convention. In February 2020 the Human Rights Watch.org noted that 'In December 2019, the Conservative government set out its priorities, which include setting up a new commission to look at human rights, the judiciary, and the courts, a move its election manifesto said would ensure "a proper balance between the rights of individuals, our vital national security and effective government".'

During the weekend of the 8th of May 2020, when I was penning this section, it was shown on the BBC that over 300 refugees were rescued from an unsafe inflatable dinghy while crossing the English Channel from France. These were the ones they caught, but it was estimated that hundreds more reached the English coast undetected. The 300 plus were taken to an immigration centre to be assessed, but other illegal immigrants will head for the cities or head for a contact they knew who had previously made it to the UK.

On 14th February 2020, UK prime minister Boris Johnson's newly formed cabinet agreed to restrict the flow of low-skilled workers into Britain from January 2021. This will work the same way as the Australian system, on a point system basis. However, this won't become Law until 2021, and it will do little to correct the immigration problems that voters were facing up and down the UK in 2019. I would estimate that there are around two million illegal immigrants in the UK, and unless Boris can clear our country of these 'illegals', he will not win the next election.

Update August 2023.

The new Prime Minister Rishi Sunak carried on with this lost cause with a new catchphrase 'Stop the Boats', four years after Boris promised the same. Three Prime Ministers and two Home Secretaries later, we still allow thousands to risk their lives in small boats. It's costing you and me £6 million a day to house these illegal immigrants. A better way may be to accommodate them in refugee camps as they do in Turkey. My next novel, The Bedford Revenge, *due at the beginning of 2024, follows a Syrian family from Aleppo that falls foul of human traffickers. The novel offers a better way to deal with these immigrants, but you'll have to wait to find out what it is.*

*****

Chapter 12. UK Housing Crisis.

You may ask what the housing shortage has to do with the prison service. I can clearly state that national problems outside of prison walls usually end up inside them. Take the case of James Pringell, a lovely young man in his mid-twenties serving a 36-month sentence for theft. James wasn't married but was engaged to a local girl who had grown up with him in the small town of Wells, in a beautiful part of the north Norfolk coast.

As usual, I try to go easy on my first session, and get them to see that I'm here to help and encourage them to tell me about any problems they face while inside, and I will see what can be done. James said he had been engaged for four years, but they wanted to wait until they had a home before getting married and starting a family. He said the problem was that almost a third of all homes in the town where he lived were now second homes or holiday homes. The increasing numbers mean it is becoming even more difficult for young people to find affordable homes in the town where they grew up, as prices rocket to meet demand from out-of-town buyers. He had put his name down for a council house, but the council were no longer building homes to rent and couldn't help.

'They said that if my girlfriend got pregnant, that would move us up the waiting list,' James said. 'We are both Christians and wouldn't go against our faith to move up the property ladder. With second home buyers coming in from outside Norfolk and buying these homes, it takes them off the market for local people. It puts up the prices of property in Wells and makes them less accessible, so there is a real shortage of affordable homes. My girlfriend, who works for a local estate agent, keeps her eyes open, but even if we were to get a starter mortgage of 90%, it would still need a deposit of around £30,000. Neither of our parents had that type of money, so we didn't go on holidays, we didn't go out much, and we saved as much as we could, but at this rate, we soon realised that we would be around 40 before we could muster up that type of deposit.'

I asked James what had got him a prison sentence, and he said that in desperation he was robbing his employer to try to build up a nest egg for a mortgage deposit. He said it went well for the first six months, but as he worked as assistant manager for a large bookmaker, his employers insisted he take a two-week holiday. He said he didn't need a holiday, but they said it was company rules and he had to take two weeks off. 'I was training to become a manager, and one of my duties was to clear the cash machines at the end of the day and place the money in the safe.' He had been creaming off around £50 a day and putting that in his pocket. He hadn't realised that the machine had its in-built computer and kept a record of everything that went in and out of the device. 'It just happened to be that while I was away, the company ran a six-month audit, and it highlighted that the banking showed a shortfall of £1,300.00, and when I returned, the area manager was waiting for me.'

He said that at the court case, I explained why I was doing what I did, and the local press and TV got hold of the story and highlighted the problems facing local couples. However, when the judge made his closing statement, he instructed the jury to decide the outcome based on the evidence given, and not to base it on what they had seen or read in the local media. I was found guilty, which was the correct verdict based on the facts, and the judge said that he was disturbed by the realities of my case, but the law is the law, and as this was a controlled theft going on for six months, he had to pass a custodial sentence. James said the situation that had led him to my door would still be there when he left. The problem would, however, be much more challenging as now he had a prison sentence, and no one would trust him where money was involved. He had been ordered to pay the money back, and the state had to keep him locked up and provide him with a bed, food, and water at a cost to the taxpayer of £47,000 each year, so nothing good would become of any of it.

More on James's story can be found at the end of this book under 'Afterword: Chapter 12. UK Housing Crisis'.

Update September 2023.
I wrote back in 2019 that without people moving up the property ladder there would come a time when homes left by those who had passed would stand empty and prices would start to fall. In March, the Office for Budget Responsibility, which advises the government on the health of the economy, predicted that house prices will drop by 10% over the next two years. The current high Mortgage rates are putting off new buyers and many building societies are predicting the prices will stop falling in 2026 but unless we increase the number of homes to rent and build more affordable homes then we are all in for a rough ride.

***

Chapter 13. Austerity.

The nine years of austerity left many people earning less and less each year, and people looked at other ways to make ends meet, and many resulted in breaking the law. Many were caught and ended up in prison. Others wanted to make the Conservative government listen to their concerns, and several protests brought London to a standstill. One such case was Lewis Norton, aged 42, married with two teenage children, who came under my wing after he had been sent to prison for 32 months for GBH. He was a colossal chap who reminded me of 'Big Daddy', a famous wrestler from the past who had blue eyes and a good crop of hair that he tied back in a ponytail during the day.

Lewis was sent to me for counselling, but I'm not sure I could do much for him apart from place him in our anger management program. He had worked as a radiologist for the NHS at Northampton General Hospital for the past 20 years. Even with a criminal record, he would get back into work as there is a shortage of radiologists across the UK. I asked Lewis to explain why he had been found guilty of GBH. He said, 'I'm normally not a troublemaker and, due to my size, I seldom get picked on,' although he had to admit that he looked like a prime target for any drunk or drugged-up youngster looking for a fight. He said that he had always been big and had once gone to the Northampton Saints Academy rugby school, but after an accident on the pitch where he had crushed a disc, he had decided to give up the sport that he loved. He said that he and his wife Sharon worked for the NHS, and while the kids were growing up, he had worked a different shift pattern than his wife so that one could take care of the children. However, this put a strain on his marriage as they seldom had time together, though they stuck together for the children's sake. Neither he nor his wife was overpaid when you considered the unsociable hours that they worked, and they had both taken a pay cut over the past nine years due to a pay freeze cap of just 1% per year, which wasn't keeping pace with inflation. So, in real terms, they were working longer for less with each year that passed. He said that the UK Conservative government had set the pay cap of 1% after the terrible world banking crisis in 2008. The problem was that the cap only applied to certain groups that fell under the 'public sector', and many workers were part of the Austerity measures. The country still paid some footballers thousands of pounds every week for kicking a ball around for 90 minutes every weekend, and you also had bankers paying themselves bonuses of millions every year, even when their company was making a loss. Lewis stated, 'Austerity could only work if it applies to everyone.' I said to him that 'I also worked in the public sector and had to stick with an increase of 1% for the last nine years,' but I had to admit that I knew very little about Austerity, and asked Lewis to explain to me, in layman's terms, what it was all about.

His reply got me thinking about the measures and whether they ever worked. He said, 'Austerity is a political-economic term referring to policies that aim to reduce government budget deficits through spending cuts, tax increases, or a combination of both. Austerity measures are used by governments that struggle to pay their debts. The measures are meant to reduce the budget deficit by bringing government revenues closer to expenditures, which is assumed to make debt payment easier. Austerity measures also demonstrate a government's fiscal discipline to creditors and credit rating agencies.'

Lewis went on to explain that there isn't any proof that Austerity works. 'There was an interesting program on the BBC a few years ago that looked at other EU countries who had jumped on the Austerity bandwagon, and examined how they were performing. The countries involved were the UK, Ireland, Portugal, Spain, Greece and Cyprus. All were forced to borrow money to save their country's banking system after the time bomb went off in 2007/2008. Greece was the first, and its problems have been the longest-lasting, mainly down to the

Greek government allegedly giving misleading financial information so that that they could become a member of the EU, and then manipulating the figures to mask the extent of its deficit right up to the time when the credit crunch exposed its deep-rooted problems. All the governments, in turn, needed to be bailed out because they ran out of money or could not borrow it in the financial markets at a reasonable price, but they have, as a result, reformed their economies. The world money lenders wouldn't loan money unless the country took severe Austerity measures to bring their borrowing down.'

Inflated property prices worldwide caused a colossal property bubble, which burst, throwing the world economy into a prolonged downturn. Lewis said he wasn't surprised to see that, after years of Austerity measures which mainly affected the working classes, countries were still in a big mess. In his opinion, governments needed to raise more in taxes from the people who could afford to pay them most, and this was the rich, who paid a tax rate of 45% on earnings over £150,000. The previous Labour government raised the top income tax rate from 40% to 50% in 2010, but the Conservative government reduced the top rate to 45% in 2012. Effectively, the coalition government had given the richest people in the country a huge tax cut by scrapping the 50% top rate. Lewis, a very clever mathematician, said that when the Conservatives came to power in 1979, Margaret Thatcher's government reduced the top income tax rate from 83% to 60%. This was reduced again in 1988 to 40%, and the 'higher rate' fluctuated between 40 and 50%.

If all income over £150,000 was taxed at 60% for the next five years, it could make a tremendous difference to the country's bank balance. All payments should be included, including earnings from overseas, and the Non-Dom system should be scrapped. Anyone holding a British passport should be taxed at the correct rate; if this were done, then Austerity could work for the first time. The government's HMRC should set up a separate police force to ensure that everyone is paying their correct taxes, and a law should be introduced where advisors would also be responsible for their actions. If they advise a client how to evade paying their taxes, they themselves would face a heavy fine or a jail sentence. The whole system is in serious need of reform, and this should be a priority for the government after the Covid-19 shambles has been sorted.

I thanked Lewis for his reply and asked him to explain further why he had ended up sitting where he is today. He replied that he went on an NHS protest march past Number 10. 'The riot police were trying to stop us from protesting in front of the Houses of Parliament. The police had estimated around 100,000 protestors, but an estimated 500,000 protested. I was at the front of the crowd, and when we reached the barricade, the force of protestors pushing from behind meant that the barrier soon collapsed as we were pushed forward. Police horses were introduced, but the crowd was pushing so hard from behind that the police officers on the horses started to use their batons to strike protestors on the back. They managed to hit a lady standing next to me, and she hit the ground hard, and I picked her up before she got trampled on. The only way to go was forward, and I then came up against the horse riders and their batons. Rather than being hit, I had no option but to grab the baton, and in doing so, I pulled the policeman from his horse, and he landed badly on the curb, and severely damaged his lower back. I never intended to harm anyone, I was just protecting myself and the lady I was carrying. However, I think the judge had been told to come down hard on any protestors, as the government knew there would be many more protests in the months ahead. As I looked like the Gentle Green Giant when standing in the dock, it was assumed that because of my size I was a thug; the judge put me away for 32 months.'

Lewis also stated that he wanted to get out and back to work as soon as possible. With Brexit, several qualified radiologists from across the EU left and moved elsewhere. I knew then that I wouldn't invite Lewis to my heist in Bedford.

***

Chapter 14. Brexit.

Following on from Chapter 13, on Austerity, Lewis asked if it would be OK for him to ask me a question. I said it would be, but I don't have an answer for everything. He grinned and said he doubted that from what he had heard about me from fellow inmates. He asked me what I thought would happen with Brexit. Well, I told Lewis that I had voted to stay in the EU, but the country had decided that it wanted to leave. The initial campaign was poorly run, and the facts were unclear to British voters. I also believe that if the EU had met David Cameron's demands on open borders, we would not be leaving.

I can see the problem first-hand as the number of Eastern Europeans now being convicted should have never been let into the country in the first place. I told Lewis, 'I have friends who live in Boston, Lincolnshire, and locals were scared to venture out as groups of Eastern Europeans loitered about the town day and night. Not all are bad but loads came to our country without any respect for our laws. You only have to read the court reports in any Lincolnshire newspaper, and you'll see how many are facing the judge. You'll see loads from Poland, Romania, Latvia, and other eastern EU countries filling the pages. It was made worse by the government not providing enough funds to cover the extra cost of social housing, education, the NHS, and other vital services. In my opinion, the government should introduce a new law, and if a non-UK passport holder is found guilty in a UK court, they and their family should be deported back to their country.'

What made matters worse was that the EU couldn't help but see the horror stories of refugees drowning in the Mediterranean Sea, and the EU felt it should help. You didn't see the flimsy boats being confiscated or the traffickers being arrested and thrown in jail. They could take themselves and their boats back and forth repeatedly. If the EU had done this, then I believe that the numbers would have been reduced dramatically. And instead of allowing the refugees into the EU, it would have been better for the EU to pay countries such as Turkey to erect proper refugee camps until the wars in their own countries had been settled and it was safe to return.

In my opinion, what the EU can't allow is for Britain to be let off lightly for wanting to leave, as if they allowed this to happen, then other countries would also want out. I'm not a gambling man, but I bet the people would also vote to leave if there were an open vote in France and Germany. An EU without the likes of France and Germany wouldn't work. I felt sorry for the politicians trying to cut a deal, stuck between a rock and a hard place. During 2017, 2018 and 2019, the arguments within the Conservative Party were shameful, when they should all be supporting their fellow MPs, who are only trying to honour the wishes of the British people.

The Labour Party was also, in my opinion, out of touch with reality and was set on preventing a no-deal from happening. The Labour Party, under the poor hard-left leadership of Jeremy Corbyn, would have done better to push for a second referendum rather than play into Boris Johnson's hands, where he knew that he would win a general election when he called it. The Labour Party could have also voted for the leave deal that the Conservatives under Boris had managed to get from the EU rather than face a general election. If they had done that, they could have played a part in getting the best deal for Britain instead of handing Boris a winning hand. What the Labour and Liberal parties failed to understand was how the influx of foreigners from both the EU and around the world had changed our country. Foreigners had conquered many cities and towns, and the British public had had enough. Boris won the 2019 election with a large majority, as his key message was 'Get Brexit Done'. Voters thought voting Tory would stop the boats and the massive influx of immigrants. It did neither. One of the first things Boris did was introduce an immigration bill which would, from 2021, work on a points system like that of

Australia. Boris forgot that this would do little to correct the current immigration problem that enabled the Conservatives to win with a large majority. Unless he can fix his mistake and weed out the hundreds of thousands of illegal immigrants by the next election, the North will revert to Labour, and the country could end up with a hung parliament. Those who think Brexit has been done are in for a rude awakening once the coronavirus pandemic has been resolved.

If the EU want a hard exit, then let the European politicians meet face to face with thousands of car workers at Alfa Romeo, Audi, BMW, Citroen, Mercedes-Benz and Volkswagen, who will lose some of their jobs as the UK would be forced to place a 10% import levy on car imports resulting in layoffs. I have a friend who works for one of the leading German brands, and he told me that business had already slowed down as people were scared that the import levy on car parts would increase costs by 20%. It would not be easy to sell once they wanted to replace their car in a few years. What a mess the EU is in.

Austerity measures that underfunded the NHS, Police, and local government for nearly a decade have now been promised extra funding by Boris. The NHS will get 40 new hospitals by 2030 and fix the staff shortage as soon as possible. Police will bring 20,000 new plods, which will only replace the numbers lost under austerity. Underfunding of local governments has pushed councils to breaking point, but Boris has promised councils more money in years to come. Yet, if you ask Boris whether Austerity worked, he will tell you it had worked.

Update August 2023
The BBC reported on 4 July 2022 that the NHS won't get 40 new hospitals. The Nuffield Trust, a health think tank, did the same research. It defines a 'new' hospital as 'a new building on an entirely new site'. If you use this definition, you find that:
Twenty-two are rebuilding projects.
Twelve are new wings within existing hospitals.

Three involve rebuilding non-urgent care hospitals.

Three are new hospitals (two general hospitals and one non-urgent care hospital).

Police will bring 20,000 new plods. This is true, but you need to remember that thousands of police officers have resigned since this announcement, and the 20,000 figure will keep the statistics about the same level as the 2019 figures.

I concluded that Lewis had been in the wrong place at the wrong time, and he wasn't a threat to society, and I would push for an early release so that he could get back to working for the NHS where he belonged. I decided that I wouldn't invite him to my heist in Bedford as he would turn the invitation down.

***

Chapter 15. Covid-19.

Nearly everything that happens outside the prison walls seems to find a way to land at our gates, and Covid-19 was no exception. Within minutes of Rishi Sunak, the then Chancellor of the Exchequer, announcing the measure of financial help the government would give to the 5 million self-employed people, criminals were hard at work making false claims. The Chancellor wanted to match the 80% figure he had set in place for those who had proper jobs and were paid via the PAYE system, as the government already knew who these claimants were. The problem with the self-employed was that not all of them had been in business long enough to have a track record with the government's tax department, HM Revenue & Customs (HMRC), and would find it difficult to claim. Add to this those working in the gig community or those on zero-hour contracts, there is no easy way for those workers to claim either sick pay or get 80% of their previous monthly wages under the Coronavirus Job Retention Scheme. According to the latest Office for National Statistics (ONS) figures, 974,000 Brits were on zero-hour contracts in December 2019—a record high.

The DWP received a million new claims a week after announcing the safety net. Without a safe way for the Government's DWP overworked staff to check every claimant, benefit fraud will hit a record high. What the Government should learn from this deadly saga is that the gig community and zero-hour contracts should be banned, and everyone should pay taxes via the PAYE system.

Updated September 2023.
*Once this book was published, I sent a copy and backed it up with a separate letter raising this point to the then Chancellor of the Exchequer, Rishi Sunak. He ignored my warning letter, and as a result, **£21 billion** of public money has been lost due to fraud since the COVID pandemic began, and most will never be recovered. The National Audit Office (NAO) revealed the*

staggering increase in money lost due to fraud since the pandemic hit compared to a few years before, and it says it is 'doubtful' that the bulk of the taxpayers' money will ever be recovered. Levels of fraud rose almost fourfold from £5.5bn two years before the pandemic to £21bn in the following two years. Since his time as Chancellor, the Conservative Party thought he did well by making him Prime Minster. I can't help thinking he would have been more careful if it had been his family's billions he was spending.

Further Update: 31-10-2023.

The Covid 19 enquiry heard revelations from No10 aides, during which it was claimed that Boris Johnson said the elderly should "accept their fate" as Covid swept the country. It also emerged that Mr Cummings branded Cabinet members "f***pigs" and called for Matt Hancock to be sacked, claiming his incompetence was "killing people". IMO Boris Johnson, Matt Hancock, and Rishi Sunak (who was chancellor of the exchequer in 2020) should be charged with negligence of duty as their poor decisions cost around 236,000 lives. For this exercise I assume that 150,000 were pensioners but it could be more. Was it down to saving money as the state pension in 2020 was £175.20 a week, times that by 150,000 x 52 weeks it comes to a staggering sum of money saved each and every year. If you also consider old people in care homes at a cost of around £750.00 a week it must have been like winning the lottery ten times over.

***

Another observation regarding Covid-19 that worries me is how the Chinese communist government could trace any Chinese person who said anything about the virus that wasn't in step with party propaganda, and the individual was soon arrested. How can the British government allow Chinese companies like Huawei (state-owned) to be part of the new G5 telecoms network in the UK even though Boris's friend Mr Trump had warned him against doing so? I firmly believe that the Coronavirus (Covid-19) was a gift from China that will kill millions worldwide. It is alleged that the virus resulted from

Chinese peasants eating dogs and other wild animals. There were also rumours that the virus was man-made in China as a form of biological warfare in retaliation to America banning the G5 Huawei in the country's next generation of super-fast wireless networks, and in retaliation at the trade tariffs placed on imports to the USA from China.

What concerns many Westerners is the way the Chinese authorities dealt with Dr Li Wenliang, who had posted to a group chat with other medics about some patients showing signs of a new SARS-like illness in early December 2019, well before Chinese authorities admitted to the outbreak of a novel coronavirus. According to *The Guardian* newspaper, police detained Li a few days later for 'spreading false rumours' and forced him to sign a police document admitting that he had 'seriously disrupted social order' and breached the law. Officers said eight people had been disciplined for spreading rumours about the virus, but it was not clear whether Li was one of those. A week later, the 34-year-old doctor developed a fever, and published his account online. After being diagnosed with Covid-19 at the end of January, he died of the virus in early February. His death sparked outrage in China, particularly among internet users. Censors were overwhelmed by a wave of critical posts, including some blaming the government.

China is also accused of hiding the findings of a coronavirus expert—known as 'Bat Woman'—after she quickly identified the genetic makeup of the new strain that has infected millions. Wuhan-based virologist Shi Zhengli is one of the world's top researchers on coronaviruses and has discovered dozens of deadly SARS-like viruses in bat caves. She studied samples from some of the first people to become infected with the new and then-mysterious respiratory illness in China in December 2019, and found that it was like SARS. It was identified as a novel coronavirus. Within three days, she completed its gene sequencing, finding that it was 96% identical to a virus found in horseshoe bats in Yunnan. But she was 'muzzled', and her team was ordered not to reveal any information about the new disease, which was already spreading rapidly as China kept the world in the dark. Could an accident at the Wuhan Institute of Virology release the deadly virus to the inhabitants of Wuhan and then onto the rest of the world?

Several critics also stated that according to www.ceicdata.com, China's labour productivity dropped by 6.26 % year on year in Dec 2019, compared with a growth of 6.77 % in the previous year. Some feared that the bubble had burst, and that the People's Republic of China and its Communist Party were trying to hide the country's poor performance. Other rumours include disbelief about the number of new COVID-19 cases and deaths reported by the Chinese Communist Party, mainly when they said that there were no further cases for three consecutive days. Critics also stated that the expulsion of American journalists was to hide the truth. Two nurses in Wuhan, who wished to remain anonymous because of the sensitivity of the pandemic, told *The Financial Times* of 'hidden' infections that met the national criteria for confirmed cases but were not being recognised in the city's official count, helping to keep it at or near zero. China's National Health Commission, the government agency, is very secretive regarding the figures across China. Many critics find it hard to believe that the virus can spread worldwide, yet no statistics for the country's capital Beijing can be found at the start of the pandemic.

Other Biochemical rumours stated that China was also angry that the BBC's *Panorama* program in November 2019 had highlighted the systematic brainwashing of hundreds of thousands of Muslims in a network of high-security prison camps. Official documents, seen by *Panorama*, show how inmates are locked up, indoctrinated, and punished.

As a Christian, one theory I would like to think could be true is that God sent the Coronavirus as a wake-up call to us all. The virus spread worldwide and peaked at Easter when Christians rejoiced at the crucifixion of Jesus and His rebirth on Easter Sunday, as Jesus died to save us all. I can't help but wonder at the choice of crucifixion by the Jews, as Jesus would have died from asphyxiation as the weight of His body would have made breathing impossible, as it does with Covid-19.

One of the good things to come out of the pandemic was that it made many of us appreciate the benefit of our community and that we can still help our fellow man. It reminded us about the gift of friendship and love and how love can save us all. It could also be a wake-up call on how we are killing the planet God created for us in seven days. Global warming, plastic pollution, and the destruction of countries through civil war are all things that make God sad, and we must find a way to overcome these man-made problems. God would have also noticed some people's and specific countries' sheer greed. If you look at oil production worldwide, countries such as America, Russia and Saudi Arabia have kept the price of crude oil high (pre-Covid) so that they alone could benefit. These three countries were pumping so much crude oil that they could not store it once the worldwide pandemic was in full swing, and demand dropped to a record low.

If you look at the global banking industry, you will see that they always look after number one. Bankers pay themselves millions yearly, even when their bank makes a loss. The greedy footballers are paid a fortune for kicking a ball for 90 minutes a week. The greedy speculators gamble with other people's money by forward buying (spot-market) items such as wheat, oil, and other essential items, which inflates the price we all end up paying for our daily bread. The greedy drug barons, tobacco basses, alcohol producers and bookmakers get rich on the addiction and hardship of others. The greedy owners of companies like Amazon (owned by the second wealthiest man in the world) allegedly make him richer by not looking after the people who make a fortune for him (see chapter 26, Internet

Taking Thousands of Jobs). Who knows, but we may be thankful God sent us this message in a few years.

Several critics (me included) have moaned about the government not buying testing kits, Personal Protection Equipment (PPEs) or ventilators earlier, and that the lockdown should have started earlier. It also upset many people to learn that our airports were still letting planes land from all over the world when other counties had closed their airports. The British government arranged for flights to collect stranded people from Covid-19 hot spots around the globe, at taxpayers' expense, yet didn't quarantine passengers for 14 days upon arrival in the UK. Several flights were arranged from Bangladesh with a high infection rate, and I wonder how many Brits died because of this oversight. From June the 15th 2020, people arriving from overseas had to self-isolate for 14 days, but why would anyone bother getting on a flight only to be told to isolate once they land? This is unbelievable, and it sounds like the government doesn't know what it is doing. The old saying of 'locking the stable door once the horse has bolted' springs to mind.

Time will tell if the critics are proven right or wrong. Still, I must admit that I was upset to see Jeremy Richard Streynsham Hunt, Chairman of the Health and Social Care Committee, giving Matt Hancock, the current Secretary of State for Health and Social Care, a hard time when many of today's NHS problems were caused by the heavy-handed treatment and under-funding dished out by James Hunt when he was Health Secretary from 2010 to 2018, when he starved the NHS of funds and set the moral of Junior Doctors to an all-time low. For readers with short memories, Mr Hunt also stood in the contest to become Prime Minster but lost out to Boris.

I feel that I should also point out that it does make me cringe when politicians have been singing the praises of our nurses and doctors during this pandemic, when on 28 June 2017, Boris Johnson, Dominic Raab, Matt Hancock, Rishi Sunak, Jacob Rees-

Mogg, Grant Shapps, George Eustice, Michael Gove, Priti Patel and hundreds of conservative MPs voted against lifting the cap on public sector wages including doctors, nurses, teachers, firefighters and police officers.

***

Couldn't Care Less About Care Homes

Having had to use the services of care homes to house my wife's relatives, I can tell you that care homes in the UK have been struggling for the past twenty years or more, and the government has disregarded this valuable sector, which in my opinion do an excellent service to our country. On the 13th of May 2020, the Labour Party leader Sir Keir Starmer stated in Prime Minister's Question Time (PMQs) that the Government had said that the Covid-19 infection of care home residents was 'unlikely', in advice issued until mid-March. The Prime Minister was left squirming when confronted with the evidence, and Matt Hancock, the Secretary of State for Health and Social Care sitting next to the PM in Parliament, wished that the PM would stop digging as he was making matters worse. The only good thing from this massive cock-up was that the government would make £600 million for infection control in coronavirus-hit care homes. Two days later, Matt Hancock, the Secretary of State for Health and Social Care, stated at the daily briefing from Downing Street that he had instructed local authorities to provide a daily report from them stating more significant details from care homes in their area. Pity he didn't do this from the start as it could have saved, in my opinion, **20,000 lives that were lost due to this shocking oversight.**

Another U-turn by Boris happened on the 20th of May 2020, again after the Labour Party leader Sir Keir Starmer stated in Prime Minster Question Time (PMQs) why the government were charging workers in the NHS and care homes from overseas £620 for medical cover. These low-skilled and low-paid workers, such as cleaners, porters and others, were discriminated against, yet the doctors and nurses couldn't work their miracles in an unclean environment.

As if to prove that the Government got it wrong, the *i-newspaper* reported on the 9th of May 2020 that 'the Care Quality Commission (CQC) said it is investigating a "minimal" number of incidents where hospitals who treated individuals for Covid-19 were not tested before the patients were discharged back to their care homes.' The CQC said the incidents led to the virus being transmitted to others.

Care homes that cater for the aged population and homes that cater for many disabilities had to supply their own PPE. However, this was exceedingly difficult for them as other organisations, such as the NHS, struggled to find suppliers. The Covid-19 test was another stumbling block during the pandemic, as care home residents and staff were also pushed to the back of the queue when it came to testing. With an ever-growing aged population, the Government must sort this mess out, or more care homes will be forced to close. The problem will be that if hospitals can't release patients to care homes, then the elderly will continue to tie up much-needed hospital beds.

Another big problem for the future of care homes in the UK is the Government's new policy on immigration. On the 18th of May 2020, the controversial immigration bill was voted through the House of Commons. The new bill that will come into effect in January 2021 will work on a points system. One of the significant point scores gained by the applicant will be if the applicant is applying for a job that will pay a salary of £25,000 per year or more. Most care workers today earn a maximum of £19,000, so they will not be given a visa. This will cause a significant problem for everyone as the NHS and care homes can't run without these valuable care workers, so they will have to pay workers a minimum of £25K. This will mean that the rates charged to residents will have to rise, and the Government will, via the NHS, have to pick up the bill.

Another worrying titbit (or tidbit to American readers) I heard about some of the current care workers was that they were working two different eight-hour shifts at two separate care homes. This alone could spread the virus from one care home to another. Some care workers from overseas lived in overcrowded accommodation where several immigrant families share the same facilities. This must have added to the number of deaths in care homes.

The Government must introduce a new law covering the employment of all staff in our NHS hospitals and care homes. Anyone working in this sector must be registered with the NHS and would be paid via the various hospitals or care home, but the new NHS human resources division must be copied in on who was being paid and the hours they worked. If this were done, a simple check could be made to see if there were any duplications. Currently, the NHS and care sector rely on agency staff and pay the agency a lot extra for the pleasure. These agencies should be put out of business, as anyone wishing to work for the NHS or care home must be employed via the NHS Human Resources division. This could not be done immediately but could be introduced to start next April. I can assure you that this would save the country millions of pounds every year, and at least stop the double work that is currently going on.

Immigration and Covid-19

The Conservative Government promised the electorate that they would sort out the immigration problem. Still, the new immigration law will do little to reduce the number of illegal immigrants already in the country. The Government won the 2019 election by promising the electorate in many Labour strongholds that they would sort the problem out. However, nothing is being done to correct the problem, and everyday hundreds of immigrants are still crossing the English Channel.

This should be stopped, with the boat being confiscated and the immigrants sent straight back to France on the next available ferry. If the government fails to get tough with France, the flooding of illegal immigrants in our towns and cities across the UK will only worsen.

It was also shocking to see on Sky News on the 17th of June 2020 that the 'Home Office does not know how many people are in the UK illegally, National Audit Office report finds. It went on to state that, according to a report, 'An up-to-date estimate of the number of illegal immigrants in the United Kingdom has not been produced for 15 years.' The National Audit Office (NAO) said the last estimate in 2005 suggested there were around 430,000 people in the country with no right to remain. But independent research since has put the figure at more than one million, Whitehall's spending watchdog said. It is noticeably clear that immigration has not been checked or even taken seriously. Still, if the Government wants to reduce the number of unemployed post-Covid-19 and Brexit, they should deport these 'illegals' as soon as possible.

Should China Be Made to Pay?
No country will do well out of this pandemic, there will be a backlash, and hopefully people will stop buying anything made in China. I do hope that Western countries insist that any item made in China will need to have the Chinese flag shown on the front of any packaging so that people can easily see where the product was made and can then choose whether they want to support the Chinese Communist Party or not. Listings and advertisements on the likes of Amazon, eBay and Google should also make it clear to potential customers that they are buying a product made in China.

Were the Chinese Communist Party to blame for not acting upon Dr Li Wenliang's findings and those of Shi Zhengli, the Wuhan laboratory's globally respected expert in transmitting animal-born coronavirus to humans in December 2019? Could the pandemic have been avoided if they had made the world aware of the problems in December 2019 and placed Wuhan City in lockdown?

I'm convinced that the Western world will never get to the bottom of who was to blame for Covid-19, but what the Chinese Communist Party can't deny is that their inaction to make the world aware of the problems in December 2019 led to the deaths of hundreds of thousands of innocent people around the world and caused bedlam in the financial stability of many nations. China should be made to pay for their mistakes and when they refuse, the Western world via the United Nations should ban all flights to and from China until they pay up. If any country such as Russia uses its veto, it should also face the ban. The UK and Europe should also follow the USA and put an import tax of 30% on any item made in China.

***

Prisons During the Pandemic.

During the pandemic, prison officers significantly protected staff and inmates during these difficult times. Sadly, Catherine Kelly, who worked at HMP Manchester, died from Covid-19. Catherine was 65 years old and had worked for 12 years for HMP. Many prison officers stayed at hotels to avoid taking the virus home to their loved ones. It was nice to see that the OYO hotel group offered cheap rates to all critical workers across the UK. Hopefully, all prison officers can keep everyone safe during these terrible times.

Covid-19 Prison Update

Prison.org.uk stated on the 12th of June 2020, 'The number of prisoners who tested positive for Covid-19 flatlined in the most recent data released by the Ministry of Justice. 490 prisoners were confirmed to have had the virus across 80 prisons, with no change in 24 hours, while the number of infected staff rose by three to 964 across 105 prisons. At least 23 prisoners and nine staff are known to have died, including one prison escort driver and one NHS trust employee working in a secure training centre.'

Boris and Cummings Saga

Nothing about this saga sounds right, and it has been alleged that Cummings must have something over Boris, as people have never seen a PM take a hit to his popularity to defend the undefendable before. Was the story about Boris nearly dying from Covid-19 in the hospital a set-up? Not one paparazzi photographer saw him going in or out of the hospital, and Boris only thanked two overseas nurses for caring for him in the hospital a few weeks later. Jenny McGee from New Zealand and Luis Pitarma from Portugal allegedly nursed Boris in the Intensive Care Unit at St Thomas's Hospital. Was this spin doctoring taken to a new level?

Exiting the Pandemic

This is the most challenging stage, especially when the public is sick and tired of getting mixed messages from all sides, and it has been shown that the elite can get away freely by totally ignoring the rules, when the other 67 million of us must stick to them. Due to the sad killing of George Floyd in the un-United States of America, there were protests around the world which did nothing to stop the spread of Covid-19. For weeks we have been told that social distancing is the most important thing we can do to help prevent the spread of this deadly virus. We all know about the BAME death rate being higher than the rate for white people. So, what do many of the black population do? They go on several protests in cities nationwide and ignore the law on social distancing.

I have nothing against protesting as I have been on several protests myself, but the organisers indeed recognise that activists will use the protest to cause havoc. With football matches being shut down, the football hooligans have little to do on a Saturday or Sunday afternoon and will string along with any protest hiding in the background. After the peaceful march, the troublemakers will guide the hooligans towards Downing Street, where they know the police will rightly protect the seat of our democracy, and all hell will be let loose as a result.

As a prison counsellor, I always look at both sides of the coin as the back of the coin will be different from the front and have a different meaning/message. Slavery will always be a tricky subject to comprehend as people will have their views on whether it is right or wrong. Some would say that without slavery, there wouldn't be a race problem today as there would be very few black people in the world, as the vast majority originated from descendants of enslaved people. Had the slave trade never happened, all enslaved Black people would have led a shorter life in Africa and been killed by hunger, drought, or disease. In my opinion, modern-day slavery can be seen in the gig community, and those people who are on zero-hour contracts which should be banned. Slavery is a fascinating subject; many facts can be found at https://en.wikipedia.org/wiki/Atlantic_slave_trade.

When I was a boy, you hardly saw a black man or woman in the UK. That was until the NHS started to recruit black nurses from the Caribbean, and other organisations like the London Underground also urged black people to emigrate to Britain. These immigrants were later known as the Windrush generation, named after the ship, that transported them. Between 1948 and 1970, nearly half a million people moved from the Caribbean to Britain, as the UK in 1948 faced severe labour shortages in the wake of the Second World War. The immigrants were later referred to as 'the Windrush generation'. I do hope that we will see harmony between all races and creeds, but instead of 'Black Lives Matter' or 'White Lives Matter', we will see '**All Lives Matter**'.

Another problem that I can foresee is when the pubs and clubs reopen. With the police, paramedics, and the NHS already on their knees, the Government must ensure that night clubs must be closed at midnight (with the last orders being stopped at 11.30 p.m.), or these front-line workers will again be stretched to breaking point. There is no need to keep clubs open until the early morning hours as yobs simply stay at home drinking cheap supermarket booze until 11p.m and then head for the nightclubs already partially drunk. The 24-hour rule was introduced when the Labour Party were in power, but I don't think it has worked well for most (that's unless you're a brewer or club owner) and exiting Covid-19 may be the right time to bring binge drinking and the pressure placed on our front-line workers to an end.

Another concern of mine is that the NHS and care staff will suffer from post-traumatic stress disorder (PTSD), and I hope that they will be treated better than the soldiers and other service personnel that keep us safe and don't face the same problems as Alan Frazer did along with hundreds I have seen over the years. More about Alan's case can be read in Chapter 27.

The most disturbing thing about this pandemic to me was that families were not allowed to say their final goodbye or to hold the hand of their loved one as they passed over. With the Government failing to act quickly and stating that the infection of care home residents was 'unlikely', in my opinion nearly 20,000 lives could have been saved. We will come out of this pandemic, but whether we return to the 'normal' we once took for granted, we will have to wait and see. I pray that I never hear the phrases 'scientific advice', 'social distancing', and 'flattening the curve' ever again. This is a burden that Boris and the Conservative Government will have to carry, and hope that the British voter has a short memory.

As the virus spread across China, many Western companies who had moved their production to China to benefit from cheap labour and fewer health and safety measures were now worried about getting their products out of China. Dr Martens Boots & Shoes is a brand my friend in Northamptonshire loved. His father and mother had worked in the company's Rushden factory, but in 2004 production was moved to China and Thailand. He said that it was a way of life for the community, and, with Max Griggs at the helm, they even built a football stadium for the Rushden and Diamonds team. In 2005 owner Max Griggs sold the Club to the Supporters Trust for a nominal £1. However, without its wealthy backer, the Club struggled, and he eventually quit in 2011. In what seemed a rather bizarre move at the time, Kettering Town moved into the ground, but left in 2012, after which the ground became unused.

An article in *The Guardian* on the 30th of November 2019 stated that it was just a small question in their regular Consumer Champions column. Why, a reader asked, had her £170 Dr Martens boots fallen apart after just six months? The response was huge, with readers accusing the bootmaker of sacrificing quality, offshoring production and chasing profits under the ownership of a London-based private equity company a long way from its roots in Northamptonshire. Wikipedia state that Dr Martens AirWair International's revenue fell from US $412 million in 1999 to $127 million in 2006. In 2003, the Dr Martens company came close to bankruptcy. On 1st April that year, under pressure from declining sales, the company ceased making shoes in the United Kingdom and moved all production to China and Thailand. I told Lewis that when my wife and I went on holiday to Orlando, my wife wanted to look around the shopping malls, and I noticed that one shop was busier than most, so, being nosy, I had to find out why. It was a shoe shop, and in the window was a big stack of trainers, but what caught my eye was the big Union flag on one side of the shoe box. I asked one of the shop staff why they were flying off the shelves, and she said that people liked to buy British as it was always good quality. Pity Dr Martens and the hundreds of UK companies who moved production to China weren't there to see this simple example of why satisfied customers are more important than cheap labour.

Several critics have moaned about the Government not buying testing kits or ventilators earlier and that the lockdown should have started a week earlier. Time will tell if the critics are proven right or wrong.

In my opinion, Boris and his chancellor are doing their best to make sure that the ordinary worker won't suffer too much, but we all know who will pick up the bill in the end. Yes, you got it in one, you and me and all our children and their children for generations to come. Add this to the massive bill we are all paying for the 2007-2008 banking crisis, and it may be a good idea for the country to declare bankruptcy and start again. I would like to know who we owe these trillions to. Someone or a country had to have the money to lend to us in the first place, and it would be nice to learn how they amassed these massive sums of money.

For further reading on how top UK companies such as Dr Martens moved production to China, please read Afterword's - Chapter 15 at the end of this book.

***

Chapter 16. Non-Dom Status. Is it Right?

Roy Wilson, aged 39, married without children, was serving a three-year sentence for fraud for stealing money from some of his clients while worked for an umbrella company that helped the rich get around the PAYE system.

Note. An umbrella company is a company that employs agency contractors who work on temporary contract assignments, usually through a recruitment agency in the UK. Recruitment agencies prefer to issue contracts to a limited company, as the agency's liability is reduced. It issues invoices to the recruitment agency (or client) and, when the invoice is paid, will typically pay the contractor through PAYE with the added benefit of offsetting some of the income by claiming expenses such as travel, meals and accommodation.

Umbrella companies have become more prevalent in the UK since the British government introduced the so-called 'IR35' legislation in 2000 that creates tests to determine employment status and ability to use small company tax reliefs. According to criteria set out by the UK Department for Business, Innovation & Skills, there are an estimated four million temporary workers in the UK, of whom 1.56 million are 'classed as being in a management or senior official role, a professional occupation or an associate professional and technical occupation.' It is estimated that 14% of the UK's professional contractors currently manage their business by working through an umbrella company. Source: Wikipedia.

Roy said that he 'had always worked in the financial sector and had earnt an excellent salary'. At first, it was just small amounts to pay for his cannabis (weed), and nobody spotted a problem, but when he needed more money to fund his drug addiction, he got caught and ended up in prison. He said that he and his wife had sold their lovely home so that he could repay the money he had stolen, and this had helped him get a lesser sentence.

Having read Roy's case notes, I noticed that he lived in a nice area on the outskirts of Cambridge and lived what looked like the perfect life. He was well travelled, and he and his wife looked set up for life, so I asked him to explain further why he had become hooked on drugs. Roy said that what he was doing for the umbrella company was legally trying to avoid his clients paying PAYE like the rest of us. He said he first got angry when he saw that those who could afford their taxes were trying to avoid doing so. He said he had started smoking cannabis in the evenings, but as his workload increased, he smoked more, and it got out of hand. He said that tax avoidance was legal, but it annoyed him that the rich were getting richer, and the poor were becoming poorer. Having always paid my taxes, I asked him what got his back up, making him so stressed that he needed more drugs. He said that 'thousands of people in the UK worked for firms that helped people legally pay less tax, but this wasn't enough for some clients. The richer my client was, the greater their desire was to pay zero tax, and those who took up non-domiciled status were the worse.'

I asked Roy to explain to me what non-domiciled status was all about. He said that 'someone with non-domiciled status, sometimes called a "non-dom", is a person living in the United Kingdom who is considered domiciled, or resident, in another country under British law. This can have significant tax advantages for the wealthy. The non-domicile rule, which allows some UK residents to limit the tax paid on earnings outside the country, has been a regular topic of debate in recent years. The BBC reported that various changes have been made to how people face charges in the UK if they wish to keep their non-dom status. Still, the tax status remains, and there is an element of mystery about it—with the number of non-doms in the UK a matter of informed guesswork.'

In 2017 the Labour Party vowed to scrap non-dom status, with some caveats to protect temporary workers, if it won power in the 2017 general election. To most people, the matter of non-dom status means very little, but to any of the millions of Britain's living on or below the poverty line, it makes shocking reading. You can also get some misinformation by searching the web, so I stuck to the good old BBC, which said, 'A non-dom is a UK resident whose permanent home, or domicile, is outside the UK. A domicile is usually the country their father considered his permanent home when they were born, or it may be the place overseas where somebody has moved to with no intention of returning. That means somebody can be born, educated and work in the UK but still hold non-dom status. It also means that some may inherit their non-dom status from their parents. For proof to the tax authority, they must provide evidence about their background, lifestyle, and future intentions, such as where they own property or intend to be buried. Key to non-dom tax status is that an individual must pay UK tax on UK earnings, but need not pay UK tax on foreign income or gains unless they bring that income back to the UK.'

This made Roy Wilson incredibly angry as he saw the system as an easy way for the rich to move their money around the world without paying UK tax on their earnings. Ron said, 'Nobody knows how many non-doms there are as people do not necessarily have to indicate their domicile status on their UK tax return.' The BBC estimated that there were over 114,000 non-doms in 2012-13. There is a charge made by the UK tax authorities for a non-dom to maintain their tax status. This ranges from an annual fee of between £30,000 and £90,000 per year, but this is peanuts to a non-dom as they save millions elsewhere. According to the Labour Party, there is good reason to eliminate this scheme and replace it with one that protects temporary workers and overseas students who can legally maintain a form of domicile overseas. Individuals raised and educated at the expense of the UK taxpayer should not have a legal loophole that allows them to not contribute back to the country that created them.

Roy said a fine example of a non-dom would be our very own Lewis Carl Davidson Hamilton MBE, born 7th January 1985, in Stevenage, Hertfordshire, England. Lewis is one of the best formula one racing drivers ever and has a significant following. Lewis's grandparents moved to the UK from Grenada in the 1950s, and his father, Antony Lewis, married his mother, Carmen, but his parents separated when Lewis was two; because of this, he lived with his mother and half-sisters Nicola and Samantha until he was 12, when he started living again with his father, stepmother Linda, and his half-brother Nicolas who has cerebral palsy. Allegedly, Lewis's mother may have claimed benefits as a single mother. When he moved in with his father, he then received child benefits. If you add that his half-brother Nicolas who has cerebral palsy, would have received a lot of financial help from the state to help him cope with his cruel disability. So, what does Lewis do when he becomes a millionaire? He thanks the country that made him what he is and has cared for his family and disabled half-brother by sodding off to Switzerland and then moving to Monaco. According to Wikipedia, at the start of 2013, Hamilton took delivery of a metallic red and black Bombardier Challenger 600 series private jet, tail plate number G-LCDH. Following the leak of the confidential Paradise Papers in November 2017, it was reported that Hamilton had avoided paying £3.3 million of Value Added Tax on his private jet worth £16.5 million. The leasing deal set up by his advisers was said by the BBC to appear to be artificial and did not comply with an EU and UK ban on refunds for private use. The BBC also say that Hamilton's social media accounts provide evidence that he has used the Bombardier Challenger 605 for holidays and other personal trips worldwide. A new company owned by Hamilton, Stealth (IOM) Limited, leased the jet from Hamilton's British Virgin Islands Company, Stealth Aviation Limited, and imported it into the Isle of Man. It was then leased on to a UK jet management company that provided Hamilton with a crew and other services, which leased it back to Hamilton and his Guernsey Company, BRV Limited. Lawyers acting for Hamilton said the company made all necessary disclosures to Isle of Man officials, who approved the approach. According to Wikipedia, as of 2020, Hamilton was ranked as the wealthiest British sportsperson, with an estimated personal fortune of $285 million.

He stated that another name that keeps popping up is Sir Richard Charles Nicholas Branson (born 18 July 1950), a British business magnate, investor, author, and philanthropist. He founded the Virgin Group in the 1970s, which controls over 400 companies in various fields. According to Wikipedia, his net worth was a staggering US$4.4 billion (April 2020). Branson expressed his desire to become an entrepreneur at a young age. His first business venture, at the age of 16, was a magazine called *Student*. In 1970, he set up a mail-order record business. He opened a chain of record stores, Virgin Records—later known as Virgin Megastores—in 1972. Branson's Virgin brand proliferated during the 1980s, as he started Virgin Atlantic Airlines and expanded the Virgin Records music label. In 2004, he founded the spaceflight corporation Virgin Galactic.

The *Guardian* newspaper stated that 'from his private island in the Caribbean, Sir Richard Branson is trying to convince the UK government to give his Virgin Atlantic airline a £500m bailout to help it survive the coronavirus pandemic and the economic fallout of the lockdown. Virgin Australia, which is 10% owned by the billionaire's Virgin Group, is also seeking a £700m bailout from the Australian government. '

Due to the coronavirus, all airlines are in financial trouble, but there were a lot of raised eyebrows when Sir Richard asked the British government for a £500 million bail-out. Yahoo Finance stated, 'Rival airline boss Michael O'Leary of Ryanair accused him of trying to "fleece" the taxpayer and told the billionaire to "write the cheque himself."' Christian leaders in Britain also hit out at large firms and the wealthy for using tax havens during the crisis and warned offshore companies should not receive bailouts in a letter to *The Times*.

Why Do the Super-Rich live in Monaco?

There are three methods of becoming a resident of Monaco: 1. An authorised Monegasque employer offers you an employment contract. 2. You intend to set up a business activity in Monaco. Though the favourite way for non-dons is number 3. You can demonstrate that you're wealthy and have enough income without engaging in gainful employment. You will need to open a bank account with a bank in Monaco, deposit a minimum of EUR 500,000 and acquire a bank reference of that bank stating that you have enough funds to support yourself in Monaco. Once you have purchased (or rented) a property in Monaco, you can stop worrying about paying taxes, as there aren't many. Income tax was abolished in 1869! All foreigners officially residing in Monaco can benefit from these zero personal income tax regimes. The Principality of Monaco doesn't levy capital gains or wealth tax. Inheritance and gift tax are payable, but only regarding assets situated in Monaco. In other words, these taxes don't apply to assets outside Monaco (money in a foreign bank account, for example).

Clever individuals know how to benefit from this. Roy Wilson stated that 'the Government should get rid of the non-don status and make any person who holds a British passport pay taxes to the UK (including money banked offshore) as most people do. If they don't want to play ball, they can forfeit their British passport and reside wherever they like. If they want to return to the UK, they would be treated like any foreign visitor and must apply for a visa. The Government would have the right not to offer a visa, which could be awkward for Mr Hamilton as he may have to miss the race at Silverstone.

The message to all these non-dons is that if they want to be known as British, the country expects them to pay UK taxes like the rest of us. To make this happen legally, the Government would have to widen the scope of the law, known as 'conducive to the public good', which could be extended to consider these blood-sucking leeches.

I placed Roy on our drug rehabilitation program, but he will struggle as he was on some heavy drugs when he got caught and finds it hard to come off them. I wouldn't be inviting Roy to the heist in Bedford as he isn't reliable while he is still drug dependent.

I checked on Roy later and found that he was now selling solar power to households in the Cambridgeshire area. He said he was doing OK but felt he was selling a system that only benefitted the installer rather than the end user. He said he would be looking for a new job as soon as he had a few more months in a regular job. I wished him luck.

***

Chapter 17. The Racist Banker.

Neil Gardener was in his late forties and was married with two children who lived in Ely, Cambridgeshire. Neil left school at 16, went to college for three years, and gained a bachelor's degree in finance. He joined Barclays, where he met his wife Susan and married in 1994. Life was great as he progressed to become an investment banker, but things went wrong after he got drunk one night celebrating landing a new client who had millions to invest. He was leaving the bar when he bumped into a black woman and spilt all her soft drinks down both sets of clothing. What happened next was caught on CCTV and clearly showed that he racially abused the woman, saying: 'Go back to your own f*****g country.' He ignored another female who told him to stop his racist rant and said: 'It'll be a different story when they take over the world, and you're all wearing burkas.' As the Muslin lady was leaving, she felt a slap to the right side of her head from behind. At this point, the hotel called security, and Neil was asked to leave. The lady later reported the matter to the police, and they reviewed the CCTV, and Neil was arrested.

When his time in court came around, he thought that the barrister—paid for by his employer—would get him off with a slap on the wrist. He was shocked when he was sent down for 36 months. His employers terminated his contract, and with a criminal record, he will never be employed in the banking sector ever again. I asked Neil what he would like to train for while he is here, as he will have to start something completely new once freed. He said that he 'had always wanted to write a book about how the rich are robbing the poor, and any help with writing a book would be helpful.' I said we could enrol him on two courses, the first being anger management, and if he completes that course, I will then enter him into the writing and publishing program. Still, he will need to use a computer without an internet connection for his coursework.

I asked him, What are the things your book will cover and who will it be aimed at, as these will be the first two things your tutor will ask, so you could start by thinking ahead.' Neil said, 'That wouldn't take much time to think about, as the first part will be aimed at making the reader aware of what goes on in the international banking and investment field.' He stated that there is a very thin line between tax avoidance and tax evasion; even the brightest people still get it wrong. Tax avoidance is legal, and indeed the Government encourages you to save in a tax-free Individual Savings Account (Isa), for example. Or you could invest in a pension scheme, donate to charity via the gift aid scheme, or claim capital allowances on things used for business purposes. What many people slip up on is tax evasion. Tax avoidance currently costs the taxpayer £4bn a year, according to the latest figures from HMRC. That is nearly as much as illegal tax evasion, which costs an estimated £5.1bn. Together, they account for about a quarter of the £35bn that is lost to the Treasury yearly, otherwise known as the 'tax gap'.

Neil stated that 'The Government should consider changing the rules regarding monies leaving the UK banking system.' According to the Labour Party, he had read in an article that a mind-boggling £13 trillion of assets in significant firms doing business in the UK are squirrelled away in overseas tax havens. The £13 trillion is six times the UK's national debt and could make living in the UK better for every man, woman, and child. The UK also needs new laws to stop overseas companies from charging a high price for branded products supplied to its UK franchise or distributor. For example, if you take an international company such as Starbucks, which was publicly shamed for paying very little tax in the UK, they could charge their UK franchisee ten pence for every pre-printed coffee cup instead of the actual cost of less than a penny. This inflates their worth to the UK, ensuring that the extra cost is pocketed by the international company, which is probably based in an off-shore low-tax country. I'm sure this is done in every industry, and it needs sorting out fast.

Leaks such as the Panama Papers and the recent leak nicknamed the Paradise Papers show how companies and individuals have been depositing money around the globe to avoid paying taxes in the country where the money was raised. The Government should prioritise establishing a large department to track this money down and make the offender pay their fair share of tax. If everyone paid, every man, woman and child in the UK would benefit. What is needed is for the government to abolish non-dom status, tighten the regulation of accountants, lawyers and bankers, increase the resources available to HMRC to enforce UK tax legislation, review tax breaks for corporates and wealthy individuals, introduce a public register of beneficial ownership for trusts as well as companies, and compelling the UK's crown dependencies and overseas territories to do the same. Make mandatory country-by-country reporting for all publicly quoted companies and stop granting amnesties to those who hide their money offshore.

Neil said that he had a brother who was severely disabled, and with the change over to the new PIP system, he was informed that he could work. I'll never know how they came up with that answer, as he can't speak, is in a wheelchair and only has partial vision. My mother, who cares for him in an unpaid role, challenged the decision, and, like most cases that are appealed, the decision was reversed. If the Government spent just a fraction of what it has cost to implement the PIP system on tax evasion, the UK wouldn't have any financial problems. He said that he had once asked a very rich Lord and landowner why the benefits he gained shouldn't be spread out so that his estate and business workers got a better deal. He said that it had always been seen that by allowing 'certain people' such as himself to become rich, his wealth would be spent and therefore benefit the wider community. He forgot to state that once he had the money, he wouldn't spend it but hide it in an offshore account that benefitted him. It never surprises me how many leading business leaders want to be the wealthiest person in the graveyard.

I said I sympathised with his thoughts, as I had just been interviewing a young man who had been made redundant due to no fault of his own and was claiming Job Seeker's Allowance. He did find a new job, but he was told that if he took it, his benefits would be stopped on the first day of his employment. He said that to take the job he would need to buy some new work clothes and shoes as the firm didn't allow trainers to be worn. He would also have to pay for petrol to get to and from the workplace 18 miles from where he lived. The new job had flexible hours, so even if there was a bus service (which there wasn't), he couldn't use it. In the end, he couldn't afford to take the job as he wouldn't be paid for a month, so he returned to his old ways, ended up again with the wrong crowd, and got caught dealing drugs.

We continually hear about the Government wanting to get people back into work, yet they don't offer financial help. If the Government had come up with a way to cover his cost for the first month, it would have been much cheaper than spending £47,000 to keep him in prison for a year. The big problem is that the people making the rules have never had to sign on or live on benefits. They would make the rules more flexible and get people off the streets and back to work if they had.

Neil won't be joining me for the heist I will hold in Bedford as he is a blue-collar worker and would be totally out of place. However, I will pick his brains on how town banks work, and I genuinely wish him luck with his book.

***

Chapter 18. Racial and Sexual Discrimination.

This is always a touchy subject to raise as different people have different views on what it is. The rule has always been to treat people of all colours, gender and faiths as equals, but I can understand where things go wrong. You hardly saw a black person when I was growing up, but that was decades ago, and we are now becoming a multi-coloured country. I always ask people I know who have made a racist comment against another human being what they would do if they or somebody close to them suffered a heart attack. Would they tell the paramedic not to save a life simply because they were of a different colour or religion? Whether we like it or not, we now live in a multi-faith country, and everyone will be of mixed race in a few decades.

I sympathise with those who say that political correctness, PC, has gone too far. I have had to reprimand an inmate who was heard saying, 'We have a lot of dyke's in Lincolnshire,' after I received a complaint from a female member of staff. I couldn't do much about it as all the fens have drainage dykes, and there is a lovely village named Dyke just north of Bourne. Another word that upsets many people (me included) is the word "nigger", which refers to a black Negro, but what I find slightly confusing is why a black person can use the word—as many do in various rap songs, yet when a white person sings along to the music, they are being racist. One of the first times I heard the word 'nigger' was when it referred to a male black Labrador retriever belonging to Wing Commander Guy Gibson of the Royal Air Force and the mascot of No. 617 Squadron. Being a Dambuster fanatic, I cried as a child when Nigger got run over while his owner was fighting for his country. It looks as if the PC brigade should steer clear of Lincolnshire as it is the home of the 617 squadron, and you'll pass many dykes along the way.

If we take the good old and trusted BBC as an example, they say that they are committed to reflecting and representing the diversity of the UK. The BBC is for everyone and should include people, whatever their background. Unless you are an out-and-out racist, you can't argue with their reasoning, but the good old BBC doesn't always get it right. I'm told that non-white and non-Christians make up only 15% of the UK's population, yet I can almost guarantee that producers will ignore the 15%, and we will see more and more programs for the minority. The same applies to gay people on TV. According to an article in The Guardian, one in 50 people in the UK now say they are lesbian, gay or bisexual, about 2% of the population.

Now let me make it absolutely clear where I stand. I don't care what people do behind closed doors if they're not breaking any laws. It also annoys me when people assume that they are sharing a bed. I would rather see men or women sharing their homes rather than see two individual lonely people.

Having made that clear, I get annoyed when every show on the BBC appears to have a gay person in it, and they openly promote their sexuality. You can see them on the screen saying, 'Look, I'm gay, aren't I pretty,' and I answer to myself, 'No, you're not.' Strictly Come Dancing is a show that is, in my opinion, too PC. You had two gay male judges, but if that wasn't enough, up pops the token black judge. There is a rumour that the next series of Strictly Come Dancing will have two same-sex dancers, and, if that happens, the show will lose many viewers, me included. To me Ballroom dancing is about a smartly dressed man and a woman in a beautiful dress. I know I'm old fashioned, but I predict that seeing two same-sex people kissing on TV will shortly follow and that will be a turn-off for most.

**

Chapter 19. The Final Straw.

One thing that got my back up and helped me decide to change from gamekeeper to poacher is the greedy nature of most large companies (including state owned banks) in the UK. This, along with the loss of my dear wife (which could have been made more straightforward), the terrible way I was dealt with after serving over 20 years in HMP, and greedy CEOs and directors have made it an easy choice to set up my heist in Bedford. Nearly every private limited company (PLC) in the UK pay their top person (usually known as the Chief Executive Officer or CEO) between 100 and 120 times more than the company's average worker's pay. This can't be right, and a way to control these leeches (I call them 'The Leeches of London') must be found either by regulation or by introducing a much higher level of tax for those 'earning' more than a million pounds in any year. No man or woman can earn up to 120 times more than another person, so a new word should be used instead of 'executive' when describing these leeches and parasites. I would call these unearned salaries 'exorbitance', and perhaps the Chief Executive Officer should become known as the Chief Exorbitance Officer.

Update August 2023
If we look at the current cost-of-living crisis and use Tesco (the most significant UK supermarket) as an example, their profit for 2020/21 was £636 million, yet in 2021/22, it rose to £2.03 billion, an increase of 219.7%. The financial experts will tell you that their overall yield was below average for such a large company. Was this low yield down to the extortionate salaries paid to Board members?

Any government could help 'shame' these leeches by simply making it law that all executive remuneration schemes should be simplified, and for companies to declare how much the pay of the top three executives exceeds that of the average worker.

This information should be placed on all products and media so that people can decide whether to support that company and its products. But governments (of all colours) don't tackle these greedy bastards and, in many cases, continue to throw publically funded contracted work to them.

A recent example would be the Carillion fiasco, where even after the firm put out profit warnings (usually a red flag to investors), the Government were still arranging new contracts with them. Carillion was a massive organisation with over 20,000 employees in the UK alone, but in January 2018 the company went into liquidation, leaving many significant projects up the creek without a paddle. The BBC reported that the £335m Royal Liverpool Hospital completion date was repeatedly pushed back amid reports of cracks in the building, with the latest opening date given by the new contactor Laing O'Rourke at the end of 2020. Carillion's Chief executive Richard Howson stepped down in July 2017 after a profit warning. He had been in charge since the end of 2011. Much of the criticism has been over the size of Mr Howson's pay award in 2016, which totalled £1.5m including bonuses. He also received a salary until October 2018. Carillion's finance director Richard Adam, who retired in December 2016 after nine years at Carillion, received almost £1.1m in salary and bonuses in 2016.

It doesn't make sense to me that paying these so-called industry leaders over a million pounds a year is worth it. Another greedy CEO was 'Drastic' Dave Lewis, Tesco's chief executive, whose pay, including salary, bonus and incentives, topped £4.6m before he stood down, or J Sainsbury's Mike Coupe's £3.9m pay package as the grocer unveiled a further fall in sales. In my opinion any company paying their top staff more than this benchmark should be penalised and hit with a tax rate of 80% once they are paid more than a million. This would apply to everyone, including our highly overpaid footballers, and the

Government should ignore cries that these top earners would leave the UK and work abroad. If anyone, including footballers, doesn't want to pay the greedy tax level of 80%, then the country could live without them and would help UK-born footballers move up the ladder, and who knows, we may again win the World Cup. It was 1966 when we last grasped this trophy, and it's worth noting that the top salary for a footballer then was around £5,200 a year, which I have calculated to be about £90,812 in today's money. Compare this to today's top football earners, and you'll see that Alexis Sanchez— Manchester United (£400,000 per week) and Paul Pog - Manchester United (£290,000 per week), and the list goes on and on. Compare these salaries to that of a brain neurosurgeon, and you would see that these top Premier League players are being paid 50 times more than a leading surgeon for kicking a ball about. *Note: Rates are correct in 2019.*

The Government must stop this abuse from happening, and the easiest way to do this is to increase the top tax rate for these greedy leeches and set up a financial police force to ensure that any money earned in the UK is taxed and paid. Paying the top 5% million more than their actual worth is, to me, criminal, and they are no better than the inmates I have dealt with over the years, that I worked within HMP. The coronavirus pandemic will not change a thing to these leeches, and they will pay themselves millions while some of their employees will have to survive on statutory sick pay of £94.25 per week. *Note: Rates are correct in 2019.*

Update October 2023.
The Conservative have just announced that the cap on bonuses paid to bankers and building society staff will be lifted. This is at a time when millions of families in the UK are struggling to make ends meet. The current rules (which comes to an end on October 31, 2023) limits bonuses to 100% of the salary for employees of banks or building societies, or double with shareholder approval.

The Nat West Bank (formerly RBS) is a fine example as the Government (i.e., you and me) owns 42% of the shares. It beggars' belief that the government allow this when they are denying junior doctors, NHS consultants, train drivers and a host of other essential service workers a reasonable living wage.

***

Chapter 20. Why Hold my Heist in Bedford?

I decided to hold my heist in Bedford as it was a market town that had also seen better days and had been mistreated by the central government during the past few centuries. Bedfordshire is an English shire county around 57 miles north of central London. The Borough of Bedford has a population of just over 153,000 and is arguably the most cosmopolitan in the UK, with some 57 ethnic groups represented.

Bedford's leading employers were the brickworks, and modern brickmaking in Bedfordshire started when the London Brick Company bought up various small local companies, such as Randall and B J H Forders & Co, to create the largest brickworks in the world. London Brick employed over 2,000 people at its peak and manufactured over 500 million bricks annually. By the 1930s, there were 135 brick makers chimneys in the Marston Vale. After World War Two, bricks were under enormous demand, to help reconstruct Britain's housing stock. Bedfordshire had the clay but not the people to make the bricks, since returning soldiers were reluctant to take up such arduous labour. The brick companies looked overseas for workers and found many willing recruits, firstly among people displaced from Eastern Europe, then among Italians in the 1950s, and later Indians, Pakistanis, and West Indians. There were so many Italians that nearly 40 Italian restaurants were still open in the town.

In the 1970s, the company again expanded by buying rival companies such as the Marston Valley Brick Company and Redland Brick. However, during the 1980s, demand for bricks fell, and the decline started with the closure of the Ridgmont pit in 1983. The sale of the pit enabled the company to stay in profit but only after making 1,100 workers redundant. The brick-making sector employs around 230 people but will never again be the force it once was. Another significant employer in Bedford was the Charles Wells Brewery which has been operating in Bedford since 1876, with the Eagle Brewery producing more than 100 million litres of beer every year. In 2017 the brewery was sold to pub operator Marston's in a £55 million deal. Around 300 people employed in production, sales and brand marketing will transfer to Marston's, but the old company will still own the 200 Charles Wells pubs across the UK and France.

The River Ouse passes through Bedford Town Centre and has several Victorian gardens and memorials along its beautiful embankment. Entry to Bedford's business and shopping centre is over two bridges that cross the river, virtually cutting Bedford in half, just as the River Thames cuts London in half. Another dividing factor in Bedford is the Midland main line from London St Pancras to the East Midlands and Scotland. A smaller station in Bedford is the Marston Vale line from Bletchley through to Bedford St Johns. Several road bridges cross the Midland main line, but the main one is the A4280 which connects the town with the west.

My plan was to control the flow of traffic leaving the town over these three key bridges, which would halt traffic in the town. Each set of traffic lights would let vehicles enter the town for three minutes at a time, but only let traffic leave for two minutes. As vehicles entering the town would hit a traffic jam as soon as they crossed the bridge, they would start to block traffic trying to leave the town. Any police attempting to reach any of our six heist venues would have to do so on foot.

**

Chapter 21. Famous Bedford Clangers

The traditional nickname for people from Bedfordshire is 'clangers', deriving from a local dish comprising a suet crust pastry filled with meat in one end and jam in the other. During the centuries, Bedford has been home to some incredibly famous clangers, such as John Bunyan, who was born a few miles away from Bedford at Elstow. He wrote his famous book *The Pilgrim's Progress* while imprisoned in Bedford jail for refusing to recognise the established Church; to this day, nonconformist chapels, some dating back to Bunyan's time, are much in evidence in towns and villages all over the area.

John Howard was born in Hackney, in east London, in 1726, the son of a partner in an upholstery business. On his father's death in 1742, he inherited considerable wealth and settled on an estate in Bedfordshire. In 1773, he was appointed High Sheriff of Bedfordshire, and supervision of the county jail became one of his responsibilities. He was shocked by the conditions he found, and visited others in England, where the situation was no better. Jailers were not salaried but lived off fees paid by prisoners' family's for food, bedding, and other facilities. This system meant that poorer prisoners lived in terrible conditions. Howard's concerns led to two 1774 parliamentary acts—one abolished jailers' fee, and the other enforced improvements in the system leading to better prisoner health. John Howard visited many countries around the world to see how they dealt with prisoners, and, during a visit to Ukraine, he contracted typhus and died there on 20 January 1790. 1866 the Howard League for Penal Reform was founded in his honour.

The Bedford reformist tradition was continued by Trevor Huddleston, born in Bedford in 1913, and a statue placed in his honour can be seen at the top of Silver Street. As a tribute to this remarkable man, the statue was unveiled in 2000 by Nelson Mandela.

Sir William Harpur was a Bedford man remembered with gratitude. Born at the turn of the 16th century, he became Lord Mayor of London and founded a school in Bedford to be maintained by a rich endowment of London land. The Harpur Schools still flourish in Bedford today and are home to four public schools named Pilgrims School, Bedford School, Bedford Girls' School and Bedford Modern School are all run by the Harpur Trust charity, which has seen celebrities and politicians such as Al Murray, Alastair Cook, Christopher Fry, Paddy Ashdown, Monty Panesar and Jean Muir as students.

Ronnie Barker was born in Garfield Street, Bedford, on 25th September 1929. Star of *Porridge*, *The Two Ronnies* and countless other comedy shows and has been heralded by his fellow performers as one of the top 20 comedy acts of all time. One of the most popular TV programs watched inside the prison was the hilarious show called *Porridge* which was a comedy based on the prison life of Fletcher, a criminal serving a five-year sentence, as he strives to bide his time, keep his record clean, and refuses to be ground down by the prison system.

John Le Mesurier was born in Chaucer Road, Bedford and is most famously noted for his role in *Dad's Army* as Sergeant Arthur Wilson and had a prolific acting career starring in over 100 movies.

Another 'clanger' that should be mentioned is Frank Branston, Bedford's first directly elected mayor until his sad death in August 2009 after he suffered an aortic aneurysm. Most clangers will remember Frank for his journalistic work and being editor of the award-winning *Beds on Sunday* newspaper. One story he was directly involved with was the headline that made the nationals in 2001, where it was reported that deceased patients were inappropriately kept in a chapel of rest at Bedford Hospital instead of the usual refrigerated mortuary. This raised questions in Parliament, and the then Secretary of State for Health (Mr Alan Milburn) had to apologise to the house and assure the house that a full investigation would occur. This was just one of Frank's highlights, and I was glad to see that a new section of the A428 trunk road bypassing the west of Bedford was named The Branston Way in his memory.

Bedford Corn Exchange, built in 1872, became home to the BBC Symphony Orchestra and 1944 hosted the BBC proms; in fact, the BBC relocated to Bedford during this period and broadcasted from its Bedford studios. Many celebrities were drawn to Bedford and performed live during this period, including notable artists such as Vera Lynn, Humphrey Bogart, Gracie Fields and Glen Miller. Glenn Miller used Studio No 1 in the Corn Exchange to broadcast live to the nation during the war years, and a bust has been erected in his honour outside the Corn Exchange.

A Note from the Writer Regarding Frank Branston:
While I was the Sales Director at Goodhead Press plc, Frank was a customer of mine as we printed the Beds on Sunday *newspaper. We met up for a business lunch for four people every few months, but each time the bill kept increasing, it was a little game that we both enjoyed. I had never won but thought I stood a chance when we went to a new restaurant, and we all ordered what to me was a reasonably priced meal. Frank let me choose the white wine (as he knew I preferred white to red), and Frank chose the red. I thought I had finally won a round until I saw the bill. Frank had gone for a bottle of Château Lafite-Rothschild 1971 which cost nearly £200 (about £500 in today's money). Frank beat me yet again. Frank was not only a good client but, over the years, had become a good friend, and it's only fitting that his name will always live on. Rest in peace, my old friend.*

***

Chapter 22. Douglas Boswell, a Lifetime Criminal.

I had got to know Douglas Boswell quite well during the two times he had ended up in prison. Doug was a lifetime criminal who started his sorry life on a gypsy site in Northamptonshire, England. His family were Romani (also called Romany or Roma), a traditionally nomadic ethnic group living mainly in Europe and originating from the northern regions of the Indian subcontinent, from the Indian states of Rajasthan, Haryana, Punjab and Sindh.

Doug didn't look like someone from the Indian continent, but rather like an Italian don. He had jet-black hair, stunning green eyes and a mouth made for kissing the girls. Doug was around six foot four inches tall and weighed about 230 pounds. He told me he had had a few serious relationships, but nothing long lasting had materialised. His parents had set him up to marry a gipsy girl from another Romany family from Bulgaria. Still, after a few meetings, he said that although she was lovely, she wasn't for him, and he told his father that he would not be forced into an arranged marriage. As he had denied his father, he had no choice but to leave the camp, and he found it difficult to get a job and somewhere to sleep.

After only a few weeks, he got spotted by one of the gangs that worked in Peterborough, who dealt in all kinds of drugs, people trafficking and prostitution. After a few months with them, he was caught selling drugs and was sent to a young offenders' institute in Cambridgeshire, where he learnt all the tricks of his trade from fellow offenders. While inside, he was well looked after and respected by other inmates as he came from the Flash gang, who were well known to everyone inside. After 15 months, he was released, and he returned to the Flash gang, who made him a full member as he hadn't grassed on them when he was arrested. The gang leader Michael Flash welcomed him back but was taken off selling drugs and moved over to the territory protection group, which, as the name implied, did a wide range of things to protect the gang's territory. While in this division, he learnt how to deal with explosives, often used to send a serious message to rival gangs thinking of stepping on another gang's toes.

I asked Doug what went wrong the second time he was caught. He said he was free for less than eight months after being caught in the wrong place at the wrong time, when one of the drug drop points got raided, just after a large consignment had been delivered.

'Apart from saying that I was visiting a friend, I had no defence, and the judge put me away this time for four years. This was a short sentence compared to the other gang members, and the judge stated after passing the verdict that it was only because the police confirmed that I had not been involved with drugs since being released last time. I didn't know then that the gang boss thought the lower sentence was a reward for my supplied information. I knew my gang days were over and had to keep a close eye on other inmates as I no longer had the protection of the Flash gang, and if the boss were 100% sure that I had sold the gang out, then I wouldn't live long anywhere. I later found out that another gang member had grassed us up, and he was dealt with very quickly and deposited in the river Nene.'

Doug stated that he had served his time as a model inmate and made friends quickly. He was a fit young man and knew many people from all walks of the criminal world. Being from a Gypsy background, he was used to wheeling and dealing, and his expertise would be precious to me.

Doug had been released a few days after I had returned to duty, and I told him in one of our private chats that I was angry with the world and that I might need his services very soon. He gave me a strange look, and I told him that I was angry with the Government for not helping his wife live longer and with the new governor at the prison, and he knew that he wouldn't be staying until retirement. I told Doug to keep his head down, avoid drugs and his old gang, stay at the lodgings found for him, and keep a clean sheet with his probation officer. If he were short of money, to hang on for a couple of weeks, I would supply him with the needed money. Douglas Boswell will be my number two and the leader of team A, and I couldn't wish for a better person to carry out my heist.

***

Chapter 23. Pre-heist Meeting.

I had contacted my eighteen guests; they all had their pay-as-you-go untraceable mobile phones, and I had spoken to them personally. They were shocked at what I was suggesting, and I'm sure they thought I was setting them up, but once I had explained the two main reasons I wanted to get back at the establishment, they all said they were in. I told them I wanted to have six sets of three bank robbers on the day to hit the six largest banks, but I didn't tell them the target town. I told them that we would have a pre-meeting, and I checked which of the guest had a car as I would then get the team leader to pick the other two up, and they could all get to know each other better. Once I had set up the meeting, I would contact them again within a few weeks and arrange to meet them all for a chat.

Pre-meeting Venue

It took me several weeks to find the right venue as most had a room to hire but only had access via the pub. Privacy was the main point as I would hold a meeting at the same time as the heist was taking place in Bedford, and I didn't want the pub landlord or a nosy waitress noticing that my guest hadn't arrived.

I had chosen each team based on where they lived and whether they had access to a car, as a test to see if the three members could work together and if the logistics worked, and they would then be summoned to our planning meeting. I planned the meeting at The White Swan public house in Bromham as they rent a room for small conferences and supply coffee/tea and sandwiches. The entrance to the room is round the back of the pub, which sits next to a public car park. The good thing was that no CCTV cameras covered the small village or the pub, so secrecy was guaranteed.

When I booked it over the phone, I made up an excuse that the meeting was for a group of ex-alcoholics, and they wanted privacy. Everything should be set up and ready to go by 9.45a.m, and we would leave quietly after our meeting at around 2 p.m. The meeting room should have at least twenty chairs, and the pub would supply sandwiches and biscuits, tea, and coffee in a thermos flask ready to drink. The pub would also supply crockery and cutlery. I told the landlord that I would pay for everything in cash before the meeting, which would be delivered by a courier and needed signing for. I also told the pub owner we would use the room again if we liked the service and privacy. I asked him if he had the space available for April 28th and again on May 29th, and he said it was available. I asked him to pencil us in, and I would give a firm order for future dates if we were happy with the privacy on offer.

The pre-meeting went well, and I explained, along with the help of my number two, how the day would pan out. I told them six teams would be aimed at the top six banks. I said I had chosen each group based on where they lived and whether they had access to a car. The car owner would be called the team leader in name only as he would be an equal partner, so I didn't want any team arguing amongst themselves. The job is to slip in and out of Bedford as quickly as possible after taking money from each bank. I explained that the CCTV system in the town would be out of action, but the cameras in the banks would still be live, so they must wear disguises, with a pull-down balaclava for use in the bank. Also, at the meeting in Bromham, I explained how the day would pan out, and I made it clear that every car owner should evaluate the pick-up run for the other two guests several times so that they would arrive at the correct time on the day.

I stated that all cars should approach the Bedford area from the M1 using the A421. Your vehicle must be seen by the ANPR camera just before you reach Kempston. You should ping the camera at around 9.45a.m. before following the route to the Kempston Hardwick railway station, where you would meet up with Doug. If you are running ahead of schedule, there are several lay-bys along the A421 to pull into. Every car should be insured, taxed, and have a valid MOT, as I didn't want anyone being stopped on the day for a motoring offence. If any team leader needs a loan so that their car is legal, ask me at the end. Sticking to the times given is essential, as they should come in handy if the police ask you any questions after the raid. On the day I will collect a parking ticket for each car for attending a meeting here. I will hopefully be able to pass these on to the team leaders when we meet up at the railway station after the heist. Your alibi will be that you were attending a meeting for ex-cons, which I had planned. The meeting was a talk on what you felt needed to be done to get you back into work and to try and interrupt the re-offending pattern that many inmates follow. You can easily tell the police that twenty witnesses attended the meeting, which started at 11a.m. on the day in question. You can be honest and tell the police who you travelled to the meeting with, but don't mention Bedford if you can help it.

***

Chapter 24. My Chosen Eighteen Guests.

To make everything run like clockwork on the day, I needed to find 18 eighteen men who would find it hard to make a legal living on the outside and would be keen to earn some extra tax-free cash. Each man had his own set of problems, and before I could even plan such a heist, I knew I had to get the best men who would follow orders so that there would be truly little chance of us ever being caught. I needed a good number two who would set up the road system on the day of the heist, plus 17 former inmates to make up six teams of three bank robbers.

Over my years as a prison counsellor and an unpaid number two to the governor, I kept records of hundreds of prisoners and their trades. I wanted to use the best men for the job, but I needed to use those recently released and who found it hard to find a job. I also tried to avoid ex-cons with severe drinking or drug problems, making my job difficult as around half of the prison population had one or both addictions. I firmly believe inmates shouldn't be released on parole unless they have been free of their addiction for six months. Without this, we will never cut the number of re-offenders that account for between 28% and 64% of prison spaces, depending on specific age groups.

I have not used any of the inmates I met over the years in our Young Offender Institution (or HMYOI) as I find them exceedingly difficult to deal with, and in my opinion the system is failing them BIG TIME. I don't know how we, as a country, have got it so wrong. Young inmates' lives are such a mess, whether this is down to many of them spending far too much time on their Xbox or Nintendo games instead of getting a decent sleep and education, or whether it's down to lack of control, discipline and leadership from parents.

Young offenders are defined as aged 18-20 years of age. However, young men continue to mature into their mid-twenties. There are some critical things to consider that could improve outcomes for people in this wider age group of 18-25. I have seen from these young people that they have never considered broader perspectives or thought about the future when making decisions, know who they are and what they want to be, and can resist peer influence and temper themselves. The above two factors are called 'psychosocial maturity'. Psychosocial immaturity is prevalent in young men in custody or under our underfunded probation service. This affects how they engage with and respond to prison regimes, probation licenses and supervision.

The prison service needs to give these young men some structure, as this has been missing for most of their sorry lives so far. Placing these young men in an institution and doing extraordinarily little to turn their lives around is pointless. In my opinion, prison is far too soft on these young people, and they should be used on farms picking the crops in all weathers for five days a week. They should also be trained to become bricklayers, plasterers, chippies, plumbers and electricians so that when they leave, they can help fill the shortage of skilled labour the building industry needs. These young men should be released to the probation service on licence to work for building firms. The Government would pay the builder minimum wage (passed on to the offender) for one or two years, which would cost far less than keeping them locked up.

To do this, the whole Young Offender Institution rules must be changed, and money must be provided to employ teachers and craftsmen to train these young men. If they had a job and accommodation already set up for them once they left, I'm sure few would return to the useless and criminal lives they were leading. If the young offender breaches his release terms, they would be sent back and placed in solitary confinement until they learned better.

***

Chapter 25. Preparation for the Heist.

Before we could hold our heist at the end of May, a lot of background work had to be done. We would need the following: workshop, van, traffic lights and signs, mobile phone, handguns, and untraceable debit cards. Money wasn't a problem as my wife had had sizable life insurance, but I still had to be careful how much I withdrew in case the police checked later. I decide to make six withdrawals of £2,500 each over six weeks. I visited six horse racing venues to cover my tracks and kept the program and entry ticket. I always went in the family section as I wouldn't be staying, and it was the cheapest. I visit Huntingdon, Doncaster, Southwell, Market Rasen, Fakenham and Towcester racecourses. I didn't hang around as I have seen the damage gambling can do, but if I were ever asked why I had drawn £15,000 out, I could say I'm unlucky with the horses.

Workshop/Barn

I needed a place to store the van, traffic lights, and other equipment for the heist. It needed to be a few miles outside of the Bedford area with no major roads nearby, as I didn't want to keep pinging any ANPR cameras regularly. It took me longer than I thought to find the ideal workshop, but, in the end, I found a sizeable unused barn just outside Astwood village, just off the A 4288 Newport Pagnell to Bedford road. The old barn had a sign outside reading 'workshop to let'. It gave a local telephone number and the name of R Becket, so I assumed it was direct to the farmer and not via a letting agency as I didn't want to take that route as agencies can be very nosy. I had set up my new mobile phone with an inbuilt voice distortion app from FunCall that would not only distort my voice but also display a false mobile number on the receiver's phone. I called the number and spoke to the farmer, who wanted far too much money for this old barn. I told him that my company had a two-year contract to evaluate and repair, if needed, railway bridges in the surrounding areas. All I wanted to do was store one or two vans, the traffic control equipment, and other small items so that we do not need to wait for them to be sent from our depot in Newcastle. I said we would need it for a year or two and would make the site and barn more secure by installing new locks and CCTV cameras to deter thieves.

We would only use the site once or twice a month to avoid being a nuisance. I also said we were prepared to pay cash up front and would only show the transaction in our petty cash folder. He could do what he liked with the money. Ultimately, he must have seen pound signs, and we agreed on £200 a month or, in this case, £2,400 upfront for the year. He said he was happy with that and asked how we would pay. I knew that the barn didn't have a lock on it, so that we wouldn't need a key, so I said that if he were happy, I would send a courier over with the cash with a simple form he needed to sign to say that it was for a twelve-month contract with an option to extend it for a further year. Farmer Becket must have been one of the struggling dairy farmers you see moaning about losing money by selling milk to supermarkets on the news. I didn't care as farmers are always moaning. If I remember right, there used to be a Milk Marketing Board that set the milk price. However, this was killed off by the farmer-led Conservative Party, which introduced the Agriculture Act 1993, which ended the Milk Marketing Board and the Potato Marketing Scheme.

I arranged for Doug Boswell, my number two, to get on his motorbike and meet me at The Tea Room café in Olney. I would bring the money with me in £20 notes along with a form for the farmer to sign as a receipt and the address and name of the farmer. If questioned by the farmer, he would tell him that he was only the courier and didn't know any more. I would then get Douglas to visit the site and make it secure. He should also fit light sensors and a mock CCTV camera to keep the thieving toerags out. You really can't trust anyone these days.

Van

We would need a van to carry the traffic lights and control boxes in, and I had heard that Highways England would be selling some of their old vans at the Fleet Auction Group held in Coalville, Leicestershire. I planned with Douglas, my number two, to pick him up at the bus stop at the end of his lane at 7a.m. on Tuesday. I never pick people up from their homes as they may have nosy neighbours. Having met hundreds of criminals, I thankfully kept a database of all their details outside of prison, and I'm glad I did.

Finding a set of trade number plates that would allow Douglas to drive the van back to the barn would be easy. My contact for number plates was also going to be able to clone me a set of plates from another van still being used by Highways England once I had sent him the number plate details. This would eliminate the need to register our second-hand van with the DVLA and save having to arrange insurance.

Chatting to a police officer while waiting to collect a prisoner, I raised the subject of cloned vehicles, and he said that 'one in twelve vehicles on the road are now cloned.' I asked what the police were doing to stop this, but he said they could do little as they didn't have the workforce available. If all car registrations were entered into a national database in real time, the computer could cross reference to see if the same number plate pinged twice within ten minutes outside a ten-mile radius. Whenever a clone was spotted, the traffic police could stop both vehicles to see which one had been cloned. I didn't tell him which was the right decision as I didn't want them to find our cloned van.

Traffic Lights and Road Signs

For the heist to work, we would need to obtain traffic control systems and various warning signs, and we had two options for this. One was to go to the construction auctions and buy second hand for cash, or we could check on https://www.roadworks.org/ to see what roadworks were in place at any time, and, for those that showed that traffic lights were being used, we could go along and borrow them. If we went for this option, it would mean that Douglas would have to work the night shift until he had stolen the three sets of traffic control lights we would need. I suggested that getting four sets would be best if he wanted to take this option, so he had a backup.

He said he liked borrowing the lights best and would let me know when they had been obtained, checked, and safely stored at the barn. We would also need three roadwork tents to house the generator along with standard cones. We would need roadside message boards such as 'pedestrians this way', and it would look better if we removed a small section of the tarmac on the bridge as this would take a long time to repair. To make the tarmac removal easy, we would need a cutter like a Stihl TS 410 brick saw concrete cutter, or an angle grinder with a spare cutting disc to cut into the tarmac. You'll also need a kango hammer with a chisel head. This type of equipment can be bought easily for cash at various construction sale sites around the UK or, cheaper still, on eBay. We will need a few tests runs on the old tarmac behind the workshop, but I'm sure it will work.

Mobile Phones
I wanted to send out a heist invitation in the form of a mobile phone with a simple message stating that the phone was from someone they know and to charge the phone ready for use, and I would call them in a few days to explain more. I went for the most straightforward non-traceable cell phone I could find and pick up in the store, the Alcatel One Touch 10.16 SIM-Free Mobile Phone, which cost £16.99 from Argos or £19.99 from Tesco, plus I added £20 to my pre-paid SIM card for any calls. I didn't want to buy more than two at a time and wanted to pay cash so that the purchase wasn't traceable. It took a few weeks to get hold of the 20 phones that I would need. Once the heist at Bedford was over and everyone had been paid, I could

request the SIM card back, issue a new one, and microwave the old ones.

Handguns

I wouldn't say I liked dealing with this part of the operation, but attending the bank without one would be pointless. I only wanted untraceable replicas, as I didn't want anyone getting shot at the party. As I needed 18 of them, I thought this would be difficult, but again Doug Boswell, my number two, came up trumps as he knew a chap in London who could supply them for cash. I was surprised how cheap these were, with prices starting as low as £45 for a Colt 1911 Plastic Replica Automatic Pistol, but we would have to pay more if we needed 18. I also wanted a real gun for security measures as I didn't want any toerag stealing the money from us while it was being processed at the barn. I gave Doug £4,000 and asked him to do his best. If they were to cost more, just let him know how much more he needed.

Untraceable Debit Card

I will need to obtain one or more of these cards as I need to buy things such as train tickets online and don't want the transaction to return to me. I found the best way to do this is to get hold of a prepaid Visa/Mastercard with cash, then pay for anything with the prepaid card and then throw the card away. This isn't easy to do if you want to hide behind the card. I firstly had to register with the card supplier by using a separate mobile phone. They also need a postal address, and I used our storage barn address for this. I also needed an email address, so I went for a Yahoo email. Uploading cash and verifying it can be tricky, but I achieved this and had no problem loading money onto the card.

***

Chapter 26. Internet is Taking Thousands of Jobs.

Simon Westdale was an intelligent young man who had lost his way through no fault of his own. Thankfully, he was still single, but he had a long-time girlfriend waiting for his release. He served four years for supplying drugs and was remorseful; I had to overcome this problem as he beat himself up, which only worsened matters. I told him that everyone makes mistakes. It's how they respond to them that matters. He couldn't change the past but could start today to ensure the future is mapped out for the better. I didn't tell him that after being in prison, he would find it difficult to find work, and like most, he would give up.

He had had a steady childhood but was never exceptionally good at obtaining grades for his schoolwork and ended up with a few Bs and a host of Cs. After he left school at 16, he went to Tresham College and took a course on travel and tourism as he had always been fascinated with travel. He said that he had done well and could have studied for a further year or two and obtained an HNC/HND at Bedford College but decided against it as he was short of cash. After Tresham College, he decided that he wanted to start earning some money and found a job at his local travel agency. Still, after making it up to Assistant Manager, he was made redundant because people increasingly booked their holidays online rather than going into a shop to book. He said that this annoyed him as he had read in the travel trade press that Peter Smith from Tui Travel (better known as Thomson Holidays) was among the five highest earners among FTSE 100 firms, who made over £100 million between them in one year. Smith's pay package earned him £13.3 million, making him the fourth highest-paid boss in the UK.

Simon went on to say that being inside gave him the time to research the problem, and he confirmed that bosses were raking it in and didn't give a damn about the workers that made them the money, nor their customers, who had to pay more for their holiday to cover their greed. One of the biggest moans he had from potential clients was that the holiday price offered was too high. Peter Smith's salary alone could send hundreds of hard-working families on a yearly holiday. Smiths' earnings of £13.3 million are more than one man can spend in a lifetime, and it's alleged that many high earners are now sending their money offshore to avoid paying UK taxes. The country loses out on the tax which should have been paid, and again when the country must borrow money to attempt to balance the books. Currently, the UK debt stands at £1.84 trillion, equivalent to 85% of GDP (figures are pre Covid-19). Even with the harsh Austerity measures put in place by the Conservative government, the country's debt levels continued to grow.

Update September 2023.

The United Kingdom national debt is the total quantity of money borrowed by the Government of the United Kingdom at any time through the issue of securities by the British Treasury and other government agencies. At the end of March 2023, UK General government gross debt was £2,537.0 billion, or 100.5% gross domestic product. It does surprise me that our Conservative government cabinet is made up of millionaires, yet they can't balance the county's books.

Simon went on to state that it was challenging to get another job as all significant travel firms were closing shops and laying staff off. Thomson's most considerable competitor was Thomas Cook (Europe's second-largest tour operator), which went bust in 2019. Previously in 2011, Thomas Cook nearly went bust but was saved by its bankers, who set up a £200 million rescue loan as they had little choice in the end but to lend more money or write off the £1 billion owed to its lenders, including 17 banks.

Simon said he found it difficult to get work as 'All my expertise was in selling travel. Going to the job centre every two weeks was a real struggle as all they could offer me was manual work. After six months, I came across an advert which stated: "Couriers wanted. High rewards offered to the right people." I attended the interview and was told I could earn £400 - £1,200 weekly doing courier work in my van or a hired van. The job would be self-employed with flexible hours working for one of the largest couriers in the UK. As a self-employed courier van driver for Tip Top Express, a typical day would consist of a collection from anywhere in your allocated area within a ten-mile radius of where you lived, followed by delivery to various homes and businesses again within my assigned area. After being unemployed for six months, I was desperate for a job but didn't have much cash to buy or rent a van. Ultimately, my parents offered to help as they could see how stressed I was from being out of work. I decided to hire a van from the company, with the agreement that I find my insurance. The insurance cost me more than I expected because I would use the van for business work. However, I went to see my contact at the job centre and told him the good news, but when I asked him about any benefits until I was paid, he said that all benefits would stop the day I became "employed" as I would no longer be seeking work. I said I wouldn't be paid for a month and had to provide all the petrol for the van, so I asked him what the Government expected me to live on for the next four weeks. He said he might be able to help with the petrol cost to get me to and from work, but not for anything else. I felt down as the job centre had done nothing to help me find work, and they wouldn't help me until I had pay coming in. No wonder many people don't bother to tell them that they have started work. The rules had been written by someone who had never been on the dole or visited a job centre.

'Thanks to my parents, I managed to survive the first month, but the wages were much less than they had told me at the interview. I had to deliver up to 200 parcels daily without time for toilet breaks while earning less than minimum wage. I exceeded the legal maximum shift of 11 hours and finished my day dead on my feet. I soon realised that if I wanted to eat during the day, I would have to eat a sandwich while driving. Finding a toilet was also tricky, and I took a two litre plastic milk bottle to pee into. Any call for a number two would have to wait until the end of the day. I would also have to break the speed limits to compensate for lost time. Icy patches, traffic jams and road closures all added to my day from hell. With most courier companies only offering self-employed jobs, it saves the company from paying the minimum wage, holiday, or sickness pay. After only six weeks, I soon realised this wouldn't make me my fortune or give me the essential money to live on. You feel trapped as the company always owed you two weeks' pay, and I had heard that those who had left found it difficult to get the money owed to them. The company would always devise an excuse, such as the van needing new tyres as I had been braking too hard, or there was a claim for damaged or undelivered parcels. I didn't have enough money to pay all my bills and started to borrow money from pay-day loan shops.'

I heard that a legal firm which led the case against taxi giant Uber also represents seven drivers who alleged that agencies used by Amazon are mistreating them. Simon stated that many parcels he delivered were from Amazon, but that is where the link ends. Amazon uses outside agencies to organise and run their delivery system so that the agencies will face the courts, not Amazon or any other online retailer. Agencies and leading UK and international household names are getting away with it. It was recently reported that Maria Ludkin, legal director of the GMB union, said: 'Employers might not like paying the minimum wage or giving their workers the protection, they're entitled to in the workplace, but it's not optional. We don't get to pick and choose which laws we adhere to and don't like.' Most media coverage is aimed at Amazon, probably because they are the biggest. Amazon's US founder Jeff Bezos, 56, is the world's second richest man who last year made **£1.6million an hour** (yes, this isn't a typo, £1.6 million an hour), so he perhaps can afford to pay a decent wage to everyone who is part of the Amazon family. If you asked a thousand Amazon customers if they would pay an extra £1 so that the company's people handling their orders could be employed and given the legal rights they deserve, I think the majority would say yes.

The Government needs to act on this 'new way to shop' as Amazon will eventually close all high street stores, and delivery to your door will become a way of life. They can blame the international banking crisis for missing the start of the revolution, and maybe Brexit and Covid-19 for currently taking up time. However, they must do what the electorate wants sooner rather than later, offering a fair deal. It was reported in the *Daily Mirror* at the end of January 2018 that DHL drivers were told to take a £2,000 pay cut or lose their job. This is from a company that made a £41 million profit in 2016. DHL deliver for some of the UK's leading companies, such as M&S, House of Frazer, O2, eBay, Argos and KFC. Regarding KFC, perhaps I should say that they are supposed to deliver, but hundreds of KFC outlets had to close as DHL failed to deliver on time. Only in this country could you have a chicken outlet without any chicken. I wonder how many of these top companies' clients are aware of the shocking action taken by DHL. I think the name DHL must mean **D**elayed **H**and**L**ing. It worries me that if these drivers/couriers are pushed so hard, they will be forced to speed to cover the ground, and as they are so tired from working long hours, a fatal accident is just waiting to happen.

In my opinion, we need an independent body set up under the Health & Safety department to test whether it's possible to deliver 200 parcels safely in a day. One of the biggest challenges facing UK workers is the ever-growing number of people having to accept a zero-hour contract between an employer (or its agency) and a worker whose employer is not obliged to provide minimum working hours. In contrast, the worker is not obliged to accept any work offered. The employee may sign an agreement to be available for work as and when required so that no number of hours or times of work are specified. Depending on jurisdiction and conditions of employment, a zero-hour contract may differ from casual work. They are often used in agriculture, the courier industry, hotels and catering, education, and the healthcare sector. A Channel 4 documentary employed secret cameras in Amazon UK's Rugeley warehouse to document worker abuses. It claimed that Amazon used 'controversial' zero-hour contracts to reprimand staff and was 'tagging' employees with GPS and subjecting them to harsh working conditions. Of course, Amazon said many of those on zero-hour contractors were happy and denied that the company reprimanded staff. You may be surprised to learn that Amazon is not alone, as many of the country's largest retailers use them. Wikipedia stated that Sports Direct, a retailer, has 90% of its workers on zero-hour contracts. J D Wetherspoon, one of the UK's largest pub chains, has 24,000 staff, or 80% of its workforce, on contracts with no work guarantee each week. 90% of McDonald's workforce in the UK—82,000 staff members—are employed on a zero-hour contract. Burger King franchisees and Domino's Pizza operations extensively use zero-hour contracts in the UK. The Spirit Pub Company has 16,000 staff on zero-hour contracts, and even Boots UK have 4,000 staff on zero-hour contracts. In the UK, zero-hour contracts are controversial.

British business leaders have supported these contracts, stating that they provide a flexible labour market. They may suit some people, such as retirees and students, who want occasional earnings and can be entirely flexible about when they work. Trade union groups and others have raised concerns about the possibility of management's exploitation and using such contracts to reward or reprimand employees for any reason, meaningful or trivial. They also raise concerns about how workers can adequately assert their employment rights or maintain decent employment relations. Apart from the months of December, July and August, zero-contracts should be banned as they can lead to poor working relations between the worker and the employer. Time will tell which way the UK decides now that it's left the EU, but for now, it's wait and see.

Simon sat between a rock, and a hard place and couldn't escape his modern-day slavery contract. He had heard several other drivers were also delivering drugs to addresses and collecting the cash as they went around their route. This worked well; he was making enough money to repay his parents and build a nest egg for the next rainy day. However, the police had got to hear about the use of couriers for the delivery of drugs, and he was pulled over one evening and found to have drugs ready for delivery, and he had over £200 in notes on him. He was charged with supplying drugs and got four years.

In my opinion, the Government needs to set up an all-party committee to save our shops once the Covid-19 pandemic is under control, as many of our high streets will never be the same again. Far too many jobs have been lost with store closures well before the pandemic, and many shops will not re-open after the lockdown is lifted. The main two reasons for these closures were the crippling business rates and the high rental cost. The government has given a business rate holiday on some shops, but not all. The high rental/lease cost needs to be lowered and based on retail values; some are ten years out of date. The Nottingham Trent University wrote in its Expert Blog dated 6th of April 2020 stated, 'Intu, the owner of, amongst others, the Trafford Centre in Manchester and Nottingham's Victoria and Broadmarsh Centres, and which has £4.5 billion of debts, was on the brink of collapse even before coronavirus took hold.' Intu owns about 20 of the UK's top shopping centres, and it's not sure Intu will survive. Smaller store owners in British high streets are also in a financial mess, and the future of our shops is unsure.

Local councils are being strapped for much-needed cash from the Government, and many will increase parking costs to try to get in the extra money, but in my opinion, they may be killing the goose that laid the golden egg. Many people have switched to online shopping, which will only increase even after the lockdown is lifted. What in my opinion needs to be done is for the Government to introduce an online delivery tax of £2 per order and the monies raised to cut business rates, make parking for shoppers free for four hours and give the local councils funds to compulsory purchase empty shops and rent them out at a more manageable rent. The council could also modernise the accommodation above the shops and rent these out to needy locals.

Home delivery isn't being monitored or regulated, and anyone with a car or van can become a delivery driver for the likes of Amazon or its agency. Many TV programs have covered the problems created by zero-hours contract drivers and the gig economy, and the latest Ken Loach film, *Sorry We Missed You*, is worth watching. All media alleges that drivers don't have time to stop for a toilet break and rely on a milk bottle, and many work exceptionally long hours without a break. Tired delivery drivers are a ticking time bomb just waiting to explode, and it could be one of your loved ones being killed in the explosion.

Some cars and vans used to deliver parcels don't have proper insurance for business use, and many speed to ensure they hit their delivery target. Many older readers will remember the carnage caused by lorries being driven by drivers falling asleep at the wheel before the introduction of tachographs in the late 1970s. Lorry drivers can only drive for four and a half hours before taking a 45-minute break. The government should ensure that deliveries should be made in vans owned by the company and that the van is correctly insured, serviced every 20,000 miles, driven by a named driver, and fitted with a tachograph.

Any person involved with deliveries within the UK should be fully employed by the company and not be part of the gig economy. It's not as if the owner of Amazon, Jeff Bezos, can't afford to pay a decent wage, holiday and sickness pay, and PAYE to the people who make him more prosperous, as he is THE SECOND RICHEST MAN IN THE WORLD.

Simon was released a few months before I was forced out, so I contacted him via the usual mobile phone method. He agreed that he would be available for the heist in Bedford as he couldn't get work and could see that it was the only way out of his current nightmare. Simon Westdale will be my second guest for Team A.

***

Chapter 27. From a Hero to Inmate.

Alan Frazer had post-traumatic stress disorder (PTSD) after leaving the army. Alan was a likeable chap who, since leaving the military in 2010, had been sent to prison no less than three times for mainly petty theft where he was trying to get money for booze; as he said, 'It did help to keep me warm on the cold nights when I was sleeping rough.' The country's homeless figure continues to grow as little is done to correct the situation. I firmly believe that homelessness/sleeping rough should be seen as a health problem, and every town in the country should provide suitable accommodation to suit the individual's needs. Those that don't follow the rules and continue to sleep rough should be sectioned and forcibly placed in a shelter.

The Guardian newspaper reported in February 2020 that 'the government has been accused of dramatically under-reporting the scale of rough sleeping following council data showing numbers almost five times higher than Whitehall estimates. On the eve of the housing ministry's annual snapshot of rough sleeping, which last year said that 4,677 people slept outside, yet the council data showed almost 25,000 people slept rough in 2019.' As a country, we are failing dismally on the problem of homelessness, but it need not be like that. *HuffPost* reported in February 2019 that Finland's much-lauded "housing first" approach has been in place for over a decade.

The idea is simple. To solve homelessness, you start by giving someone a permanent home with no strings attached. If they want to drink, they can; if they want to take drugs, that's fine too. Support services are available to treat addiction, mental health and other problems and help people get back on their feet, from assisting with welfare paperwork to securing a job. The housing in Finland is a mix of designated standard apartments sprinkled throughout the community and supported housing: apartment blocks with on-site services built or explicitly renovated for chronically homeless people. For example, a Salvation Army building in Helsinki was converted from a 250-bed emergency shelter to an 81-apartment supported housing unit. If Finland can do it, Great Britain, the fifth most prosperous nation in the world, can do it too.

In my opinion all addictions should be treated as a health problem, as placing these people in prison doesn't work and never will. It also costs around £47,000 a year to keep them in prison. On Alan's third visit to the prison, he fell under my wing, and I worked with him to get him off the booze, and hopefully keep him off it once he was released. Alan had seen service in the Bosnia War and Iraq. He was a highly trained bomb disposal officer, and what he didn't know about making and dismantling incendiary devices wasn't worth writing about. He was happy when he was tinkering about on a project, and I put him on a course that could see him partly trained as an electrician's mate before leaving prison. There was a shortage of electricians, and he should have no trouble getting work once he left, but his having been sent to prison three times will put many employers off.

Within a matter of days of me leaving the prison service, Alan was released, and found lodgings in Newport Pagnell. He had tried to get work for about three weeks when I contacted him, and he was again down in the dumps but was still sober. I sent him a welcome invitation and spoke to him within a matter of days. We agreed to meet at the coffee shop in Olney to discuss what we could do together. We met on a rainy Monday afternoon, and I told him what had happened and how disappointed and angry I felt. I said I had a plan that wasn't legal but could bring us a nice financial reward and great satisfaction. I asked if he would be interested, and he said he would be pleased to help as he had nothing to lose. If he got caught, he knew he would have a roof over his head, be fed well, and be kept warm for the next ten years.

I explained my brief plan to him and said he would be responsible for the small explosive device I needed to kill off the CCTVs and the six dummy timer boxes we would leave behind after every bank raid. I also explained that we would need an incendiary device for the old house on Clarence Street. I said that he would have to be careful about buying in any of the explosive devices as we didn't want them coming back to any of us. He said, 'I have mates in the forces who would supply anything we need for cash.'

I explained my idea to kill the CCTV cameras, to gain access to the control box and place a small incendiary device that a mobile phone call would trigger. When it exploded, it would spray mercury across the terminals and short-circuit the system. I also said that apart from the mobile phone activating the small bomb, he needed to find a way to trigger the device if, by lousy luck, someone checked on the box between the time the small bomb was planted and the actual detonation time. He said that sounded simple enough and 'could easily be made without causing any unwanted attention'. I told him that the device needed to be as silent as possible as we didn't want the police being drawn to that part of the town as someone had reported hearing a bomb go off. Alan said that he would investigate it and get back to me. Before parting, I handed him £2,500 under the table and said there was plenty more if he needed it. He should keep in touch, but only via the phone I gave him. I asked him what means of transport he had, and he said he had his motorbike still stored up at his mother's farm from when he was inside. I said that was good as I may have a few courier jobs that need to be done soon, and the cover of his helmet would help. Alan Frazer will be part of my Team A.

***

Chapter 28. Underage Sex and Incest.

Barry Swift was in his mid-50s and starting to lose his hair, but he had kept himself in shape and looked considerably younger than his years. He had been found guilty of having sex with a fourteen-year-old girl. He was married with three grown-up children who had all left home, and his wife for 31 years was standing by him. I had a description of what he had been convicted of, but in all my consultations, I like to take my patients back to their childhood, as this is where most disorders start. Being a prison counsellor, I saw a wide range of sex offenders, and I had to try to help them understand that what they had done was wrong and try to find a way to put them on the straight and narrow, so that after they were released, they had a good chance of never reoffending. Although we had to deal with the inmates that were allocated to us, I never liked dealing with sex offenders that had done terrible things to incredibly young children and even babies. I had to spend time with them, but I didn't have to listen to them.

'So, tell me, Barry, when did you first become aware of sex?' Barry said that he first became aware when he was about eight. He lived in a house with his large family of mum, dad, two brothers and six sisters. The house had a long garden with several sheds and many fruit trees. One of his older sisters had invited some of her schoolmates around to play in the garden, and the game they played turned out to be doctors with a lot of show me yours, and I'll show you mine. 'I remembered that my older sister had persuaded one of her friends to show me her privates, hoping I would show all the girls mine. I looked at the young girl, who was very pretty and had lovely long golden hair that went a long way down her back, and she had started to blossom with her tits just beginning to show. I was too young to get turned on, so I never showed them my privates.'

He went on to state that his older sister Belinda left him alone for a few years until he was 12, and again, he ended up in a shed with his sister and one of her friends. However, by this time, he had started to get a woody and play with himself; his sister made him lie down on the floor, pulled his trousers down and made him get a boner. What surprised him was when his sister took his cock in her mouth and started to move it in and out of her lips and suck simultaneously. 'I was in heaven, but to my surprise, she stopped, got on top of me, put my penis in her wet vagina, and started moving up and down. A short while later, I told my sister that she had to stop as I needed to pee, but she just said it would be all right and to pee in her. I now know that I was then having my first orgasm but was still too young to produce any juice.'

Barry said that his older sister never left him alone after that, but 'she stopped when I told her I was now producing some cream. It was obvious that my older sister had had sex for a few years, and I didn't realise until much later that my father and my older brother were also having intercourse with her. Looking back, I can now see that I came from an incestuous family, and at the time, I never knew that it was wrong. Growing up in a large family, love and attention was very thin on the ground, and I suppose having sex was a way of feeling that you were loved. It wasn't until much later in life that I realised my father abused all my sisters, although it wasn't spoken about then. What convinced me that it had happened was when my father died, and three of my sisters wouldn't go to his funeral. They told my mum they weren't well, and I never thought much about it then. Years later, when my mother died, the same three sisters were again ill and never come to their mother's funeral.

'I asked my older sister Belinda what she thought was going on. It was then that my worst thoughts were confirmed. My sister told me that "Dad sexually abused all of the girls" and that "Mum must have known what was going on," and three of my sisters also blamed her for not stopping it, and that's why they never showed up at either funeral service. I asked my sister why she thought that Mum never told Dad to stop, and my sister came back with her theory that Mum had produced eight children and didn't want any more, so she let Dad abuse the girls so that she could rest. My sister also said Mum never left Dad because she had nowhere to go, and deep down, she still loved him.'

I asked Barry if it was the incest that had led him on the path that ended up with him sitting in front of me rather than sitting at home with his wife. He said that he had never thought that young girls were sexy and that he wasn't a paedophile, and before I asked the obvious question, he said that he had never abused his daughters and would 'take a lie detector test to prove it.' I told him I wasn't here to judge him, but I had a duty to try to find out what had led him to my door so that when he left, he didn't return a few months later. Barry said he was never attracted to young girls but didn't like big tits either. Perhaps his first experience in the garden when he was eight had set in his subconscious mind that budding girls were his favourites. Barry said that although he had been caught out with his victim, he honestly thought that she was 16, and he had been too weak and couldn't say no to the temptation.

He was honest and said that when he was released, he would ensure he didn't fall into the trap ever again. He would give young ladies a very wide birth. Barry asked me if I thought that incest was 'common amongst large families.' I told him it should be me asking the questions and not the other way around. He stated that he felt guilty for not doing something about the incest problem once he had heard the sorry facts. I said that in my opinion, incest was a massive problem in society. It didn't just affect large families, nor did it have any class boundaries as, in my time as a prison counsellor, I had faced the problem far too many times.

I went on to explain that in my opinion it was a genetic problem that did pass down through the generations and that some families accepted that it was part of family life. Some victims accepted the problem, but as he found out, three of his sisters never forgave his dad or mother. I suppose that better education could be the answer, and children as young as six should be told that their body is theirs alone, and that if anyone tried to touch their private parts, they should tell their teacher about it. I also said that easy access to porn on the web was a problem as some websites had sex between young and old look as if it was a normal thing to do. You also had the problem of girls' and boys' bodies maturing at a young age, and the old saying 'curiosity killed the cat' was probably true. We ended our session with a warm handshake, and he thanked me for being honest with him, and I said likewise and, 'It's good to talk.'

On checking up with Barry after his release, he sadly informed me that his wife hadn't waited for him, and they now live separate lives. He had difficulty finding a job at his age and was happy to help me and bring in some extra cash. Once Barry had left, I had 15 minutes to grab a cuppa before my next session, and I sat back and thought about the problem society faces with paedophiles and wondered if we would ever find an answer. I knew an ex-primary school governor who spent a few years with us for importing a child sex doll from China. He had been arrested at border control when they seized the three-foot-high doll. Police visited his home and found two more dolls dressed in children's clothes, and he had had sex with them. I have always had a niggle in the back of my mind that him taking out his warped passion on a piece of plastic would help prevent him from raping a child. I'm not condoning what he did, but in my time in various prisons, I have known chaps serving less time for interfering with real children. Barry Swift will be my team leader for Team B.

***

Chapter 29. How Gambling is Ruining Lives.

Pete Griffith was 67 and born in Bourneville, Birmingham, England. Pete had been married twice but is now single. He has no children or contact with any of his previous wives. He was the only son of Jack and Mary Griffith, who had met when working for Cadbury's in the chocolate factory in Bourneville near Birmingham. Cadbury's rule was that married women should be at home and not at work. It does make you think that the Cadbury brothers got it about right as they also provided medical care, housing, education, leisure facilities, and much more and, in its heyday, was the best place to work. Pete said he had a wonderful childhood until he was around 12 and his dad suffered a terrible road accident and could no longer work. The family then moved to Coventry. Pete's parents died about ten years ago, and he currently lived in a council flat in Rushden, Northants, but he would have lost his flat by now and would have to start all over again when released.

To be able to see forward, one must also look back. This is my rule when performing the counselling part of my job. If I'm going to stand a chance, I must get to the bottom of the problem and therefore ask each client why they became an addict. Pete told me that he started gambling when he was 12. A local café had pinball machines where you could put a shilling (5 pence) in the slot, try to get the week's highest score and win five pounds worth £100 in today's money. A fiver in those days was a lot of money, and many kids would play every day after school. Some would even skip school to try to win. Many stole from relatives or would take empty beer bottles back to the off-license and get a few pence back per bottle so they had money to gamble. This was when recycling was at its best, as milk was delivered to your house in the morning and the empties collected the next day instead of what we have now, where plastic bottles end up either in the landfill or in the sea.

At another counselling session, I asked him to explain a little more about how he became addicted to gambling. Pete had already mentioned what he did as a child, but I needed to know what went on in his adult life. He said he 'had worked in a shop that gave you half a day off on Mondays, Wednesdays and Saturdays. In the weekday half-days off, there was little else to do, especially during the winter,' and so he spent his time and the little money he had betting on the greyhounds or horses in the local betting shops. He said that he had never smoked or drank as he had seen far too many people become addicted without realising it, but it didn't dawn on him that he was also an addict.

Pete soon realised that he never stood a chance of winning significantly, and if he hit the jackpot with a good run, it was never enough to change his life. He joked about how he noticed far too late that in a betting shop there would be three or more windows where you could place your bets, but only one window that paid winnings out. I asked Pete if he still gambled, and he said not anymore. It's a mugs game, and the Government doesn't do anything to stop it. He said that when he was a young teenager, there were no betting shops on the high street, and bets were placed with a bookies runner who would either be in the local pub at lunchtime or at your place of work. In 1961, the law changed, allowing betting shops to open but not display the fact in the shop window. He said he could remember when you had to pay a tax on your winnings, or the bookie would let you pre-pay the tax when you placed your bet. Chancellor Gordon Brown introduced the betting tax in 1968 but abolished it in 2002. The reason was the move to offshore betting, where punters didn't have to pay tax. Instead of the betting tax, bookmakers would be taxed on their gross profits at a rate of 15%. Gordon Brown – or his advisers – didn't consider that many of the UK's top betting firms would become off-shore companies in countries with a low corporation tax rate, and the UK would end up with zilch.

Modern betting shops are very user-friendly, and you can lose money on many bets or coin machines. Pete stated that he disliked the coin machines as they were set up only to pay out about a third of their takings in prize money. He believed that the percentage was laid down by one of the Government quangos, but it should be clear on the machines what percentage of takings are paid out. He said he had also tried poker on the web and bingo, but he woke up one night and kicked himself for being such an old fool. He realised that with the casino knowing what cards they give you, they always had the upper hand. Many casinos would let you have a win now and again to keep you hooked. Bingo was just as bad as they also know what numbers they are giving you and everyone else in the game. They just set up the computer on their end to maximise their winnings. He was annoyed to see one day when he bought one of the UK's national tabloids, an advert for bingo where it stated clearly that they pay out five million pounds in prize money every week. What the Government should make them also say in the advert is how much money gamblers put in the pot before they paid out the five million. If they told the truth, it would be around £20 million in and £5 million out. He reckons that they should also be made to add that 'Anyone who gambles are a big fool' but felt that this would be asking too much.

I asked Pete what he felt should be done to stop others from following in his footsteps. He clarified that a total gambling ban would never work, but punters should be told the truth about how much the machine will pay out for every £10 put in. He said that if punters could see that they would only ever pay out 34% of monies gambled, they would probably keep their hard-earned money in their pockets. The same applies to online casinos, bingo operators and The National Lottery. He said that there should be a tax of 20% levied on any betting. This way, the William Hills of the world would have to declare their income and pay the 20% to the tax office. Punters would then know that if they were gambling a pound, only 80 pence would be staked, or they could pre-pay the tax when placing their bet. For £1 bet, they would need to part with £1.20.

I asked him if he felt 'punters would just gamble on the web where there wasn't any tax to be paid.' Pete replied, 'Such overseas websites should be blocked, and Australia will require overseas companies to collect goods and services tax, GST. This GST differs from VAT and will be placed on luxury items such as gambling, booze, cigarettes, et cetera.' The USA introduced the Unlawful Internet Gambling Enforcement Act (UIGEA) in 2006 to give more weight to the Federal Wire Act of 1961. The overarching purpose of the law was to prevent gambling companies from partaking in 'restricted transactions,' which means they cannot accept payments related to wagers using the internet from overseas players. If they did, they would run afoul of any extant federal or state laws.

Pete said the UK needs its own UIGEA, which would be one of many tools to restrict online gambling. The UK may also need a backup plan to prevent monies from being paid to overseas companies involved in gambling. The bank or card company should charge an extra 20% which is paid directly to the UK tax authorities. A team of cyber detectives would need to monitor what was being paid out. Pete said that the man or woman in the street doesn't realise how profitable betting companies are. According to *The Guardian* newspaper, the Bet365 boss netted £323 million in a single year. The 2018/2019 year saw Bet365 customers stake £64.49bn on sports over the 12 months, a 22.7% improvement on the prior year. Just think what good the Government could do with 20% of £64 billion annually. Pete did admit that he didn't know how much of the £64 billion came from overseas punters, nor how much the company paid in tax, but he would find out and let me know.

Pete stated that any addiction, whether gambling, drugs, smoking or alcohol, should be treated as a medical condition, and the NHS should support addicts. Gambling ruins thousands of lives every year, and at least the betting levy of 20% would help cover the cost of any treatment. He said the Conservative government would be reluctant to do this, as they receive donations from gambling/betting organisations. Although Pete is getting on in years, I have asked him to join me in the heist I have planned in Bedford. He willingly accepts as he is a beaten man and doesn't care if he gets caught and sent back to prison, as at least he will have a roof over his head and three solid meals every day.

Pete Griffith will be my second guest on Team B.

To read another sad story about how one punter took his anger out by stopping the Derby and more on 'skin betting', which is hitting youngsters hard, please go to Afterwards - Chapter 29, Gambling Extra, which can be found at the end of the book.

***

Chapter 30. Buying his Council Home.

The third member of Team B will be William (Bill) Bennett, who was married to Sophie and had three children aged 5, 9 and 13. Bill had an excellent job at the Thomas Cook travel agency, but when the big bosses decided to close several branches in 2014, he was made redundant. He and his family had brought their council house (even though the mortgage repayments would be twice that of the rent he had been paying) like millions of others who thought they were doing the right thing. This was fine while he had a job, but with no income, he soon got behind with the mortgage, and in the end, he was forced to give up the house that had been his family's home for over 20 years and his late mothers before him.

When he and his wife visited the housing department of his local council, they first argued that he had made himself homeless and they couldn't help. Ultimately, the council had to give in as he had three children, and they put them up in a B&B, costing more than his mortgage had ever been. Six months later, he was rehoused by the council but miles away from his previous home, which meant the children had to change schools and his wife's part-time job would be lost. Bill finally got another job, but it wasn't in travel, as most travel companies closed shops and cut the holiday price on their website.

His new job was acting as a relief postman, and one day he had to deliver an oversize letter to his previous home, which sent shivers down his spine, but he couldn't risk losing this job, so he took a deep breath and rang his old doorbell. He was surprised to see an Eastern European lady, which by the name he assumed was from Poland, and he asked her if she had bought the house. No, she said, her family was renting it, but they were looking for somewhere cheaper. He made up the story that a friend had once lived in the house, but he couldn't afford it and had to move. He asked the new tenant how long she had lived there, and she said, 'only two months' as they had to 'save up the £650 a month payment in advance plus a month's deposit.' Bill was shocked and angry that his home had once been a council home with affordable rent, only to be convinced that he was doing the best for his family. He wanted to get a foot on the property ladder, only to find out that not only had the council lost a valuable home to rent out, but he had also lost. The only person who has gained out of all this was the private property baron who had brought the house at a low rate and was now renting it out and raking in the money. 'I couldn't help thinking of the old saying where it states, "The rich get richer, and the poor get poorer".'

I asked Bill why he 'got angry when he spoke about his former home.' Bill said that the three-bedroom council home had been in his family for over 40 years, and it was the banking crisis of 2008 that started the country's downturn, which affected thousands of families with many smaller companies going bust, yet not one of the wankers had ever suffered or been brought to justice. The crash had been like an earthquake, but the aftershocks did the most damage. The British Government put in millions of taxpayers' money to save the day and became the main shareholder of some banks. One of these banks was the Northern Rock which the British government stepped in at the eleventh hour and saved the bank from going under.

Bill went on to say that what the Government should have done was to instruct Northern Rock to take over mortgages like his and to set up a deal that kept a roof over his and his family's head and saved the council from having to pay more money to keep them in B&B accommodation. I asked Bill why Northern Rock would want to take over a dodgy mortgage for someone who couldn't pay. He said that they wouldn't, 'But what the Government should have done was to bring in a new law that building societies could not foreclose on a mortgage but instead sell the property and mortgage to Northern Rock at either 80% of the home's current value or if the mortgage had been partly paid off by the current owner, and the outstanding balance was less than the 80%. They should transfer the mortgage to Northern Rock at that level. Northern Rock would then deal with the situation by postponing repayments or taking the interest-only payments until the owner was back on their feet. This would have been far better for thousands of families forced into a situation caused by a third party, i.e., the banking community.'

Bill said that since being behind bars, he had done a lot of research and found that in 2007 analysts such as Morgan Stanley thought there could be a 25% decline in house values in two years. The International Monetary Fund estimates that British house prices were overvalued by 30%. The Financial Services Authority (FSA) says a million people face losing their homes over the next 18 months. Northern Rock was the first banking casualty; the buy-to-let flat specialist Bradford & Bingley was the second; others will follow as this second mortgage-related financial shock shreds banking balance sheets and undermines confidence in the financial system. The then housing minister Caroline Flint's see-through cabinet briefing papers revealed the problem (although, curiously, she didn't see fit to tell the country the news herself). Indeed, the government was still actively encouraging first-time buyers into a market it knew was collapsing. Ministers should be precisely doing the reverse: warning young families not to take on mortgages for flats that will assuredly land them in negative equity.

Iain Macwhirter of the *The New Statesman* warned, 'This is going to be far, far worse than the housing recession of 1990-92.' Fuelled by irresponsible bank lending, UK house prices nearly tripled in the decade to 2007—a more lunatic rise even than in America. British prices have been running at nearly eight times average earnings against a historical average of 3.5. This was never going to be sustainable. In August 2007, the bubble burst, and a combination of related events conspired to turn this boom into an epic bust that would likely consume the British economy and lead to depression. You may think the credit crisis is over, but the real crisis is just beginning. Myra Butterworth, Personal Finance Correspondent for *The Telegraph,* wrote in January 2009 that 'more than 1,000 homes being taken back by lenders every week despite several new schemes announced by the Government to help struggling homeowners to keep their properties.' The article stated, 'The figures are expected to get even worse, with the Council of Mortgage Lenders predicting 75,000 homes repossessed in 2009.' According to Britain's largest building Society Nationwide, house prices saw their biggest annual decline in 2008, with the average cost of a UK home falling 15.9% to £153,048. It is the biggest annual drop since records began in 1952. The stock of possession cases remaining unsold has also risen sharply from 12,837 at the end of September 2007 to 27,123 a year later—an increase of 111%." First, the banks found that because of the US subprime mess, they couldn't borrow cheap money from the international markets anymore, so they cut back on lending and increased rates.

Banks such as Northern Rock, offering 'suicide loans' of up to 120% loan-to-value, stopped lending altogether. Not surprisingly, people stopped buying. The number of first-time buyers in March 2008 was the lowest ever recorded, with fewer than 18,000 in the UK. Bill said he had read thousands of articles from a wide range of professionals, yet they still needed to devise a plan to resolve the problem. What happened in 2007-2009 could happen again (post-Covid-19), and the Government should put his suggestion into law so there was a safety net for any family suffering eviction.

I asked Bill what made him 'turn from a law-abiding family man to a criminal in such a short time.' He said that his relief postal job was on a zero-hour contract, and, after the holiday period, he was told there wouldn't be any work until December. The house the council had found his family was on a very tough estate that was a dumping ground for families like his, and he needed to get enough money to move his family to a more quality area. He only wanted a few grand to pay the deposit and cover moving costs. He had a lot of time on his hands as he only had to sign on every two weeks, and he started up a window cleaning round to try to make some extra cash. It soon took off as he only canvased better areas, and was doing okay until the rainy weather set in. He didn't know that one of the houses he was cleaning was owned by the manager of the job centre. He hadn't declared any extra income, and the job centre took him to court. He explained to the court that he was trying to get enough money to move his family to a more quality area, but the judge wasn't interested and sentenced him to 18 months.

I asked Bill if his wife and children were keeping in touch (I knew they were, but we never let on that I already knew the answer)' and he said that his wife came every few months but didn't want the kids to see him while he was in prison. He said his wife had forgiven him, but they were 'worried about the future now that he had been in prison.' I felt sorry for Bill (although I was meant to remain neutral). I could understand how he and his family were feeling. All he had done wrong was to try to buy his council house and make a better life for his family. In prison, new skills can be taught so that when someone leaves, they have a better chance of securing work. Bill lived in a horticultural part of England, so I suggested he look at the Horticultural or Garden Centre worker's course. There is a national shortage of horticulturists in the UK; therefore, he stood a better chance of getting a job when released. However, Bill didn't complete the course as he was found to be dyslexic, and he left prison with little chance of getting a job. He had had to return to the tough estate he hated and found it challenging to find work. He was pleased to hear my voice and was willing to join the heist in Bedford. William Bennett will be my third guest on Team B.

Update: August 2023.
The Right to Buy has always been controversial, and many of the Council houses sold to tenants at a discount rate helped balance

the Council's books and did not provide money to build more social housing. The next Government must make it law that any borrower can ask to pay interest only until their finances improve. This would save the local authority paying for families housed in B&Bs or hotels. The Government must realise that many couples started married life in a cheaper council house, giving them money to save towards a mortgage deposit. Unless we can get more people on the first step of the ladder, no one will be moving up the ladder. When older homeowners die, there won't be anyone near the top of the ladder able to buy these surplus homes.

***

Chapter 31. Prison is a Dumping Ground for the Mentally Ill.

James Burley was just one of the many inmates at my office door who shouldn't be here. During my 20-plus years as a prison counsellor, I have seen a massive increase in the number of people sent to prison suffering from some form of mental health problem. Many of these prisoners are a danger to themselves but are no danger to the public and shouldn't be in prison. Mental health appears to be at the bottom of the list, with the NHS and local governments being underfunded for the last decade. If the mental health problem could be controlled or fixed, then it would be in everyone's interest to release these sick patients back into the community under strict supervision, where instead of costing the taxpayer around £47,000 every year to keep them locked up in jail, they could be contributing to society.

One sector under the mental health umbrella is ex-soldiers suffering from post-traumatic stress disorder (PTSD). One such prisoner that fell under my control was James Burley. James saw action in the Afghan War and in 2007 was sent to fight in the Badlands of southern Helmand. James had always wanted to be a soldier and joined the Midland Regiment after leaving college. He was trained to manufacture and dismantle incendiary explosive devices, which came in handy several times during his time with the army. During one of our chats, James told me he was doing well until a six-month tour in 2007, where his unit, the 2nd Battalion of the Midland Regiment, fought many pitched battles against a well-armed and ruthless Taliban force. His platoon knew that the enemy would take a particular route—after evening prayer, to where they were waiting to pick off any troops returning to barracks. James had been instructed to build an incendiary explosive device to take the Taliban out.

However, a young child who had been taken ill was being rushed to the local doctors, and her father took a shortcut directly along the route that we had set the bomb. The device exploded, killing the child and two adults. About a week later, during an ambush, James' best friend was killed along with the platoon sergeant and several other close colleagues were seriously injured. It was later reported that it had been the largest ambush suffered by British troops during the 11-year war. James told me that the death of the child and his best friend started a downward spiral as he quickly developed a drinking problem, became violent and increasingly withdrawn. Despite displaying the classic symptoms of post-traumatic stress disorder (PTSD), he received no help or counselling from the Army, and instead he was sent back to Helmand in 2009 and again in 2011.

Looking at his case notes, they plainly stated that since returning home, LCpl Burley had suffered from hallucinations and violent episodes and constantly heard voices inside his head. He had committed acts of self-harm and had developed a deep hatred of Asians. It was there in black and white that he had PTSD, and why he had been sent to prison rather than a hospital beats me. I requested to speak with James' parents to see if they could throw more light on what had brought about the change in their son, and they were delighted to hear that someone was taking an interest in him and planned to spend a few hours with me after visiting their son next week.

James' father, John, who lived in Matlock, Derbyshire, strongly believes his son's mental health was destroyed by the failure of the British Army even to acknowledge that he was ill. John said that the British army sends 18-year soldiers into battle to kill, watch their mates being killed, and expect them to carry on without help when they return home. 'We thought the army would care for our son's health and well-being, but we were wrong. There was ample opportunity for them to help, but they didn't. We tried several times to speak to James, but he refused to admit he had a problem or talk about the events in Afghanistan. When he was home on leave, he would get into fights, and was arrested once, but the charges were dropped, and the problems were passed back to the army, but all he was told to do was pay some compensation." His dad said that after speaking on the phone to James in January 2012, he called and spoke to his commanding officer and told him that he firmly believed his son was a danger to himself and his colleagues. He was flown back to Britain under military escort, but when he arrived at his barracks, he was accused by a senior officer of being a coward who had let down his friends. The same day he was given a medical assessment by the base GP, who said he was 'fine' and could leave the camp. Back home on leave, he had nightmares where he dreamt of killing his parents and younger brother.

With continued pushing by us, he finally underwent a psychological evaluation where it was accepted that he had severe PTSD and was prescribed antipsychotic drugs. The army then started to medically discharging James, but we were told this could take up to a year. Once he was released, he came home, but even with all the antipsychotic drugs in his system, if he saw an Asian person in the street, he would try to vomit on them. The stress on the family was indescribable. It was for this problem that James ended up in prison. He saw a group of young Asian men one night and attacked them; even though he was outnumbered, he still broke a few noses before being arrested and charged with GBH. The CPS decided to drop the racist charge as they felt it was in the best public interest as it would look bad in the press and do little to help either party. When the case came to court, James had already agreed to plead guilty, and when the judge issued the sentence, he said that he would have preferred if James had claimed insane, as it was clear to him that James needed medical help. He also said that the public also needed protection. As there were no available beds at a home for the mentally ill, he would have no choice but to send James to prison for 24 months with the proviso that if a bed became available in a secure mental hospital, James could serve his time there.

James' dad said he had made an official complaint stating that the army had been negligent by not diagnosing James' suffering from PTSD. The reply I got was short, and it just said that Government data published by the National Audit Office, compiled from Ministry of Defence records, suggested that only one soldier in a thousand suffered from PTSD. I told James' parents I had noticed a sharp rise in ex-soldiers ending up in prison. I pointed out that new research produced by the Centre for Medical Health Defence at Kings College in London found that 40 out of 1,000 service personnel suffered from the condition, rising to 70 out of 1,000 for those serving in a combat zone. Mr Burley said that their local solicitor is now acting on their son's behalf and is taking the army to court for negligence in not diagnosing PTSD earlier. She will argue in court that the number and frequency of operational tours military personnel are expected to complete are taking its toll. Lessons from the past are still not being implemented at ground level, and the MoD must take action to ensure we are not sitting on a mental health time bomb.

I thanked James' parents for providing me with the background on how their son arrived at my door and promised them that I would do all I could to try and get James the medical help he deserved. Once James was released, he went back to live with his family. His local community mental health team was treating his PTSD, and he was making some progress but still relied on his antipsychotic drugs to get through the day. He found it exceedingly difficult to get a job as no employer wanted to take the risk of him attacking any Asian customers.

I told James I would keep in touch, and he would be coming to the Bedford's heist. James Burley will be my team leader for Team C.

***

Chapter 32. Children Need to Know Who is Boss.

Ken Shoemaker was an out-of-control young adult who thought he could get what he wanted by having a tantrum. That was until he met a judge who had seen far too many spoilt brats and was left with no choice but to show Ken there were rules and everyone needed to play by them. We all need rules; without them, everything would be bedlam. Just think of driving your car to the shops. You assume that everyone will drive on the same side of the road as you and at the correct speed limit. If everyone decided they wouldn't follow the rules, then no one would ever reach the shops alive.

As a prison counsellor, I have seen far too many out-of-control young adults. Ken Shoemaker was a fine example as he was undoubtedly an uncontrollable child who had never been disciplined and had grown up not knowing right from wrong or understanding the meaning of the word 'no'. He was like many other youngsters allowed to eat and drink what they wanted, and their bodies proved that they went for the sweet options. Right under their parents' noses, they had gone for sugar-loaded food and drink, and sugar had become their drug of choice. Sugar gives you a short-term 'high', but there is always a low after any 'high'. These children are becoming addicts at an incredibly young age. As they age, many add drugs, booze and cigarettes to their list of goodies, as their brain is always seeking the next 'high'.

Hundreds have passed my door in recent years, and they may as well have a ruddy great warning sign across their forehead which states, 'diabetes welcome'. Many of these little porkers will develop diabetes and be on prescription drugs for the rest of their lives. Some of them will lose a limb, but they won't be able to join the 'I've lost a leg—isn't that sweet' club, as with over **175 new members every week,** the membership secretary is overloaded. You or your children must kick the sugar addiction before it's too late.

I'm talking about discipline, not child cruelty, as the latter is against the law. Smacking a child has been seen by many as child cruelty for decades now, but I'm not sure if we haven't created a bigger problem for society by being too PC. We all need to draw a line in the sand and know that if we cross that line, we would be in trouble. Mild smacking is allowed under a 'reasonable chastisement' defence against common assault, but very few parents smack an unruly child these days. There are, however, more ways to ensure that a child doesn't cross the line. The withdrawal of games, mobile phones and TV for a few hours or days usually does the trick, yet many of today's parents don't use any form of punishment and just let their children run wild. Many bad parents allow their children to play war games on their computers. The child can also see adult material and join groups such as Faceache, Twotter and a host of other groups where many young people get bullied and, in some sad cases, the child hangs themselves as they can't take it anymore.

Smartphones are just as bad, and parents must insist that they don't take the computer or phone to bed with them as they will not get any sleep and their school grades will start to tumble. Education at home and school should make children aware of the wrong side of the internet and social media. They need to be taught how to reply to emails that are not nice and turn the ruddy contraption off or block the sender. I've lost count of how often I have seen a young child in the supermarket having a paddy just because Mummy said no when the child wanted a bar of chocolate. I feel like telling the mother to take back control as, if she can't control her three-year-old, then she has no chance when the child becomes a teenager.

The rules of life are simple. As a child, you must be educated and do as you're told. As an adult, you must work until retirement age, and as a pensioner, you should sit back and start to enjoy life. Without discipline or sticking to the rules, a child will not learn enough to get a decent job when they grow up and will do low-paid manual work until they retire. Retirement will be miserable as they never earn enough money to start a separate pension scheme, and they will scrape by on the state pension until they die. It, however, need not be like that if parents draw a line in the sand from the word go. The likes of Ken Shoemaker would never have ended up in jail, and I would probably be out of a job.

I sat Ken down and tried to unravel where it had all gone wrong in the vain attempt to try and turn his life around. I asked him about his early years at home and school, but I already knew the answer as I have had hundreds of 'Kens' sit in front of me. He said he didn't like school and started to skip school when he was around eight. He said he had an easy life at home as he always got his way. I asked him what he did with himself during the day, and he said that he mainly spent time on his Xbox. He said he liked the war and violent games like *Fear 1*, which made him feel good when he killed. During his teen years, he was expelled from school several times, and his mum and dad were warned that they could be taken to court if the problem continued. He didn't care if they went to prison as he could look after himself by then. I asked him where he would live if his mum and dad were in prison, but he hadn't thought about that. He never thought about the consequences of his actions.

I asked him what he thought the school could have done to ensure he turned up daily. He said that he had made his mind up that education was a waste of time as he would probably end up being a professional footballer or winning *The X Factor*. I asked him why he 'hadn't achieved any of those goals.' He said he did go for a trial with the Cobblers football team in Northampton, but as he smoked every day (including cannabis), 'they weren't interested.' I asked him about his work when he officially left school. He said he 'did nothing.' I said, 'Haven't you ever worked since leaving school?' He said that he did get a job at McDonald's, but it only lasted three weeks before they sacked him 'due to poor timekeeping.' I asked him how he survived on the Job Seekers Allowance. He said he 'did a few jobs for cash in hand and made up the shortfall of cash by selling dope to anyone who wanted to buy it.' In the end, he got caught several times dealing, but this was the first time he had to serve time. He just thought they would keep letting him off with a slap on the wrist.

As a prison councillor, I see more and more of these 'uncontrollable kids' that turn into uncontrollable adults. As the regional rep for the Prison Officers Association, I had a Young Offender's Institution in my region, and the Governor had told me that the problem kept growing year after year without anyone doing anything about it. It's clear to me that more guidelines should be made available to parents informing them of the law relating to smacking a child and suggesting other ways to keep control of their young. The education authority must act fast when the child starts skipping school. If the child doesn't want to go to school, they should be forcibly taken as it's the law that they must be educated. Schools should not be able to expel a pupil as this is just moving the problem along the line. Instead, every school should have a 'sin bin' class to house the school's troublemakers. The children in the sin bin should have breaks from the other pupils at different times. They should, however, arrive and leave at the same time as the rest of the children. If this didn't bring the child back in line, they would be sent to a residential school in the county, and if their behaviour got better, they could return to the mainstream school but under close supervision.

Any teenager who didn't find work within four weeks of leaving the education system should be given a free bus pass to get to and from the Job Centre 'every weekday' to sign on. If a local business required casual labour, they could call upon these unemployable youngsters to fill the part-time vacancy. There would be an incentive for the job seeker for any casual work done. The employer would only be allowed temporary jobless staff for a short period as some would use the route to get work done cheaply rather than take people on full-time. I had mentioned this idea to several people in my local Job Centre and got some silly objections put in the way. The usual one was 'Who would manage the jobless drop-in centre?' I answered that some older unemployed people could be paid a higher benefit rate for helping. It would also give the unemployed adult work experience and help them feel part of the community rather than sitting at home doing nothing.

Lazy school leavers have far too much spare time to join gangs and create societal problems. The young men who sleep around without taking any protection, and some of the young girls welcome the attention and are quite happy to get pregnant as the baby will give them a free benefit ticket for the next 16 years. There needs to be a system that deals with these young studs and slags. The single mothers and their offspring should be housed in a block of flats that are warden controlled. The block should cater for ten young mothers at a time. There should be a ban on male visitors after 6 p.m., two young mothers should be trained as childminders, and the other eight mothers should be forced to work. Getting pregnant at a young age shouldn't be a fast track to social housing and benefits for decades to come.

At present, there are far too many teenage girls sleeping around and expecting the taxpayer to pick up the bill. The Child Support Act of 1991 was a great disappointment and was replaced in 2012 with the Child Maintenance Service (CMS). If the sperm donor (so-called father) doesn't pay, then he can be sued by the authorities, but little can be done when they don't pay. In the real world, the sperm donor should pay 14% of his weekly salary for his first child, raising it to 19% if he sired two or more children. The CMS has legal powers to get the child maintenance paid, but this is only good if the sperm donor has money and is at work. If the sperm donor has zilch, they can't get blood from a stone. They may get a percentage of the stud's Job Seekers Allowance paid to them, but with the present system that allows a layabout to sign on every 14 days, there is little incentive to get work.

Unmarried Mothers

I should explain that I'm not having a go at single mothers in general, as there are many cases where the mother had been in a relationship, and her partner dumped her and the child. Some unfortunate single parents have lost a partner who served in the forces, and many more sad cases where the state should do all it can to improve the system for these ladies. There are what I would call "opt-out mothers" who use a baby to get the benefits system to work better for them. In *The Daily Telegraph*, Myra Butterworth ran a piece called 'The benefit of being a single mother'. In the article, she mentions two young ladies and decides that a single mum's life has its attractions—financially. Myra wrote about how single mums can manipulate their status to their financial advantage, as two of her best friends fell into this category. She wrote, "One of the girls enjoys the support of more than £1,000 in working tax credits to top up her part-time job working several days a week for the council (where she finishes at 4.30 p.m. on the dot and has a gold-plated public sector pension). Her income also includes child maintenance from the father and child benefits. It makes for a rather attractive bank balance as her take-home pay equals a £70,000 per annum salary. The other is in a similar position but doesn't work, so a beautifully located house is thrown in. *The Sun* newspaper said in an article called 'I'm entitled to every penny' that Emma Lawlor, 27, first became pregnant when she was 17 and has been a full-time mum ever since. In the article, Ms Lawlor says she puts her kids first and that making her benefits stretch far enough to give them everything they need is difficult. She stated: 'I am not doing anything illegal or wrong. I must look after my kids; I love them all and treat them occasionally. It's stressful looking after my five kids on my own. I buy a few takeaways for them because sometimes I can't face cooking, and yes, I do smoke, but I can't cope otherwise.'

In 2016 the Government reduced the benefit cap from £26,000 to £23,000 in London and £20,000 elsewhere to stop those abusing the benefits system. It was rumoured that the Government also considered stopping child benefits after the second child. It is said that this would hopefully stop mothers on benefits from having an extra child. It increases the family's income. If introduced, the start date would be 12 months from its introduction. The child benefits cap would only affect newborn children and not current families with more than two children.

Introducing the sign-on daily system will take some managing, but the savings would be more significant than the current bill. I would have a bet (but I'm totally anti-gambling) that the jobless figure would be cut in half within six months of such a scheme being introduced. Signing on should be at 8.30 a.m., and the day would finish at 5 p.m. The Job Centre would need to move to a building that gave the space for some activities such as snooker, table tennis, etcetera, along with a tea/coffee facility and a soup and sandwich option at lunchtime. The Job Centre could assign casual jobs to anyone attending, such as picking up litter, cleaning up graffiti, mowing a pensioner's lawns, and other things. The rules would be strict, and if a claimant failed to turn up, they would not be paid any benefit for that day. The only exception would be if they were genuinely ill and would need to supply a signed letter from their GP stating such. Things like having a hangover or claiming they can't work as they are cannabis dependent will not be allowed. The country needs to get these young people working; if it doesn't, it will pay for them for the rest of their useless lives. The scheme will require much planning, but sitting on your backside isn't an option. For those that live in villages that don't have a bus service and is more than three miles from the Job Centre, there would be a need for the jobless to be able to sign on at the local post office or store.

Every unemployed person would be supplied with a 'Jobs 4 all' card (like the plastic driving license) and with this card they would be able to get free bus rides to and from the Job Centre or use it to sign on for the day at the local post office or shop. As well as the card, the new system would also need to have a fingerprint recognition check system else the yobs would get someone else to sign on for them. If they lose the card, they will be charged £10 for a new one and lose two days' benefit as they cannot register for work electronically. If someone needs help mowing their lawns, painting a fence, general cleaning, or ironing, they could record their need via the 'Jobs 4 All' website or post and a suitable job seeker would be sent out to do the work. They must show their 'Jobs 4 All' card and get the homeowner to sign that they have done the work. Job seekers should know that if they abuse or steal from the homeowner, they will end up in prison for a fixed five-year term. It's time to get tough, as having one and a half million people unemployed can't be tolerated any longer. Post Covid-19 unemployment will shoot up and only add to the problem.

I firmly believe that first offenders should be placed in a prison farm environment where the rules are better suited to get these offenders used to a working environment. They should be tagged, and if they work hard, they could gain benefits such as home weekend leave, a drink and video on a Friday night, et cetera. If the offender doesn't want to play ball, they should be isolated until they agree to work. There should also be training programs to teach these offenders a trade such as bricklaying, plumbing or any profession that the construction industry is crying out for. The scheme should also work with the construction industry to provide jobs for these offenders. The Government would subsidise their salary for the first year as this would cost less than keeping them behind bars and becoming regular re-offenders.

Ken Shoemaker will be my second guest on Team C.

***

Chapter 33. Autistic Sibling Problems.

One inmate that caught my eye was Glen Toogood, who lived in Bedfordshire. Glen was in his early 40s when he first came to see me for counselling, and he was a clean-shaven man with mousy blond hair and stunning sea-blue eyes. It was a wonder that he was still single as I knew from his records that he wasn't gay, yet he appeared timid, and perhaps that was the reason he never married. This was his third time in prison but the first time he came under my wing, and he had been caught again for dealing drugs.

During the sessions, I tried to get a breakdown of the inmates' childhood, and Glen said that one of his worse childhood experiences was to do with his brother Tom who had autism. I told him I also had an autistic brother and could understand how hard his childhood had been. Glen said that his brother 'was born with a bent spine and had surgery in his first year of life to try to correct the problem but with little success. Apart from this, he seemed like a normal infant, but that ended when he was around 20 months old when we were told he also had autism.' He said that he had felt that his brother got all the attention and that his parents didn't see him hurting and feeling left out of things. He now understood why his parents had to give all their time to his brother, and once he left school, he had a lonely life as he lived with his parents and brother in a small village on the fens. He couldn't drive (and even if he could have, he certainly couldn't afford a car), and eventually, the Job Centre sent him to a residential college for training as a chef. He liked cooking and did well on his course, but he was lonely, and his roommate at college introduced him to cannabis, which was the slow path to becoming a junkie.

I thanked Glen for his honesty but was unsure how I could help him as this was his third time in prison, and, as he was now in his forties, getting a job on the outside would be difficult, but all we could do was try. I put him on the drug rehabilitation course but wasn't expecting a miracle. It would be hard for his parents to cope with one child in a residential care home and another in a more secure care home called prison, so I hoped some good would come of it. To my surprise, Glen did well on his drug rehabilitation course, and when I checked him out a few months after leaving us, he was still off the weed, but finding a job was nearly impossible.

More on autism and how it affected Glen, and his family can be read in the 'Afterword' section at the end of the book.

I like Glen and could understand the poor deck of cards he had been dealt, so I invited him to the heist in Bedford.

***

Chapter 34. Neo-Nazi Supporter Needs Extra Protection.

Geoff Laxly, aged 35, was born in Harrow and educated to a higher level at the Whitefriars School before joining the Nationwide Building Society when he left school at 16. Geoff never married but had lived with a few ladies along the line, but none of them stayed around for especially long as they soon realised that he loved football more than them. He was a Millwall supporter and got into trouble fighting other football rivals regularly. He openly told me he wasn't there for the football, but being a football hooligan gave him great satisfaction after a dull week at the bank. He claimed that he was also a racist, which is what put him in prison.

He was on my list to try and put him on the right track so that, when he left prison, he would leave a better man than when he came in. I had dealt with a few neo-Nazi supporters before, but Geoff would be a complex case.

He was a founder member of the National Action group, which is now banned in the UK, and a member of the National Front, which is believed to be one of the longest-running neo-fascist hate groups in the world. Unfortunately, violent racism and neo-Nazism are experiencing a terrifying resurgence worldwide, mainly thanks to the internet. I asked Geoff what had led him to become a member of such extreme groups, and his answer shook me as he felt he was 100% right in doing so. After leaving school, his family moved to Boston, Lincolnshire, famous for the Pilgrim Fathers, who set sail from Boston in 1607 to find religious freedom in the new world that we now call the United States of America. Many people think that the Pilgrims set sail for America from Boston. Still, they sailed from Boston to Holland, and a few months later, the English Separatist Protestants later crossed the Atlantic to New England in the USA. Geoff said he wasn't always a so-called white supremacist, but when the likes of Romania joined the EU in 2007, everything changed in Boston. He said that since 2007 eastern Europeans could catch a plane to the UK without requiring a visa. This open-door policy was fatal for many cities and large towns across the UK as it let thousands of undesirable men and women into the country. There was no check on anybody's criminal record, and we opened the door to welcome murderers, rapists and even child molesters.

This has resulted in Boston becoming the most segregated town in the UK. Many immigrants headed for Boston as they knew that there was work for anyone who wanted to pick the likes of Brussel sprouts, and in many cases, it was cash-in-hand. The local authority had to provide housing and education for thousands without a penny extra being paid to them by either the UK Government or the European Parliament. Geoff felt it was like your next-door neighbour tipping a bucket of shit over your garden fence daily. Locals accused the Government of 'dumping' asylum seekers in Boston at the same time as substantial public service funding cuts. Nearby towns of Wisbech and Spalding suffered the same problems as immigrants are tempted by the area's abundance of agricultural and factory jobs.

Geoff wasn't surprised that Boston led the way in voting for exit in the EU Referendum. English Defence League (EDL) marched in the town in October 2016, unsettling many migrants and stirring up ill feelings. Geoff said he was proud to have marched shouting 'Get the immigrants out.'

In a way, I can understand his concerns. Still, there is a legal way to get your concerns over rather than join nasty groups such as the National Action Group, which, like all terrorist groups, use social media to get the wrong message across freely. I asked Geoff if he agreed to what the NA group did after the terrorist murder of Jo Cox MP in June 2016. The National Action shared photos of her killer Thomas Mair with the caption: 'Don't let this sacrifice go in vain!' They tweeted things like 'Only 649 MPs to go' and 'Jo Cox would have filled Yorkshire with more subhumans!' Did he also agree with National Action members also celebrating the terrorist attack on the Pulse nightclub in Orlando last year, where it shared images of a police officer's throat being slit? He showed no remorse and would be a tough case for me.

Geoff's affiliation with National Action led to him being charged under the Terrorism Act 2000 and sitting in front of me. The likes of Geoff Laxly are hard work as the prison service must segregate them from other prisoners for their safety. He wouldn't last a night if we didn't, and many would say that he shouldn't be segregated and that he should be made to face what he calls the 'subhuman'. We must protect every prisoner even if it goes against what we believe, but we have a moral duty of care. I tried all my usual tricks, such as asking what he would do if he had a car accident and needed life-saving surgery, but the nurse was from Eastern Europe, and the surgeon was from Nigeria. Would he say, 'Please save me,' or would he stick to his morals and tell them to fuck off to where they came from? They never like to answer, but it would take more than a tricky question or two to change the likes of Geoff Laxly.

I also made Geoff aware that the USA has some of the world's most prominent 'white supremacy' groups, yet nearly 96% of today's Americans come from immigrant stock. It worries me to think about the future: unless the powers do something to bring us all together, there will be more significant divides. I also asked him if he knew that in the First World War, 75,000 Indians died in France fighting for Britain. And the same number wounded? And in World War Two, they killed about the same number of soldiers but also lost nearly two million civilians. He never replied.

The ethnic communities also need to do more to integrate within the UK. I can remember when the City of Leicester was mainly white. Still, during the 1960s and 70s, the Asian community started to take over city sectors by buying homes in a particular postcode area. Wherever you look, you can see separation in any city. The new City of Milton Keynes is a fine example, as many of the districts have been taken over by non-whites. An old friend of mine used to have a council house, but he moved out as the estate had been taken over by people arriving from Somalia. I don't have all the answers, but something must be done before it's too late.

Geoff Laxly will not be invited to the heist as I am concerned that he may be too wild for the job at hand.

***

Chapter 35. Mickey Mouse Approach to Credit Cards.

James Smith, 32 years old, was a likeable chap who had gotten into debt after borrowing more than he could pay back. Instead of declaring himself bankrupt, he got into drugs and later sold drugs to feed his habit and help make money to pay off his mounting credit card debt. He had to declare himself bankrupt when caught and found guilty of drug running. He is currently serving a five-year sentence, but he was worried that if he didn't cure himself of his addiction, he would leave prison and return to dealing again. He wanted to get off drugs as his wife still loved him, and he wanted to make up for some of the damage he had done. His wife and children had lost their home, as he obviously couldn't keep it once he was declared bankrupt.

I asked James why he hadn't sought advice on his mounting debt problem before it reached the critical stage. He said he didn't want to admit to a stranger that he had well and truly cocked up. He told me that at the start it was easy, as he was in an excellent job as a retail store manager, and he wanted to take his family on the holiday of a lifetime to Florida as his two girls were Disney-mad—the holiday cost around £2,500, which he paid on his credit card. The holiday was great, but tickets for all the attractions and eating out pushed the cost of his holiday to over £3,000. In the beginning, paying back the interest wasn't too difficult, but when his wife was made redundant, he only had his income to try to pay for everything. He really maxed out on his credit card, so he got another one and then a few more later to try to keep afloat, but with the interest they were charging, he just kept digging a bigger hole for himself and his family.

I had seen James' problem far too many times and wondered why the Government hadn't developed a safety net that would be better than losing his home and liberty. What, in my opinion, the FCA and the Government should introduce was a safety net plan that would give the debtor a better way out of the dire situation they had gotten themselves into. How it could work is that the debtor could apply for the safety net route either via the court or a body such as the Citizens Advice Bureau. The debtor or his advisor could choose one of the credit card companies to consolidate all his debt. The debtor should go for one which offers the lowest APR, and that company would take over all the debt. He would then be given a debit card to pay his bills, and a plan would be put in place to repay all his debt but at an affordable level. He would agree not to take out any further credit cards or debt until he was free of the safety net.

I explained to James how people must realise the dire consequences before falling into the credit card trap. Suppose you borrow £2,500 (let's, say to pay for a super 50-inch TV) as many people fall for the sales pitch where they state that it would only cost you £50 a month. Most people would think, I can afford that, it's not a problem. They do not realise that they will end up paying more in interest than for the original cost of the television. It is a common mistake to let yourself get used to paying only the minimum amount that is due on your credit card bill. Most credit cards have an annual percentage rate (APR) of around 18% (store cards are considerably higher). A minimal payment is typically determined using a percentage of your entire balance. The rate is usually about 2% but can vary depending on the card issuer. For the £2,500 plasma television, 2% of your original debt would be £50. With an APR of 18%, your payment would cover £38 in interest and just £12 towards your £2,500 liability. After the first payment, you would still owe £2,488. If you paid only 2% of your total balance due every month, paying off your debt would take 334 months. In other words, it would take 28 years to pay off a £2,500 liability. The television will probably have stopped working long before you have paid for it. Even if you decided to pay for 28 years, you would also have paid £5,897.00 in interest. Your actual cost for the plasma television would end up being £8,397.00.

I'll never know why this isn't being taught in schools rather than the useless algebra. Teenagers need to be taught the basics of life, such as how mortgages work and whether they will ever earn enough to take a mortgage out. How much will smoking 20 cigarettes a day will cost them in a year? The answer is that with a packet of 20 Dunhill International costing around £13.00 daily, they would be spending a staggering £4,745.00 a year on their nicotine addiction. It will be not only bad for your health, but also for your pocket. The same goes for a bottle of wine a day. This addiction would cost you around £2,190.00 a year and won't do your liver any favours. I was once told that if an adult couldn't last a day without an alcoholic drink then they are an Alcoholic. Sorry, James, for having a rant, but it makes me angry why we let children leave school without learning the basics. It also annoys me that MasterCard charges the supplier around 2.5% of the price to process the payment. This is on top of the 18% APR MasterCard charge the cardholder.

In January 2018, the UK Government brought into law where the seller could no longer charge the cardholder the 2.5% as a fee, but all that will happen is that the seller will add the 2.5% to the price. The likes of MasterCard have always charged this fee, even in the good old days when the shop had to place your card and a payment slip in a machine to emboss the slip. The shop had to log all these slips onto a banking slip, and his bank would then have to log the transaction and process it for payment manually. Nowadays, no one must write or log anything as it's all done by computers, yet they still charge the same rate as they did back then. It's about time the Government took on the big boys and got them to levy a smaller charge.

But back to you, James. What will your job prospects be once you are clean and set free? James said he 'hoped to train for a trade to do with construction. Either sparky or plumber would be lovely. I don't think I'll get a job in retail as they don't like employing convicts for obvious reasons.' I didn't argue that point, but I told him I would investigate getting him a start on one of the much-needed trades within the construction industry. I would also be keeping a close eye on his addiction.

I'm glad James got on top of his drug addiction, but he wasn't inside long enough to qualify as a sparky or a Sparky's assistant. He said that the Job Centre had told him about a training scheme which was mainly done at home, and after 12 months you could pass the exam and become a Sparky's mate. You could then continue with the course while being employed, and, hopefully, after a further 12 months, he could become a certified electrician. I asked him why he hadn't taken up the course, and he said that it would cost him £36.00 every week and he didn't have that type of money as he only got a Job Seeker's Allowance. Why the Government hadn't paid for the course beats me as it would be far better than paying him benefits for the rest of his sorry life, and more cost-effective if it kept him out of jail.

I was pleased that James had kept clean, and he accepted my offer to be a guest at the Bedford Heist, as he could then afford the training course to become a fully qualified electrician. James Smith will be my team leader for Team D.

*** ***

Chapter 36. Money Laundering is a Growing Problem.

Steve Marshal, who had been sent inside for money laundering, was as black as the Ace of Spades and was currently serving a four-year sentence at Her Majesties Pleasure for money laundering and fraud. Although initially from Nigeria, Steve came to Britain as a young child with his family in 1969, escaping the Nigerian civil war. His family changed their name to Marshal as soon as possible as they didn't want anyone from Nigeria to find out where they had moved to as some would like to settle old scores.

When a prisoner falls under my watch, I try to re-educate them and change their way of life so that they contribute to society instead of always taking. It was challenging to place Steve on any training course as he only wanted to do the same course, he had done the last time he was inside. This was at another prison in the north of England where he was put on a design and printing course, which he found extremely helpful as it helped him improve at the forgery side of his illegal business. I laughed when he said he would be 'eternally grateful to the British prison service for providing him with new and better skills.' I told him he wouldn't be so lucky this time, and he ended up helping in the prison's kitchen.

As with all prisoners under my care, I asked him what had led him to his current way of life. He said that his family were housed in Manchester, and when he left school, he joined a local print and design company and was quite happy with life until he lost both parents in a car accident when he was just 20. The house they called home was a modern three-bedroom house on the outskirts of Salford. His parents had a mortgage on the house, which was more than he could afford, so it ended up being sold, and he did raise just over £50,000 from its sale. He wanted to do something with the money and needed a roof over his head, so he ended up leasing a rundown printing shop in Salford with a lovely flat above the shop. Things went okay for the first few years, but once large companies started trading on the web, he couldn't match their low prices and started losing money quickly.

Then, a contact he had made at an ex-pat do held at the King's House Conference Centre in Manchester suggested that he did some work for them. 'I knew it was iffy, but when you were down on your luck, there was little I could do but to go into partnership with them. I had to sack the two staff as they weren't in on the plan, and my new friend replaced them with four of the team who knew the game well. We started by printing cheque books and made a lot of money producing forged chequebooks for a wide range of false accounts. It was easy to get the client's details on many debit cards, and showed the client's name, account number and sort code. These details were supplied by another Nigerian group who were scanning cards when someone used a cashpoint.

'This went well for a few years, but the banks were getting wise to our scheme, changing the paper used, and introducing more security features. The paper wasn't too much of a problem as we could make this in Eastern Europe, but one shipment from the paper mill was traced to our shop, and the police raided us. I ended up serving three years as I had told the court that I had been forced to do what I did or my family back in Nigeria would be killed. The course I took was beneficial, and within two weeks of being released, I was back printing new forged cheque books for the same people, but this time it was based in Rochdale, which was a depressing part of the city.'

I asked Steve what went wrong this time around. He said he was only charged as a worker this time as he didn't own the printing outfit. 'I tried to use the same excuse as last time, and I think this helped keep the sentence down.' He stated that some companies monitor cheque fraud and act as an early warning system for their members. 'They found out that we had just hit a few companies who banked with the Royal Bank of Scotland,

and somehow they traced it back to our set-up.' Steve would be released in 2020, and I told him just before he left that I may need his services later, but I couldn't tell him more at that time as I was unsure if I would invite him to the Bedford heist.

In the end, I made Steve a full member, and he would be busy on the day robbing one of our target banks and helping us launder the money so that we only got back genuine untraceable notes. Steve Marshal will be my third guest for Team D.

***

Chapter 37. Allegedly Robbed By the Bank.

Jacob Henningsson was born in Jamshog, Sweden, but moved to the UK in 2002 to teach Mathematics at Christ's College in Cambridge. Probably the most famous Christ's College student ever was no less than Charles Darwin, best known as an English naturalist, geologist, and biologist, and for his contributions to the science of evolution. Jacob settled down and married an English girl in the village of Grantchester in 2004. He later sired two lovely girls named Katarina, after his mother and Carol, after his mother-in-law. Everything was rosy, and he settled into the British way of life and became well-known for his work at Christ's College, Cambridge.

While in Cambridge, he met up with other tutors from the various colleges. He started a small firm as a joint venture, and developed a software program that would help teach mathematics to students with a learning difficulty such as dyslexia. They set up the company with their own funds, but to get the product to the world's marketplace, they would need a worldwide patent which would not come cheaply. They decided to approach the Royal Bank of Scotland (RBS) for a loan, and based on their standing, they borrowed £100,000 to gain the protection and patent they desired. Things went well, but the cost was spiralling out of control, and they needed to go back to the RBS and ask for a further £50K to see the finished and fully protected product reach the market.

They didn't realise simultaneously that one of the RBS subsidiaries, Global Restructuring Group (GRG), was being investigated as several complaints had been received alleging malpractice. GRG was responsible for overseeing the small business clients that had gotten into trouble. Still, critics alleged it was deliberately putting businesses under, so it could take control of them cheaply and sell on for a profit. The bank denied the severe charge that it sought to profit from deliberately putting companies out of business. Still, Buzzfeed's investigation (a global team of investigative journalists) and exposure on the BBC Newsnight programme had forced the bank to acknowledge for the first time that something went wrong in its treatment of Britain's small businesses. The RBS denied any wrongdoing. More than 16,000 companies' worth £65bn ended up on GRG's list of assets, and in 2011 GRG netted £1.2bn in profits.

After listening to Jacob's story, I fully understand why he exceedingly hated banks. He had lost the goose that would lay the golden egg and net him and his company millions of pounds for years. I asked him what had caused him to be serving at Her Majesty's Pleasure and sat back to listen to his story. Apparently, after losing the company, he started drinking, eventually leading him to lose his job at Christ's College, Cambridge. He continued to drink, and he lost his lovely house in Grantchester and his wife and children, who had moved in with his wife's parents. One night he was sitting in his bedsit in Cambridge drinking, and on the tv screen he saw a news report about the RBS titled 'Bankers from another planet'. The program questioned why a bank (of which the British taxpayer owns 80%) with losses of £5 billion could justify obscene bonuses of up to double its bankers' annual salary. It made him mad, and, as he was out of whisky, he just got in his car and drove to a 24-hour supermarket to buy more.

On his way back, he travelled along Trinity Street in Cambridge, spotted the RBS branch, and saw red. He aimed his car at the large window and drove straight at them, not caring about the consequences. He wasn't injured badly, but the bank's front was demolished. He was charged with criminal damage and drunk driving, but the killer blow was dangerous driving and hitting a tourist he hadn't seen, who lost a leg. 'As you know, I got five years, meaning I would be out after serving 33 months if I behaved myself.' Jacob was probably the cleverest inmate I had ever met, but apart from trying to sober him up, there wasn't any course I could put him on as he didn't want to learn a new manual trade.

Instead, he did agree to teach other prisoners' mathematics, which would be challenging. Having agreed with the governor, he allowed him to teach basic maths to fellow inmates, and he was good at what he did. I suggested a teaching career, but he said that apart from his two lovely girls, kids scared the hell out of him. I did sit in on one of his sessions, and it was clear that he had a gift, but he also understood those that were useless at maths. He said that one of the easiest ways to teach was to start at the beginning, as once a student had mastered the basics, the rest would follow. Jacob was also helpful with another significant problem every prison in the world was facing, and that was to do with mobile phones. After drugs, one of the 'must have' items in prison were a mobile phone. These were smuggled in the same way as drugs were. Female visitors would shove them in places we couldn't check with a brush down, and once passed, security would retrieve them and sell them on. Some correctional officers were as bent as the inmates and could obtain anything an inmate wanted.

Update:
In the UK, 20,000 mobile phones and sim cards were recovered as prison contraband in 2016. In 2017, a prison in Bristol added telephones and computers which were not connected to the internet into the prison cells to combat illegal mobile phone usage. The UK Parliament passed a law which would allow mobile phone operators to jam cell phone signals in prisons later that year. The legislation also enabled prison officers to use devices which detect mobile phone usage.

I was sorry to see Jacob leave, as were many fellow prisoners he had helped understand maths. When I checked on Jacob a few months after he had left prison, I was pleased to hear that he had kept away from the booze but sad to hear that his wife was getting a divorce, and he was only allowed to see his daughters once a fortnight.

As he struggled, I asked him if he wanted to join the heist in Bedford, and he jumped at the idea. Jacob Henningsson will be my team leader for Team E.

***

Chapter 38. Couldn't Care, Wouldn't Care, If You are 18.

Rees Jones, aged 22, from Corby in Northamptonshire, England, through no fault of his own had been pushed from foster home to foster home since he was eight as both his parents were sent to prison for drug dealing. Rees ended up in a residential care home in Northampton after being arrested for drug offences at 13. He ran away more times than he can remember and always ended up in the area of the town known as Sammy's End. Drugs were always available, and, if he couldn't steal to get money, he would sell his body to the never-ending number of males cruising the run-down streets. He could always guarantee being picked up as he was a young-looking, slim child; that was always a benefit.

I asked Rees what went wrong when he left his residential care home in Northampton at 18. He said that 'there should have been some support, such as a personal adviser, but it all went wrong, and due to councils not having enough money to employ care staff, I was lost amongst the ever-growing numbers of kids leaving the care system due to them reaching 18. I had been found a flat, but it was on the Bellinge Estate in eastern Northampton. Bellinge and its neighbouring Ecton Brook estate were built in the 1970s and 80s as new towns to house the overspill of London and other areas, now council estates. Bellinge had suffered from severe problems in the 1990s and became one of the most crime-ridden estates in England.'

The Bellinge estate had cleaned up its act since then, but it was still not a nice place to live. Rees said that there was a support system for young people in foster care or residential care, but there is something wrong with the system as a third of young people are ending up on the streets within their first year of becoming an adult.' I pushed him to try to help me understand what had gone wrong as I could see that he was provided with a flat, yet he still ended up in prison. He said that when he left residential care and was given a home, he had no idea how to budget his benefit, and he soon got behind with his electricity bill and rates. His power was cut off due to non-payment, and the council would take him to court for the rates.

He said he was never shown how to make and stick to a budget at school or before leaving care. This was probably because the benefits he would receive weren't enough to cover the bills, so they couldn't show a way to budget without showing in black and white that the benefits he would get would never be enough. 'If I could find a job, it would be a low-paid job, and even if I worked 60-plus hours a week, I still wouldn't bring in enough to break even.'

I asked Rees why he hadn't contacted one of the organisations, such as the Roots Foundation, who were there to help young people like him. He said he 'didn't know about such organisations and should have been told they existed.' He had a friend in a foster home since he was nine, and under the Government's Staying Put legislation, which came into force in 2014, he can now remain until he is 21. Being in a residential care home didn't give him the same option. He said he had done some research in the library, and, after this system was introduced, 75% of young adults decided to leave their foster home once they turned 18. It looked as though many of the 75% had only been in a foster home since their early teens and hadn't had the same time to bond with their foster parents as a child of, say, seven did.

Money (or the lack of it) plays an essential part, as when his friend was in foster care, his foster parents would get paid £429, consisting of a £214 fostering fee and £215 maintenance. However, when the same child turned 18, the money dropped to £120 weekly. Around 10,000 16 to 18-year-olds leave foster or residential care annually in England. With a third of these teenagers ending up sleeping on the streets, that's over 3,000 more youngsters heading for a drug and alcohol-dependent life which will result in the Government spending a fortune to keep them alive. Something needs to be done soon, or many more will end up in prison, costing the British taxpayer £47,000 yearly. I placed Rees on a drug rehabilitation programme, but, as soon as he leaves, I'm sure he will be back on the streets carrying on as before and again sitting in front of me.

I had a job locating Rees as he had moved out of the apartment he had been given when he left, but I just had to ask around the rough sleepers in Northampton to find him.

He accepted the offer to join the heist in Bedford. Rees Jones is my second guest in Team E.

***

Chapter 39. How Do We Deal With the Mentally Ill Inmates?

Lenny Adams reminded me of John 'Goldfinger' Palmer, the infamous 1983 Brinks-Mat bullion robber, although a jury found him not guilty in 1987. Like John Palmer, Lenny was also from Solihull, Warwickshire and had the same 'smart' look about him, but his eyes gave him away as they always read 'DANGER' to me. Lenny had always suffered from mental health problems and had had a miserable childhood, as his condition was not diagnosed until he was age 34. Older men had abused him, and when he reported it to the school, he was told not to be silly and to act like a man.

Lenny had been in prison too many times and was in the wrong place, as prison staff are not trained to deal with mental health problems. During my twenty-plus years as a prison counsellor, I have seen the number of prisoners suffering from mental health problems rise tenfold. We used to joke about it, with young officers stating that Maggie Thatcher had closed all the mental institutions as she didn't want to end up in one. As the years passed, prison was the only option open to the courts as they had a duty to protect the public. People like Lenny should be treated and cared for in a hospital close to where they have family and friends, but during the past decade more mental health patients in England were sent for 'out-of-area' treatment.

This, in many cases, made their condition worse. Still, due to funding cuts and a desperate shortage of beds, it meant doctors were often left with little choice but to call hospitals around the country in a bid to secure a bed and suitable treatment for patients suffering from severe mental health conditions, including schizophrenia, psychosis and anorexia. Attacks on prison officers have risen over the past decade. This overload of prisoners with mental health problems has done little to end the rising number of prison officers suffering from stress and anxiety attacks. Mental health problems and depression will affect over 25% of people at some time during their lives, and if treatment isn't provided quickly, the situation worsens. Mental health has suffered when hospitals and health trusts try to balance their budget. The biggest problem is that the people who make the laws know sod all about the everyday issues facing their constituents.

If I ruled the world, I would make it compulsory for every MP to spend a Friday and Saturday night at their primary A & E department to see first-hand what damage cutbacks are causing ordinary people daily. They would also see the problems caused by drugs and drinking, and I would guarantee that after a few nights at the sharp end, they would have a different view on the NHS, drugs, binge drinking and many other problems. It would also benefit society if they spent a shift or two with their local police force. They would then see the issues facing police forces in every part of Britain, along with the time the police force spends trying to sort out domestic abuse, homelessness, people with mental health problems, and drugs and alcohol abuse, and that's before they even try to catch criminals.

The Government's Gestapo division (the DWP) keeps getting matters concerning mental health wrong. The current well-publicised Personal Independence Payment (PIP) problems continue to discriminate against people with mental health problems. In December 2017, the High Court ruling declared that this policy had been 'blatantly discriminatory' against people with mental health conditions and was unlawful because there had not been any consultation. Paul Farmer, chief executive of mental health charity Mind, said in *The Daily Mirror*, 'This ruling is a significant victory for people with mental health problems. If the ruling is allowed to stand, then more than 160,000 people with mental health problems will be able to access the support they should have been entitled to all along.'

Ultimately, we see all the country's problems end up at our prison gates, and it is only getting worse. The prison service is at breaking point, and the number of prison officers per inmate is getting to a crisis level. Something needs to be changed, or more and more officers will leave the service and the dream that Tony Blair had about 'any system of justice should not just be to punish and deter, but also to rehabilitate, for the good of society as well as the criminal' will be lost forever.

Lenny accepted my invitation as he said he needed the money, but I didn't ask him what for. Lenny Adams will be my third guest in Team E.

***

Chapter 40. Another of Our Professional Prisoners.

Mike Hood was 47 years of age but looked a lot older and was a professional prisoner. I named Mike and other inmates like him "professional prisoners" as they have made it their life's work to be in prison. They know they will get housed, clothed, and fed and their addiction treated, so why live as a 'free' man where they will struggle to find a job and to live off the minimum benefit money provided? Over the years, I have witnessed the steady rise in the numbers of some of the regular offenders asking the judge if they could be placed in a particular prison and have the cheek to request a specific cell or wing, they would like to be housed in when they arrive there.

This culture needs nipping in the bud and a new training system to ensure every inmate leaves prison with a new trade. There is a national shortage of qualified staff in the construction industry, which needs more electrician's mates, plumbers, bricklayers, plasterers, chippies, and workers in many other trades. Farming is a sector that is crying out for horticulturists, and workers with a wide range of farming skills such as Agricultural Engineers, Poultry / Broiler management skills, Herdsman, etcetera.

Update August 2023
Once the war in Ukraine ends, there will be a massive rebuilding program, and people in the building trade will be offered work at a high wage and the UK will face a shortage of craftsmen and women. If we are ever to house the younger generation, the UK needs to build more homes and tempt young people to climb the housing ladder.

There are different types of prisons in the UK, and an excellent example of an open prison would be the HMP North Sea Camp, a category D prison in Lincolnshire. I had met the governor, Graham Blatchford, who, like me, began his career as a prison officer and, over 26 years, worked his way through the Prison

Service ranks. He is candid about his objectives and priorities. In my opinion, the best use of an open prison is to make the first-timers work. Many have never worked hard in their lives and found it hard to take and follow orders. Placing new offenders in a closed prison, they will soon learn how soft it can be. They would be placed in a cell with their TV and will possibly learn new tricks from other inmates.

Open prisons are better if the community understands what we are trying to do. You must have an open and honest approach to the local community. This is about preparing people properly for work once they return to the community.

I asked Graham what he thought had gone wrong at HMP Ford open prison in West Sussex, where inmates had rioted. He said it had a bad reputation as it was easy for inmates to get hold of booze and drugs, and when the governor tried to tighten up on these two matters, the inmates rioted. He did go on to state that a recent inspection found that the new governor had addressed the problems which caused the riot in 2011, and that it had made a lot of progress in preparing prisoners for the outside world. In my opinion, a more educational role of prisons should be made a priority instead of spending over a billion pounds on building new prisons. A new system must be found where training is prioritised, and the last few years of an inmate's prison sentence are spent working and living in the community. They would be tagged and must follow strict time schedules and curfews. After two years in prison, any new employers of such reformed prisoners would be financially rewarded as the cost would be far less than it would be to keep them locked up.

If prisoners break the relaxed rules, they will be arrested and sent to a hard prison. The softer prison option should be a thing of the past. I firmly believe that any prisoner who is an addict (drugs, alcohol, gambling etcetera) should not be released back into the community until they have controlled their addiction and has been clean for six months. I strongly disagreed with the old IPPs (Indeterminate Sentences for the Protection of the Public) as it was not managed correctly. Still, with an addict, it was easier to see whether they had beaten their habit and could survive outside. I'm convinced that we (the prison service) have got it wrong in the past and had given up hope of ever breaking the mould that kept returning the same prisoners to us on a regular basis. We may as well do away with prison gates and replace them with revolving doors.

Young offenders serving less than 12 months should only be sent to open tough prisons, and the long-term prisoner (excluding the obvious murderers, rapists etcetera) should be moved to a prison to start their retraining to make it in the real world. If you send a young offender to a closed prison, they will be more trouble to the prison officers as they have not yet learnt about rules and discipline. It was rumoured that these young hooligans caused the riot at HMP Ford open prison in 2011 as they all thought they were still above the law. The open prison route had never happened to Mike Hood as he was a professional prisoner and had spent more time in prison during his adult years than he had spent on the outside. Before being sent to prison the first time, he was training as an electrician's mate; he should be able to continue his training at an open prison before being released. Mike was released from prison in January 2018, and I helped set him up in a halfway house where another of my team would watch him.

I'm glad to hear that he is doing well, and Mike Hood will be my team leader for Team F.

***

Chapter 41. A Runner in More Ways Than One.

Tony Weston was 36 years old and married, with two young girls. He lived in a small village called Lode in East Cambridgeshire on the southern edge of the fens. It lies just eight miles to the northeast of Cambridge. The village had an aged population and one pub (that had since closed), but it did have a post office and a small general store. Tony said that he was a keen runner, and he first found the village when he entered the village's yearly half marathon. He fell in love with the place and was happy to see a three-bedroom bungalow come onto the market when he and his wife were looking for their forever home.

Tony's wife Jenny suffered from panic attacks and had an immune deficiency and poor lungs (COPD) since she was a teenager. Jenny had been on tranquilisers and other medication ever since. Due to his wife's poor lung condition, she needed to rest every afternoon, so they wanted a quiet village. Tony had moved there in 2006 and purchased his first home with his wife Jenny, and at first it was everything you could wish for in a lovely quiet village on the edge of the Fens. At the time of buying, they did not plan on having children, but to everyone's surprise, his wife gave birth to two lovely daughters in September 2008. There wasn't a school in Lode, but the Bottisham Community Primary School is only a five-minute drive away, and it always gained good Ofsted reports. Tony went on to tell me that he had a standard upbringing and had done well at school, and after college, he worked for a large manufacturer of farm machinery.

When he was 21, he got caught with cannabis and was given a caution. He tried to kick the habit but failed dismally and ended up in court for supplying a class-A drug. He had been visiting a mate who was his supplier when his mate's house got raided, and, as his mate's phone number was on his mobile several times, they assumed he was part of the supply chain, and he was put away for 40 months. I asked Tony what started him on drugs. He said an old saying goes, 'Be careful what you wish for', he had always thought it was a load of rubbish until he met his nightmare neighbour next door.

'The family consisted of mum, dad and two noisy teenage boys. The family had lived in the village for generations, and his neighbour's brother was on the parish council, and his wife worked for the district council. After only a few weeks in our new home, the amplified music from the teenage boys was deafening. I visited my neighbours, and the man of the house wasn't at home, so I spoke to his wife and explained that due to my wife's medical condition, she had to sleep for a couple of hours in the afternoon, so could she ask her sons not to play loud music between two and five in the afternoon. She said that she would discuss it with her husband when he returned.

'Within 30 minutes, there was a knock on my front door, and I was expecting to see my neighbour, but instead, it was their son, whom we called drummer boy. He said they had lived in the village a long time and wouldn't be told what to do by any newcomer. I asked him why he couldn't agree to play loud music at a set time each day, but he said he would play music when he liked. For the next few weeks, the loud music got worse, and I had no choice but to ask the local environment officer from the council to get involved. He said he would write to the family and gave me a load of sheets to log down every session's start and finish times. We logged the times down, and the worst spell was during a two-day school holiday where they played loud music 19 times. The worst thing about the situation was not knowing when it would start. If it were a lovely summer evening, we would sit out on the patio, but no sooner had we settled than the loud music would start. There was a tall brick wall between their house and ours, so I'll never know how they knew we were outside in the garden. After a month, we sent the forms back to the council but didn't get a reply from them.

'I chased the council and spoke to my MP, and after her intervention, the council came around and set up a noise monitoring recorder. If the monitor heard a noise, the recorder would wait 30 seconds before recording. For that week, there were a lot of stop-and-start sessions that only lasted 20 to 25 seconds, so they must have been warned by someone in the council that we had a recording device installed. After a week, the council collected the kit, and the noise started up again, only this time it would be louder and more frequent. A year passed, with us hoping our neighbour's boys would grow tired and move on to other things, but this didn't happen. I returned to the council, and we started the whole process again and logged every noise nuisance. The council then decided to install the sound recording system again, but I told him what had happened last time and that if we only got 20 to 25 seconds again, I would call the police. The officer from the council set up the system yet again and said that we needed to ensure that everything was correct at the time of recording, as it must be like for like.

'During that week in June, we had a heatwave, so when the wife went for her afternoon kip, I opened the bedroom window to try and get some fresh air into the bedroom. After a week, the officer collected the machine and said he would report back when it was analysed. I was still waiting to hear back, so after two weeks, I called him. On the fifth time of calling, I managed to speak with him, and he said he could hear the noise, but I had cheated by opening the bedroom window. I reminded him that he had said that the recording should be accurate, and I told him it was. He said I had ruined our chances as I opened the window. I said that most people in the UK would open their bedroom window during a hot spell, but he wasn't budging.

'It was making my wife's condition worse, so I got our local solicitor involved, and he set up a meeting in Bottisham that all of our neighbours attended along with the boy's grandmother, who said that she had taught the two boys that they were good boys. My solicitor went through all the log sheets that I had kept a copy of, and he said that on paper, it looked as if there was a noise problem, and suggested that a curfew be set between 13.00 and 16.00 hours every afternoon. The boy's parents had said they had never had a problem with the boys, and one was due to start university soon. I didn't mention the noise they made on an evening when their mother was working the late shift at the local supermarket, and the boy's father was out drinking. They would gather in the street with their mates, and although underage, they drank cans of beer and threw the empties into my garden. Other neighbours had also complained, but they didn't stand up to them as I did. The meeting and the following letters cost me nearly a grand, but I thought it would be well spent if it stopped my wife from killing herself, as the constant noise made her suicidal.

'Things quieted down, and the curfew was honoured, but the loud music would start again as soon as it was over. One summer afternoon, my neighbours were having a party by their pool in their back garden, and the music got loud. Another of my neighbours had called around and heard the noise, so he picked up a plank of wood, started banging loudly on their wall, and told them to turn it down. The only response we got back was a load of verbal abuse, and the boys' dad threatened to come around and knock my f**king head off. They, however, did turn it down, but this was mainly due to his wife coming home after a long shift at the supermarket, and she would have heard the loud music when she entered our street.

'Things continued but only improved after one of the boys left for university. However, the day after his return, they held a party to celebrate one of the son's birthdays, and the loud music continued until the early hours. I let this go as it was a birthday celebration, but on the next day, the loud music started at 1500 hours and continued non-stop for nearly four hours. I called the police and explained what had happened, and a police officer came around. I told him that he had just missed the mammoth session, and he went around to our neighbour's door and knocked loudly, but no one answered. When the policeman returned to our house, I said that I hadn't seen the boy leave, and no sooner had I said that I noticed the boy walking down the street. I told the policeman that he was walking down the street and the copper went after him. He called the boy back several times, but he just kept on walking. This upset the policeman, and he caught hold of the boy and made him return to his house. I assumed that he was reading him the riot act. After that, things went incredibly quiet, but even to this day, my wife can't settle as she expects the loud music to start up again. It was only due to the neighbour threatening violence that the police would take it seriously, and if he hadn't, we would still be facing the same problem now.'

Tony went on to say that the council was useless, and it annoyed him that the environment officer for the council was as helpful as a chocolate teapot. Noise nuisance is a significant problem nationwide, and the Government must do something to correct this injustice. I asked him how this had ended up with him sitting where he is now. He told me that a few months after the police had become involved, he had been visiting a local village fete, and he saw the useless environment officer strutting around, but what made him see red was the person he was holding hands with.

'None other than my neighbour's sister-in-law worked for the council. They were in it together, and I just lost it and punched the officer, and I was arrested for GBH. The court listened to my story but found me guilty, and, as it was an officer for the council I had assaulted, the judge said that he could only offer me a custodial sentence. As this was my second time in court, I got 36 months.'

Tony added that he was worried about getting a job once released, as he had been in prison twice. I said that I would do what I could, but only after he had completed an in-house anger management course. Tony finished the course, but there wasn't enough time to complete another course which was to be released in 2020. Just before leaving, he came to his last appointment with me. He smiled when he told me that his wife had said in her previous letter that the problem had stopped but only because the teenagers had moved away. She believed that the older boy had been sent to prison after being found guilty of supplying class A drugs so that he made enough money to feed his habit. The other son had been given an Anti-Social Behaviour Order (ASBO) and had since moved away. Tony said that it was apparent to most people that the teenagers just ran wild, and if the boy's parents had laid down the law (when it was obvious that there was a problem), the boy's lives could have had a better outcome.

I caught up with Tony, and as he hadn't found any work, he accepted the invite to join us in Bedford. Tony Weston will be my second guest on Team F.

***

Chapter 42. When a Bottle is Your Best Friend.

John Tredwood was a 39-year-old alcoholic who had hit rock bottom several times and ended up in prison twice during the past six years. John was born in Nottingham and spent most of his young life growing up in the St. Anne's area of the City. Nottingham is like any large city in the UK: you can be disadvantaged from birth depending on which area you are born in. John, who looks like the infamous Curtis 'Cocky' Warren, has the dubious honour of being listed on two high-profile lists: *The Sunday's Times*' Rich List and Interpol's Most Wanted. The notorious drug trafficker earned his nickname due to this brazen criminal activity, which included a £31 million cannabis smuggling operation on the island of Jersey only a month after he was released from a Dutch jail.

I asked John to tell me his life's history, and it made me sad to hear what he was born into. He said that when he was thirteen, friends would make fun of him if he didn't have a drink. 'I just gave in because it was easier to join the crowd. I was unhappy and just drank to escape my miserable life. I went out less and less, so I started losing friends. The lonelier I got, the more I drank. I was violent and out of control. I never knew what I was doing. I was ripping my family apart. Eventually, I was kicked out of the family home at age seventeen; I was homeless and started begging for money to buy booze.

'After years of abuse, doctors told me there was irreparable harm to my health. Many of my first concerns were about drinking, and everything else came second. I realised that when I did not drink, I had a sense of panic and would start shaking. I couldn't go for more than a few hours without a drink. When I was 26, I got arrested for being violent after another down-and-out tried to steal my bottle of cider. I did him a lot of harm, yet I can't remember anything about it as I was drunk. I was charged with GBH and sent to prison for 30 months, and hoped I would get some counselling once inside to help put me back on the right track. I served my time, and when I got out, I found a place to live and a job. But after just two days, I was back on the booze.

'During the next few months, I went to work drunk, blacked out in clubs and bars and can't remember getting home. Ashamedly I slept with someone and could not even remember the person coming home with me until we bumped into each other the next day. I have destroyed two relationships because I hurt them so much through my drinking, but I put drinking first. I spent the next eight years in and out of detox and hospitals, trying to figure out what happened to me and how I couldn't quit. It was the worst and longest nightmare. My addiction built steadily; before I realised it, I had become a morning and afternoon drinker. I carried on stealing to feed my habit, and in the end, I got caught, and this time, I was sentenced to five years.

'You know that and more about me than I can remember myself.' I asked John if he wanted to stop drinking, and he said he had little choice while inside as most jails are mainly dry. 'In some open prisons, the rules are relaxed, and, in a few cases, prisoners carry on the practice of brewing hooch with varying degrees of success and a high capture rate by prison staff – the smell of the fermenting brew usually gives the game away.'

John did unexpectedly well on the long detox program, leaving prison free of his nightmare. On checking on him after a few weeks, I found that he was still free of his addiction but was finding it difficult to get a job, so I have sent an invitation to John to join me on the heist in Bedford, and I'm glad that he has agreed to come along.

***

Chapter 43. Why I'm Going to Get My Revenge in Bedford.

After reading how these men went wrong and how little we as a caring society do to help mend these broken human beings, I hope you'll understand why I have decided to try and open the eyes of those we elect to serve us. While working in Her Majesty's Prison service, I have seen what is wrong with our society today. I get angry knowing that the rewards would be great if our leaders tried just a little to fight all addictions. It sickens me to read that the government spent over 108 million pounds of our money on attempts to stop sick and disabled people from getting the benefits they were entitled to. The Department of Work and Pensions (DWP) spent our money appealing against disability benefits over two years.

This sickening waste of money is even worse because the claimants won most cases. It has been clear for years to those who are sick or disabled and those that care for them that there was something seriously wrong with the system they were forced through. Even when the United Nations said they were deeply concerned, the Government ignored them. It's common knowledge that over two years, over 2,000 people had died after being passed fit for work by some unelected pen pusher.

Iain Duncan Smith, the then minister in charge of this fiasco, stood down, demonstrating that, after all, he did have a conscience, but he should face charges and be brought before the Court of Human Rights at the Hague. Instead, what the conservative government did was give him a knighthood. I, for one, will never call him 'Sir'. If you compare the treatment of the sick, disabled and poor in this country with the soft treatment given to the tax evasion of some of the super-rich, then deciding to set up several special heists across the UK was easy for me to make.

My second in command, Douglas Boswell, has started to call me Robin Hood, and I tease him by calling him Friar Tuck. I don't mind the name, but this time it's for real, and I will enjoy taking money from the rich and giving it to the poor. Enjoy my heist in Bedford.

***

Chapter 44. Heist time – Let the Entertainment Begin.

With all the pre-planning done, it was the day of the heist, and I was sure it would work fine. My number two, Douglas Boswell, Simon Westdale, and Alan Frazer will start early as they need to set up the traffic lights as early as possible. The CCTV cameras would still be working, so they must look as if they are genuine workmen and wear some form of disguise as they will be caught on camera. The first set of traffic lights would control the flow of cars across the river Ouse on the A4251 road. Doug had positioned the van facing north so it would be pointing to the next set of lights that needed setting up. Both Doug, Simon and Alan would set up the builder's tent on the pavement, and the generator would be set up and connected to the traffic lights about ten meters on either side of the tent but not placed in the centre of the road until one was showing red. The other end, now green, would be moved to the middle of the road, and both men would place cones and warning signs and ensure that every item was weighed down with sandbags, so they didn't blow over.

The traffic light system we had borrowed from around the country did have a pre-emption system that allows the regular operation of traffic lights to be pre-empted, allowing emergency vehicles right-of-way, but this had been turned off as we didn't want the fire engine, ambulance or police getting through quickly. Once the lights were working, Simon got out the Angle Grinder and cut a strip of tarmac about 12 inches wide from the centre of the road to just under the tent. Doug would then get the Kango hammer with its chisel head and remove the top layer of the tarmac, leaving it visible at the side of the shallow trench. It only took 25 minutes to complete the work before moving off to the railway bridge that crossed the central London to Scotland line. This road was vital to control the number of cars and trucks leaving the town. The road was the A4280 which ran from Bedford to Northampton, and it was easy to repeat their success with the first bridge. The next target was the main

A6 road bridge crossing the Ouse. They set up the usual traffic lights system and headed a few yards north to tackle the CCTV camera control box.

**

Chapter 45. Heist Time - CCTV Camera Control Box.

Like all main towns and cities, you couldn't spit on the pavement without it being recorded on a CCTV camera, and the police use these rather than having a police officer on the street. Bedford is no exception and has over 100 cameras covering the town 24/7. The police monitor Bedford CCTV cameras at an office just south of the river Ouse. To make the crossing of the river, all cameras north of the river, i.e., in the town centre, are brought together in a control box just north of the A6 river bridge, which sits just south of St. Paul's Square. The green box looks like those you see from BT at the end of most streets, where all the phone lines come together before being sent to the central exchange down a fibre optic cable.

Incendiary Bomb in Clarence Street.

One more thing that needed setting up was the incendiary bomb in Clarence Street. The derelict house at the end of Clarence Street needed to be set up and ready to explode at 10.00 a.m. We took the van to the address and found a parking lot outside the house, and Doug soon gained access via the rear of the property. As soon as we entered, we could smell death. We hadn't expected to find anyone inside, but to our dismay, there was a tramp who, when we tried to wake him up, we discovered was dead. He must have died during the winter from the cold, and we were uncertain what to do. Doug said that we would carry on as planned as we had no alternative, so Doug and Simon covered the two floors with five gallons of petrol on each floor while Alan set up the timer on the incendiary device that would explode at 10.00 am on the dot. Once done, we repaired the lock on the rear door, but before leaving the house, we fixed the 'Police – Crime Area – Do Not Cross' tape to the front and the back entrance.

My Day as Heist Organiser.

I had an early start, mainly because I was so excited that I couldn't sleep. I drove around Bedford just after 8 a.m., checking out the work that Doug and his team had done, and. even at this early hour, traffic was starting to back up. I then headed for The White Swan public house in Bromham, as they rent a room for small meetings and provide coffee/tea and sandwiches. The entrance to the room is round the back of the pub, which sits next to a public car park. In the morning I made sure that I visited the pub for a quick coffee at around 10.30 a.m. as I wanted them to be able to say to the police that I was there, and after my coffee I went to the meeting room and moved a lot of chairs around and poured a lot of teas and coffees and then emptied the cups into a sink at the back of the room where there was a small toilet. I tipped many of the sandwiches into a carrier bag and would feed the ducks later.

The room looked as if a meeting had taken place for around 20 people, which was important as it would give everyone an alibi for the day. They would all tell the police that the reason for the meeting was to see if any ex-cons would be interested in starting a group to help each other. It was being arranged by Lucas Payne, who gave an example of a similar scheme that had worked for ex-cons in the States. After leaving the meeting room, I returned to my car and purchased six more parking tickets from the machine, as these would be given to each team leader. After that, I headed north out of Bromham and took the country lanes back to Kempston Hardwick station to wait for the safe return of my guest.

The A-Team.

After setting up the traffic lights and setting the incendiary devices, the A team members headed back to the workshop to remove the angle grinder and Kango hammer, sweep the van out and load the 18 large suitcases. We also smartened ourselves up and put on our robbery clothes and disguise. Thankfully one of the team could get us trainers, which had a raised platform making us three inches taller than usual. They took a bit of getting used to, but we managed not to fall over. We also wore a lot of padding to make us fatter than we were, but it made Doug look like Father Christmas. He said he didn't care if it stopped him getting recognised. We all added caps or hats and wore sunglasses. Every guest to the heist had been told to grow a beard if they didn't have one and, if they usually had one, to shave it off for the day. A couple of the robbers couldn't grow a beard quickly, so they had been supplied with stick-on beards for the day. After the heist, they were to leave these in the suitcase's side compartment when returning to Kempston Hardwick station.

We then grabbed a cup of tea and ate some cereals Doug had laid on for us before heading off to meet all the others at the railway station. As a precaution, Doug used his car to the station as it needed to ping the ANPR camera on the A421 just before it reached Kempston, so that if the police checked later, they would see that his car was where he had said it was. Alan would drive the van to the Kempston Hardwick station via the back roads.

Heist Day 9.30 am.

The central police station for Bedford is in Greyfriars, but many activities were moved to the much larger and more modern Kempston police station, which is southwest of Bedford town. In recent months the police chief has been contacting the local press (along with anyone willing to listen), repeating his warning that he "cannot keep people safe anymore", and attacking spending cuts he claims have left him with too few officers to respond to 999 calls.

Well, I was listening, and I hope he won't have too many officers available when our heist is in full swing. Precisely at 9.30 a.m., the CCTV control centre called the sergeant on duty and said that all the CCTV cameras were no longer working and that they had contacted the company to find out what had gone wrong. The bad news was that the company couldn't get anyone out until later in the day, as they were also facing problems in Norwich. The Norwich problem had nothing to do with us, but it was welcome news.

***

Chapter 46. How the Team Made it to and From Bedford.

The team players will arrive in five vehicles carrying three people in each. Their cars will be parked behind the uncrewed railway station in Manor Road Kempston, where they will be met by my number two, Douglas Boswell and his two team members. Each of the six groups of three will be handed a suitcase, numbered 1 to 18, so that when returned, we can easily see who got the most out of the heist. The various suitcases contained the tools of their trade. Each included a replica handgun, skin-colour surgical gloves, and printed notices they would need once they were in the bank. The team leader had notices that would be fixed to the outside bank's doors and ATMs. The team leader also had the 'Police – Crime Scene – Do Not Cross' tape pre-cut to fit the entrance to the bank.

The train to and from Bedford station is used by many holidaymakers travelling from Bedford mainline station to London Luton airport, so people in the town with suitcases wouldn't seem out of place. The miniature railway station the guest will use is on a line that had originally run between Oxford and finished in Cambridge. The line was called the Varsity line. The Oxford to Bletchley part was closed during the Dr Richard Beeching massacre of railways, which happened at various times during the 1960s. The Bedford to Cambridge section was also closed in the 1960s but left the Bletchley to Bedford part (known as the Marston Vale line), which was probably saved due to the vast brickworks in Marston.

During the early millennium, the route slightly changed, and, instead of starting in Bletchley, it was relocated to the larger Milton Keynes Central Station. The other end of the line finishes in Bedford St. Johns but stops at the central station in Bedford for a few minutes. The line had been managed by several consortiums but was taken over in December 2017 by the London Northwestern Railway. There are talks to reopen the route from Oxford to Cambridge, but this has been talked about so many times that I'll believe it when I see it.

The train the team will be taking is the 10:03 from Kempston Hardwick to Bedford Main Line station arriving at 10:15. The cost would be only £3.00 return (off-peak) per guest, which I had already paid, purchasing online using my untraceable debit card and printing off the vouchers. The Kempston Hardwick station is about half a mile outside the village of Kempston, so it is seldom used. The benefit is that there is a tiny and free-to-use car park with no CCTV to worry about, so we can be in and out without being logged in. On arrival at Bedford station, they will leave the central station in groups of three, rather than a group of 18 which could easily be picked up if the police checked the station's CCTV later. Those with their target bank being furthest away would go first, followed by the second team and so on.

Once outside the station, they could all head separately to their target banks at a stroll but avoid any ATMs along their route. Many have independent CCTV coverage, which the police can check later to show anyone using or passing by the ATM. They don't have to worry about broader CCTV coverage as these would have been disabled by the time they arrive. All teams must arrive at their bank by 10.45, and the group leader should open the side pocket of his suitcase, remove the two printed A4 messages, and attach these to the bank's entrance. It would be a simple message with the bank's logo at the top stating, 'Bank Closed until Noon Today Due to Computer Failure. Do Not Enter Before Noon.' This should give enough time for customers inside the bank to leave. At some time between 10.45 and 10.58, a similar notice should be placed at any ATM. At precisely 10.59, the team leader should let his two teammates enter and then attach the tape across the entrance, which states, 'Police Crime Scene Do Not Cross'.

They should enter the bank as a team, and the deputy team leader will show the first bank teller the pre-printed message which states, "This is an armed robbery. Do not press the alarm button. Move away from the counter and tell the other tellers to stand back from the counter but stay in position". You then show the second message sheet, which informs the bank teller that they now need to open the door to let the team through to the back of the bank. Once inside, one of the team goes behind the counter and demands that the teller empty the contents of their till into the suitcase. At the same time, the other two team members gather all the other staff and get them to assemble in one room which the team leader controls. When all are assembled, he demands the bank manager take him to the safe, open it, and place all the money in the suitcase. When all the money from the bank safe and the teller's stations have been collected, the team return to the room holding all the staff. The bank manager is then told to leave with the team leader and the unused suitcase and proceed to the ATMs, where the money is removed and placed in the third suitcase. Once this has happened, everyone returns to the holding room and hands one of the staff a message to be read out loud. The A4 sheet states, *"Please read this out to everyone. All mobile phones must be placed in a bin. The bin will be left outside the room. All computers, fax machines and landline phones should be switched off and disconnected from their power supply. You will see that we have placed a timer just inside the door. This must not be touched until the countdown clock shows 00.00. This timer is a small-time bomb, and, once set, it will detect any phone or computer signal in and out of this room, and it will also detect any change in room pressure, so do not open any doors or windows until you see the clock is showing 00.00. It will also detect any loud noise, so do keep quiet. Thank you for your money."* Doug asked again if all phones had been placed in the bin. Everyone nods their heads to say yes. The three bank robbers leave the bank and take separate routes back to the station for their return train ride to Kempston Hardwick.

***

Chapter 47. Heist Day 10.00 am. Clarence Street Bedford.

At 10.00 a.m. a device controlled by one of our mobile phones triggered an explosion and caused a large fire which should draw the police away from our main area. The main fire station is situated south of the river, and, with the traffic control in place, they will struggle to get to the fire north of the river Ouse. What we want to happen is for the police to tie up any available officers at the scene of the bomb explosion and fire at Clarence Street and to keep them busy for at least the next couple of hours. With the planned delay the fire crew still hadn't arrived by 10.20, and the fire had taken hold and started to spread to the next terraced property. If luck were on our side, it would take them hours to control the fire as it spread from attic to attic along Clarence Street. Police were busy getting people to evacuate houses and move the cars parked along the narrow street. They were not quick enough for the first two cars and a campervan, which probably contained two calor gas bottles as the flames shot across the three-foot pavement, and soon had both cars and the campervan alight.

After only a few minutes, the first car's petrol tank exploded, throwing flames in all directions. By 10.40 a.m. the fire crew were still struggling to get across the river Ouse, and once they had crossed it, they were met with cars in both directions blocking the road, and they had nowhere to move to. My plan was working better than I could have hoped. At just after 10.45, police finally managed to get some homeowners to respond, but there was one old lady who couldn't be moved as she was bedridden, and it would need both the fire service and ambulance crew to move her safely. A paramedic on a motorbike arrived more quickly than the ambulance, and he rushed in to see the overweight lady. The ambulance had the same problems facing the fire crew, but they arrived five minutes after the paramedic. However, they could do little until the firefighters arrived, as they needed the lifting gear to move the overweight lady. The fire was now only two doors away, and the police insisted that all persons be cleared, and only when the fire crew arrived would they go back in.

The old lady was now panicking, and the paramedic gave her a sedative to try to help relax her. He told the policeman who had joined him that he wasn't leaving and wouldn't go. He said that the poor lady was obese because she had been reliant on steroids for over 25 years due to a low immune system, but she had not been told from the start that the steroids would make her gain weight. The officer tried to plead with the paramedic, but he wouldn't budge. The policeman knew he couldn't change the paramedic's mind and left the scene. A few minutes later, the second car's tank blew, spreading the fire closer to the old lady's house. If that wasn't bad enough, the calor gas bottles in the campervan exploded and set more cars and homes alight on both sides of the street. The paramedic got hold of a couple of blankets and soaked them in the sink, and, after wringing them out, placed them over himself and the old lady. Five minutes later, the house was ablaze, and still no sign of the fire crew. The police spoke to the paramedic via his control room and told him to get out as the house was burning and the old lady's home would soon be gone. He said that he was staying put and killed his phone. He could feel the heat from next door, even though the dividing brick wall, and he knew that unless a miracle happened, his and the old lady's days were numbered.

***

Chapter 48. Bedford's Gangs.

As with any town or city in the UK, Bedford has its fair share of gang culture, and, based on the county's population in 2015, it also had the highest rate of murders in England. Bedford has two main criminal gangs, but one was severely depleted in 2017 when six gang members were sentenced to between 15 and 22 years for a 'violent' retaliation gun battle. As with all gangs, protecting their territory is a must, and the trouble between Bedford's main two gangs had been going on for several years. No sooner had the sentences been read out than other gang members stepped in to fill the vacant slots at the top, and business carried on as usual.

The gang leader was Mohammed Fazi, and he was sent to my prison, and I knew he was still controlling things from inside via his iPhone. Just before leaving, I arranged a meeting with Mohammed in the comforts of my soon-to-be-vacated office. He wondered why I had called him up, as he knew that I was leaving soon and that it would be too late to offer him counselling. He did say that he had first refused my offer of a meeting, but after speaking to other inmates, he had been told that I was straight, so he decided to see what I wanted. I didn't like the bloke as he came over as an arrogant bugger, but my meeting wasn't about making new friends. I told him I knew Bedford well and knew he was still pulling the strings by controlling his gang via his iPhone. I wasn't bothered about that as I would be leaving very soon, but I wanted to make him aware that something big would happen in Bedford, and that it had nothing to do with drugs. I didn't want to give too much away, but I had to let him in on some of the plans else he wouldn't feel safe and would instruct his gang members to take my project on.

I informed Mohammed that on the last Tuesday of the month following the second bank holiday in May, something big would happen in Bedford, and his gang may want to be part of it.

Several target businesses would be hit, and to enable this to happen the town's CCTV would be out of action from 10.30 a.m. on the day, accompanied by dire traffic problems in the town itself. A diversionary project would also be set up in the north of the town to draw the police to that area. What his gang could do is rob the two main jewellers in St. Peters Street at precisely 10.45 a.m. They should steer clear of the town centre as this would be grid-locked, but his team could enter and escape via the A4280 St. Neots road at the east of the town. They should wear a disguise as the jeweller will sound the alarm. However, with everything else going on in the town, the police will be slow to respond, and they should have a good 15 minutes to execute the robbery and make a clean getaway.

To cause more confusion, his gang should hit the two jewellers precisely simultaneously as this could confuse the police station as other alarms would also be ringing at 10.45. The police may reasonably assume that it's a fault on the system, especially as all the CCTV cameras were also down. The prime targets would be Baker Brothers Diamonds and John Bull & Co jewellers in St. Peters Street. They both stock some expensive jewellery and watches, and the gang should make a small fortune from 15 minutes of work. He asked me what I wanted out of it, and I told him I would want 20% of the take once sold, which would go towards setting up all the other diversionary precautions. He said that that answered the money side, but what else was I getting out of the deal, and why did I involve his team? I gave him a straight answer and said, 'The way the Government had failed my wife and the new governor had tried to stitch me up, I want revenge.'

I told him, 'I could set up two teams to hit the two jewellers, but the escape route would take the men away from the safe route I had planned for all my other teams.' I also told him that I wanted his gang and any other team to hit the big stores in the town centre, but this couldn't occur until after 11.45 a.m. I stated that the police commissioner had been moaning that he didn't have enough officers to manage 999 calls and that I would be proving his point.

Mohammed still wasn't sure that I could be trusted, but I said that trust was the same for both of us. He asked, 'What will stop me from becoming a grass in return for some years off me 22-year sentence?' I mentioned the name of Shuheb Alweda to him and told him I knew the truth behind his death and where he had disposed of the body. I said I knew it was his first kill to prove himself, but he had panicked and made some silly mistakes. I said that if he did the dirty on me, he would have an unhappy stay inside, with a daily strip search, and be charged with murder.

I also told him he should have confessed to all his sins before he went to court, and he would have only been given around the same number of years for both offences but would have had a clean sheet when he was finally released. This knocked the smile off his face, and he said he would help. I forgot to mention to Mohammed that his two targets would hit the panic button 15 minutes before our six teams hit their target banks. Any spare police crew would be sent to deal with their robbery first and tie up any available foot soldiers, maybe pounding the beat in the Bedford town centre. They would be sent on foot to St. Peters Street, which was far from my band of merry men, which was fine with me.

***

Chapter 49. Bedford's Gangs are Doing Their Bit.

As pre-arranged, two sets of gang members entered the two jewellery shops. The first team of three gang members entered the Baker Brothers Diamonds store, where only one young girl was behind the counter. The young lady who looked up knew immediately that the men entering the store looked like trouble. Within seconds she had a gun pointing at her head and was told to move away from the counter and open the door to the rear of the store, where they knew the higher price items would be secured in the safe. The second gang member turned the open sign on the door to closed, locked the door, and pulled the blind down. The young store assistant keyed the code into the inner door lock but must have put the wrong number in, and she was told to try again, but this would be her last chance. The gang member wasn't aware that the code the young lady had entered first wasn't a mistake, but by entering the number, it set off the silent alarm. Her second attempt let the robbers through to the safe and back office.

Two other staff members were in the rear of the store; one was an older man in his sixties and a younger Asian woman. The older man was told to open the safe but said he couldn't as it had a time lock. The ploy failed, and the second gang member hit him across his face with the back of his hand and told him he had heard that one before, so he had until the count of three or he would see his young store assistant shot. He was still shaken by the force of the backhander he had taken, but the gang member knew it wouldn't have been that hard as he didn't want to knock him out. He pointed the gun at the head of the pretty young store assistant and started counting one, two... and then the young store assistant wet her nickers. Before the gang member said three, the older man stuck his hands in the air as a sign of surrender and opened the safe.

The third gang member took the young Asian lady to the front of the store and instructed her to unlock the display counter and remove the rings and other expensive jewellery. To save time, he had been told to bring with him a long barbecue skewer, and with the top of the suitcase now open, he slid the skewer under the row of rings and lifted the complete row in one quick action, and they dropped to the bottom of the suitcase. This took around five minutes, and when he couldn't get any more in the suitcase, he and the young Asian lady went to the back of the shop to see how the others were doing. He was amazed to see that some of the top watches in the safe were from the world's most desired brands, including designers such as Rolex, Gucci, TAG, Heuer, Raymond Weil and Longines. Some of these were valued at over £20 grand, so there had to be money in the town somewhere. There were rings from designers such as Christian Bauer and the Messika brand from Paris. There was also a range of gold jewellery from Clogau Gold, Marco Bicego's, and the Italian goldsmith Fope, which offered a lovely 18ct white gold bracelet priced at just over £14 grand.

The team quickly tidied up and was about to leave when the managers phone rang. Everyone stood still as if they had been frozen in ice, but the phone kept ringing. The team leader pointed the gun to the older man's head and told him to answer it without letting on that they were being robbed. He answered, and the robbers could hear that it was the police. They listened to the message from the policeman who said, 'Good morning, sir, it's PC Gallagher here from Bedford police, and I was just checking if there was a fault on your alarm system as the John Bull jewellers down the street also went off at the same time.' With the gun pointed at his temples, the older man said everything was OK, and the alarm was constantly going off. 'When I met you in the bank last week,' he told PC Gallagher, 'I forgot to ask how your wife was doing with her pregnancy.' The policeman stuttered but said she was doing well and thanked him for asking. The owner ended the phone call, and the robber asked for any mobile phones, which he took control of and ripped the telephone line out of the wall. He told the three jewellers that they had done well, but that he would be leaving one of the gang across the street, and if they saw that they had come out from the back of the store within the next half hour, they would pay the price.

The gang's robbery at John Bull Jewellers, just a few doors down St. Peters Street, also ran like clockwork, and the second gang bagged some excellent rewards, including several Breitling watches, which sold at just over £6 grand a piece. John Bull stocked a superb selection of valuable watches but lacked the quantity of gold jewellery that Baker Brothers Diamonds had. But even so, it would make a good morning's work. I had already informed the gang's leader where to tell his staff to deliver their haul so it could be fenced. Most of the more expensive watches would be sent overseas as they would make more money from the wealthy Russians. I had already told Mohammed that he must make it clear to his gang members that they were not to keep anything as a memento as they didn't want the police to find a stolen watch around one of his member's wrists.

The route I had given him was the safest way to turn the goodies into cash, and the process should take no more than three weeks. I knew that he would check out the name I had given him, but he would find that I had given him an introduction to one of the best dealers in the country.

***

Chapter 50. Party day 10.50 a.m. Greyfriars Police Station.

At the Greyfriars Police Station, the duty sergeant was made aware that the alarm system for both jewellery shops in St Peters Street had been activated. The control room manager wanted to know if he should ask a crew to attend. The duty sergeant said it was strange that both alarms went off simultaneously, but that it was probably due to the same fault they were facing with the CCTV system. He told the control manager to see if he could get one of the officers attending the Clarence Street explosion to investigate, but not for it to take priority. He said that if there were any community police officers in the town centre, they should make their way to the jewellers to see if they had a fault with their alarm system.

PC Gallagher informed the duty sergeant that he thought something was wrong at the Baker Brothers Diamonds store as he had phoned the owner to check. Still, he sounded strange, and asked about his wife's pregnancy, but everyone knew he didn't even have a partner, let alone a pregnant wife. He told the PC to get hold of any available policemen and direct them to the jewellers in St. Peters Street as soon as possible. Still, the duty sergeant knew that with the explosion in Cavendish Street, all available staff would be tied up there.

The police finally arrived at the jewellers at 11.06 a.m., but the robbers had long gone by then. The staff were shaken up, but the Asian woman from the Baker Brothers Diamonds store said she thought she recognised the voice of one of the robbers as she had met him at a nightclub only a few weeks ago. She said she liked him, but her friend told her to stay away as he was a gang member dealing drugs and other nasty things. The police rushed around to where they knew the gang would be hanging out, but when they arrived, they found a group of young men playing snooker, and were informed that they had been there all morning. The officers searched everyone but could find no trace of expensive watches or jewellery on them. It's an excellent job that the gang's boss ensured that no one kept any item, as if they had, they would be spending a long time behind bars. The haul was well on its way to north London, and no trace of it would ever be seen in Bedford again.

***

Chapter 51. The Clarence Street Fire continued.

At Clarence Street at around 10.40 a.m. the fire engine's siren could be heard as it moved along the street but not too close to the fire. The fire chief asked the panicking policeman what the situation was, and he was informed that there were two people still in number 7, but the old lady was disabled and bedridden, and they would need their special lifting gear to remove her safely. The fire officer soon got his crew to start putting water on the house and the one next to it. He told the police officer that he couldn't risk sending men into the house as they would be in too much danger as the roof on number 7 looked ready to collapse. Within a matter of minutes, the roof of number 7 Clarence Street and the house next to it, number 5, collapsed into the top floor of the houses. It would be a matter of minutes until the roof and attic space on the remaining terraced houses (row houses, to our American readers) would collapse like a set of dominoes falling one after the other. What made matters worse was that it looked like the street had been used as a free car park by people working in the town centre, and none of the cars could be moved. Some workers would have a long walk home at the end of their shift in the town. The fourth car was also well alight, and the petrol tank exploded, sending flames to the other side of the street, and setting more homes on fire.

Clarence Street looked like a scene out of Aleppo in Syria after the troops had flushed out ISIS. Still, unlike Aleppo, the residents of Clarence Street would be re-housed locally. Still, using the Grenfell Tower disaster in London as a guide, they would stand more chance of being rehoused in Aleppo than in the fifth most prosperous nation on earth. With the explosion of the petrol tanks on the cars parked along the street, the fire spread along both sides of Clarence Street. Most of the terraced houses had been converted to flats, which had made the developer a nice little packet, but none had any form of fire protection as they didn't need it. Many of the apartments were then rented out by local agencies, and, with the influx of EU citizens, many flats were overcrowded, with sometimes three or four families living in one flat. The police or the fire service couldn't find out who owned what and had done what they could to clear everyone out of their homes, apart from the old lady and paramedic in number 7. However, none-EU citizens shared some of the flats, and no one answered the front door just in case it was a person from immigration control on the other side.

All the fire chiefs could do was aim water at the roofs and the houses on fire, but he had no chance of controlling the fire as he had to pull back to the Filler Hill Road end for their own safety. By 11.00 a.m., the scene was ablaze, and one older man who had been rescued from number 11 Clarence Street told a local reporter from *Bedford Today* that it reminded him of the bombing of Albert Street, Bedford during the Second World War. He said that he had been only nine at the time, and Bedford was bombed regularly by German aircraft with a few bombs left over from their main bombing run, which would have been to one of England's northern cities. Thankfully, my parents owned a shop with a large cellar, and we all slept there during the night.

It wasn't until around 11.15 a.m. that the fire was controlled with backup fire crews arriving from St. Neots, Sandy and Biggleswade. They tackled the blaze from the Queen's Street end, but again they faced access problems caused by parked cars. It makes you wonder how many other streets in the UK had the same problem, and no doubt that there would be an expensive and slow public enquiry which would hopefully bring new laws into place so that every street in the land would be able to be accessed by a fire crew, should the need arise.

It wasn't until 11.25 that the rescuers managed to get into number 7, where they were expecting to find two dead bodies, which they did. It was impossible to check what was left of the bodies as they had been partly cremated by the intense heat of the fire and crushed by falling debris. Undoubtedly, the paramedic would be rewarded posthumously for his bravery, and maybe, as a result, all paramedics would be paid better for their fabulous and dangerous job.

***

Chapter 52. NatWest, 81 High Street, Bedford.

Six groups are doing the hard work of robbing the central banks, and the first team's target was the NatWest bank in Bedford High Street. The team to hit the bank comprised of Douglas Boswell, Alan Frazer and Simon Westdale, all of whom had helped me get everything ready for the heist. The bank has easy access via double large doors to a modern-looking interior. When the team arrived, the bank was busy, so they attached the 'Bank Closed until Noon Today' notices and the notice stating that the ATM was closed until noon due to a computer problem. They then waited 15 minutes for the bank to clear. At precisely 10.59 a.m., Alan and Simon enter the bank, followed a minute later by Douglas, who had just fixed the 'Police – Do Not Cross' tape at chest level across the bank's entrance. Alan went up to the first teller and instructed her to stand away from her side of the counter and to tell the next teller to make her way to the door, which led to several large rooms at the rear, with the safe being in the next room to the manager's office.

The teller who opened the door was told to return to her position behind the counter, and to keep her hands out to her side. Alan knew that he was now in control of the front part of the bank, and Doug and Simon would take control of the rear. Doug started to round up all the staff at the back of the bank and got them to sit on the floor in the room at the back of the building. Once they were all gathered, a bin was passed around to collect all their mobile phones. The manager and his assistant were told to disconnect any form of communication in the room, including any computers, fax machines or phones. They were told this was very important and would be told how important it was before they left. Doug then told the manager to follow him, and, once outside the room, he was asked who had the keys to the two ATMs, which were filled from inside the bank. He said he had the keys and was told to hand them over to his assistant, who would now continue to the front of the bank, where Alan would be waiting for him. The manager was then taken into the safe room and told to open the safe. The manager said he couldn't do that as it had a time lock. Doug chuckled and told the manager to stop delaying the inevitable as he knew he was telling a porky pie. Once the safe was opened, Doug instructed the manager to place all the notes in his suitcase except the old paper notes, which were no longer worth anything. He was also told to put all the foreign currency in the case.

At the front of the bank, Simon was systematically getting the tellers to remove all the notes for each till, including the locked drawer just below the till, which held a backup supply of notes. Once the tellers had placed the bank notes in Simon's suitcase, they were guided to join the other bank members at the rear. This left Alan at the front of the bank with the assistant manager, who was told to open each ATM, remove the notes, and place them into the suitcase. Before leaving, all employees were now in the rear room, and Doug produced the dummy timer bomb from his suitcase and placed it on top of a filing cabinet so everyone could see that the countdown clock had been started and was currently showing 60 minutes. Doug explained to the bank staff that they shouldn't move until the countdown clock shows 00:00. The device has three trigger settings, and No.1 will detect any loud noise – so no shouting. No 2 will detect any signal sent from any computer or phone, and No. 3 checks the room pressure – so once we have left and started the countdown, don't open any windows or doors, or you will kill everyone in this room. Before leaving, I asked again if any mobile phones hadn't yet been handed in, and one of the tellers held up her phone, which was placed in the bin outside the room. On leaving the bank, the three robbers split, and slowly made their way down the High Street, crossing into Silver Street and then along Midland Road to reach the station.

***

Chapter 53. Barclays Bank 111 High Street, Bedford.

The team to hit the Barclays Bank was made up of James Burley (No. 1), Ken Shoemaker (No. 2) and Glen Toogood (No. 3). The Barclays Bank sits in a corner position facing the busy high street. The bank has automated glass doors, and we must be cautious when placing the do not enter before noon A4 laminated sheets. Thankfully, the automated glass doors are set back about three feet from the main two wooden doors, so the team only had to close one and place the sign on it. We arrived as planned and closed one of the doors at 10.45, but only two tellers were working their tills which had caused a line to form, of customers who were all waiting to be served. James attached the bank closed notices and the notice stating that the ATM was closed until noon due to a computer problem. At 10.55, a smart-looking man arrived at the door holding a Costa coffee in his hand and was shocked to see the sign stating that the bank would be closed until noon. James pointed out the sign to the man, expecting him to walk away like others had. However, the man holding his coffee said, 'I am the manager, and everything was fine 20 minutes ago.'

The manager started to enter the bank, and James followed him in, pointed his gun into the man's ribs, and told him that his bank was about to be robbed and he would have to casually turn around and wait with us for a few minutes. Thankfully, the manager complied and watched more customers leave the store. I know he wanted to try and call out to anyone, but with every client that exited the bank, I dug the barrel of my gun into his ribs. At 10.59, Ken and Glen took over control of the manager and stepped into the bank. I was seconds behind them after fixing the 'Police – Do Not Cross' tape across the entrance, closing both wooden doors behind me.

Ken walked the manager to the first teller window and informed the young lady that this was a robbery and to stand back from her till and tell the other teller to do the same. When they complied, Ken took the manager to the security door, which led to the back of the bank, and told him to enter his code and continue. James joined Ken and was not surprised to see several rooms and offices in use. James decided that the room at the back would be best to store all the bodies in, and both robbers, with the manager's assistance, started to round up all the Barclay staff and placed them in the rear room. Ken kept guard on the staff, and James took the manager to the room that held the safe and told him to open it. The manager did not hesitate and was told to place the money in the suitcase as well as the foreign currency. James then asked the manager for the keys to the ATMs, which he provided. James wasn't worried about the extent that the manager was helping them. Still, James had noticed that the second teller had given the manager a nod, which was their signal to make the manager aware that she had activated the silent alarm. This did not worry James, as he knew that the other five banks would also be activating their silent alarms and that the police would think the system had a fault.

James returned the manager to the rear office, where he could join his staff and the two tellers from the front. Once they were all gathered, a bin was passed around to collect all their mobile phones. The manager and his assistant were told to disconnect any form of communication in the room, including any computers, fax machines or phones. They were told this was especially important and would be told how important it was before they left. James then handed Glen the keys to the ATMs and told him to be quick. When Glen returned with his suitcase full, he produced the dummy timer bomb from his suitcase and placed it on top of a filing cabinet so everyone could see the countdown clock showing 60 minutes. James explained to the bank staff that they should not move until the countdown clock showed 00:00. This small countdown box held an explosive that would kill everyone in the room. He explained to the bank staff about the three trigger settings. Before leaving, he asked again if any mobile phones, tablets, or iPads had yet to be handed in, and three staff members held up their phones which were placed outside the room. On leaving the bank, the three robbers split up and slowly made their way down the high street and then along Midland Road to reach the railway station.

*∗∗

Chapter 54. HSBC Bank, Bedford.

The second team's target is the HSBC, also called the Household Bank which is situated close to the main police station but isn't in direct view. The three guests are Barry Swift (No. 1), Pete Griffith (No. 2) and William Bennett (Bill) who was (No. 3). The big problem with this bank is that it's a modern complex and has floor to ceiling windows through which nosy members of the public can easily see what is happening inside. The entrance was easy to manage as it was a single door, and we could easily manage, so they attached the 'Bank Closed until Noon Today' notice and the one on the ATM stating that the ATM was closed until noon due to a computer problem. As these three guests were in the public view, they needed to look smart so that they could pass off as a detective. All three had to visit the charity shops to pick out a suit as they never wore a suit in their normal life. As with all the other targets, timing was essential, and at 10:59 Pete Griffiths and William Bennett entered the bank, followed a minute later by Barry Swift.

Pete went to the first teller/cashier window and pointed the gun at her and told her to stand back from the till and to tell the other tellers to do the same. Bill Bennett then instructed the first teller to open the door to the bank's rear. Once in the rear Bill and Barry soon spotted the manager's office and Bill headed straight there. Barry's job was to get all the other staff to congregate in a small office at the rear. A bin was passed around and staff were told to place their mobile phones in the bin but not to worry as they would be left outside the door. He also told them to disconnect all phone, fax and internet connections in the room. While all this was happening, Pete was busy at the front instructing all the three tellers to fill his suitcase up with goodies. After he was sure that they had tipped everything in, they were marched to the smaller office at the back. Bill had asked the manager to open the safe, but he hesitated and tried the old-time lock excuse, so bill pointed the gun to his head, and although the manager had pissed his pants, he told him this would be his last chance. Once the safe was open, the manager was told to fill the suitcase with notes and foreign currency, of which they had a large number of Euros which was probably due to the high level of Italians that remained in the town. Once that was done, he called for No. 2 to join him, and he asked the manager for the key to unlock the ATM machine and handed it to Barry.

The ATM had just been filled up to replace the money that had been withdrawn over the bank holiday weekend, so it looked like a tidy sum. When all three guests returned to the back room, Pete produced the dummy timer bomb from his suitcase and placed it on top of a bookcase so everyone could see that the countdown clock which was currently showing 60 minutes on the clock. Doug explained to the bank staff that they shouldn't move until the countdown clock is showing 00:00. This small countdown box holds an explosive which will kill everyone in this room. The device has three trigger settings, No.1 will detect any loud noise – so no shouting. No 2 will detect any signal sent from any computer or phone and No. 3 checks the room pressure – so once we have left and started the countdown clock don't open any windows or doors or you will kill everyone in this room. Before leaving he ask again, is there any mobile phone that hasn't yet been handed in, and two staff members held up their phones which were placed outside the room. On leaving the bank the three robbers split up and slowly made their way down Allhallows and then along the Midland Road to reach the railway station.

***

Chapter 55. Lloyds Bank 34 High Street, Bedford.

The team to hit the Lloyds bank was made up of James Smith (No. 1), Geoff Laxly (No. 2) and Steve Marshal (No. 3). Like all teams they had arrived outside the bank at 10.45 and attached the 'Bank Closed until Noon Today' notice and the one on the ATM stating that the ATM was closed until noon due to a computer problem. The outer door led to an inner door which was made of full-length glass, but thankfully the windows of the bank were higher up, with frosted glass at the bottom. This would limit the visibility of our actions from outside. There were a few customers inside the bank, and they were slow to clear. One lady did approach the bank and, having read the 'Do Not Enter' message, considered that it must apply to everybody else and not her, as she tried to barge pass Geoff, who told her that there was a queue, which she could join if she wished, but he made it clear that there would be no queue jumping. She said a few words in German that he could not understand, and she wandered off down the high street mumbling to herself.

At 10.59 James and Steve entered the bank and Geoff followed after fixing the 'Police – Do Not Cross' tape across the entrance closing both wooden doors behind him. There was still an old lady being dealt with at the second teller window, but we couldn't wait for her to leave, and exactly at 11.00 a.m. James pointed his gun towards the first teller and told her to stand back and tell the other teller to do the same. James then told the first teller to unlock the inner door, and Geoff pointed his gun to the old lady who tried to scream but only got half of it out before she fainted and crumpled out cold on to the floor. Both Geoff and Steve picked up the old lady and carried her into the rear of the bank, but just stood there until James pointed to a rear room which was empty. They lay her down and started to gather up the manager and all other staff, checking every room, and the toilets to make sure no one was hiding. James had to keep an eye on the tellers as well as keeping an eye open for what was happening in the rear of the bank. James then instructed the tellers to place all notes and £2 coins in the suitcase, but they said that they didn't have a key to the lower drawer that held even more notes. James knew that the tellers also had the key for the drawer, and he pointed his gun at the brow of the first young teller, who, despite wetting herself, produced a key and completed the task.

The second teller follow suit but thankfully didn't pee herself. Once they had done their part, they were led to join the fellow workmates, but the first teller begged to be allowed to go to the toilet to clean herself up but was refused permission. With everyone safe, the manager was taken to the safe, and he opened it without a fuss, and loaded all the money, both GBP and other currencies, into the suitcase. He was then asked for the ATM key and was returned to the storeroom to join the others. I passed the keys to Steve, and he knew that they were for the ATM and left to grab his goodies. Meanwhile a bin was passed around those in the storeroom, and everyone was asked to put their mobile phones and any electronic equipment into the bin and were told that they would be left outside the room for collection later. Steve returned, pulling his filled suitcase behind him, and Geoff then produced the dummy timer bomb from his suitcase and placed it on top of a table so everyone could see that the countdown clock, which was currently showing 60 minutes. Geoff explained to the bank staff that they shouldn't move until the countdown clock is showing 00:00. He also explained about the three trigger types. Before leaving he asked again if there were any mobile phones, tablet or iPads that hadn't yet been handed in, and one staff member held up his mobile phone, which were placed outside the room along with the rest.

Just as we were going to leave, a young lady, whose name on her badge was Shirley, asked permission to check on the old lady. We agreed but told her to hurry up. She said that she had been trained by the company as the bank always had to have a medically trained person working at the bank. After running a few checks and feeling her pulse, she said that the old lady hadn't fainted but had had a stroke and needed urgent medical attention or she would die. Geoff instructed his colleagues to carry the old lady out to the front of the bank and place her just outside the main door and then to come back for their cases. I informed the others that we had called for an ambulance, but they were not to move until the countdown clock showed zero. I then set the clock and we made our way to the station. Geoff called for an ambulance, saying that an old lady was outside the Lloyds bank in the High Street, but she had had a heart attack. The operator asked for more information, but Geoff told her that he was just a passer-by and didn't want to get involved. The three men separated and made their way back to the railway station.

***

Chapter 56. Royal Bank of Scotland.

The fifth group of robbers visited the Royal Bank of Scotland branch, which is situated on Mill Street. The three guests will be Jacob Henningsson, Rees Jones, and Lenny Adams. I was looking forward to the boys paying a visit to the RBS, as this bank has pissed me off more than any other. They used to have a branch in the small town I lived in, but they closed the branch down, making a good friend of my wife's redundant without a thank you from anyone. In chapter 37, you would have read the sad story of Jacob Henningsson, whom the bank allegedly robbed after setting up his company. And the biggest dislike is the way the company has been allowed to be poorly run. The British taxpayer had to fork out £45 billion for an 84% stake in the company during the financial crisis of 2008. This in my opinion was money well spent, as the consequences of not doing so would have made the world recession of the 1930s seem like a picnic in the park.

However, in 2016 the bank made another loss of £7bn – so chalking up some £58bn of losses since 2008. As with the other five banks robbing the RBS following the tried and tested rule of engagement and entered the bank at 11.00 a.m. on the dot. However, there was still one customer at the first teller's counter, and he had already pointed a gun at the young lady and told her to fill his bag with notes. Jacob approached the man, who looked as if he was high on drugs, and pointed the cold barrel of his gun at the robber's neck and told him to place his weapon on the counter and step back. So shocked was the scruffy man that he put his gun down and ran out of the bank empty-handed. We let him go and informed the teller that the real robbers had arrived, and she was to open the door and let me and my colleagues in. This she did, and everything went as clockwork, and we picked up the first robber's handgun, made a sharp exit, and had a quiet stroll back to the railway station.

***

Chapter 57. Santander Bank, Midland Road, Bedford.

The sixth set of robbers hit the Santander bank on Midland Road and part of the largest shopping centre in Bedford, the Harper Centre. Santander UK plc is a bank wholly owned by the Spanish Santander Group. When the bank started between the years of 2007 to 2010, it had some terrible reviews and an inferior relationship with its customers. However, a survey in 2014 ranked their satisfaction higher than any of the other leading high-street banks. It had a nice spread of customers, and, being a European bank, always had an active foreign currency section, so the team were expecting to get a fair share of Euros for their effort today.

The team for this bank was Mike Hood, Tony Weston and John Tredwood. When arriving at 10.45, the team was shocked to find that there was a large protest going on when they arrived at the Harper Centre, organised by the Save Our Oceans group, which was trying to get plastic banned by forcing manufacturers to recycle their plastic so that it didn't end up in the sea. Although the team were keen to play their part in recycling, they were there to do a different type of recycling themselves, and welcomed anything that would keep the police off their backs. As with all our banks, the formula worked fine, and our three modern-day merry men conducted their task and headed back to the railway station with smiles on their faces.

***

Chapter 58. The After Effect of the Heist.

In the late morning, the traffic in Bedford was still bad and the police were running around like a chicken who had just had its head chopped off. At 11.00 a.m. on the dot, the duty sergeant at the Greyfriars Police Station had been made aware that six banks had triggered their silent alarm, but he just assumed that this was a fault in the system. Even if he had wanted to check them out, he didn't have any spare officers to investigate. Several were still helping at the explosion and horrific fire in Clarence Street. Other officers were trying to protect the Environment Secretary George Eustice from an angry crowd in the Harpur Centre, and his only foot officer was now investigating the jewel robbery at the Baker Brothers Diamonds store in St. Peter's Street and his detectives were now chasing the gangs as information had linked one of the robbers to the raid at Baker Brothers Diamonds.

At around 11.30, the lonely community constable who had been sent to the jewellery raid was now told to get back to the town centre to see if he could help at the protest in the Harpur Centre. On his way down the High Street, he noticed the 'Police Do Not Cross' tape at the entrance to the Barclays bank. He found it strange that there had been no mention about a bank raid on his police radio, so he thought it best to check with base. He called the duty sergeant and told him what he had found, but the sergeant could only say that there had been several of the bank's alarms going off, all at 11.00 a.m., so he told the community constable to stay in front of the building until he had checked with the detectives to see if they knew anything about it.

After only a few minutes the duty sergeant was back on to the young community constable, telling him to stand guard on the scene and let no one enter or leave until the CID turned up to investigate. About 20 minutes passed and still no sign of the CID, but he assumed that with the traffic at a standstill it would take time to get through. Five minutes later, DCI Jimmy Mercer arrived and showed his badge to the young officer. He had also brought his partner with him, who also showed her card, and the young constable made a note of both their names and time of arrival. Both detectives entered the bank, and neither could see anyone. They progressed to the rear of the bank and passed the room which held the safe, and noticed that it had been left open, and in the last office they noticed that all the staff were in the one room, and it looked as if all their mobiles had been binned outside.

The lady detective went to open the door, but DCI Jimmy Mercer pulled her hand away from the door handle as he had a gut feeling that something was wrong. One of the captives jumped to his feet and waved his hands, shooing them away. Both detectives stood back, and the man inside then put a finger to his lips. He then got hold of an A4 sheet of paper and wrote on it in big letters that there was a bomb inside. DCI Jimmy Mercer turned to his pretty assistant and told her to go outside the bank and call in the bomb disposal team, and then to stay outside and try to cordon off 100 meters either side of the bank. The young detective then called the duty sergeant and broke the news to him, and requested back-up so they could cordon off the high street. He said he would send any available officer to assist.

As they had already called the bomb disposal team in earlier that morning, the duty sergeant already had their number and called them back in. The duty sergeant also contacted his officer, who was leading the team trying to protect the Environment Secretary George Eustice that two bombs had now been located in Bedford, and the town was now in major alert as he feared that it could be a terrorist threat. The minister was whisked away and headed on foot to the Bedford Blues rugby ground where a helicopter was waiting to take him to safety.

Back at Barclays bank DCI Jimmy Mercer wrote back a note asking where the bomb was and how did they know that a bomb was placed in the room. The manager wrote back stating it was a timer bomb that was on countdown and couldn't be made safe until it showed 00.00. This writing took time, but after being told to be quiet, there was no other way. DCI Jimmy Mercer asked the manager what was showing on the clock now. He wrote back '29.16'. The DCI wrote back asking why they couldn't leave. The reply said that the device could detect change of pressure in the room, also any loud noise and any mobile signals. Seeing the bucket of mobile phones outside, he now understood more. He wrote back to stay calm as the bomb disposal team were on their way and they would be able to defuse it. He also wrote that he needed to check outside but would return in a few minutes.

At 11.52 he came back in with a bomb disposal officer in his heavy protective gear and asked for all the facts. DCI Jimmy Mercer told him that the manager inside the room had said that it was a bomb placed on top of a cabinet that could be triggered by any loud noise, change in room conditions and any mobile signal. The bomb disposal chap said that he had never heard of a bomb with multi trigger options, and he thinks that it would probably turn out to be a dummy. With just five minutes to go until the alleged bomb would be made safe, it would be best to wait outside. I was told to leave but he would remain. At exactly 12 o'clock there was a shout of joy as the clock hit 00.00. There was a rush for the door, but the bomb disposal officer told them to stay where they were just for a few more minutes until they had the bomb safely within a bomb-proof case. This happened within three minutes, and the staff were let out.

Some dived for their mobile phone to call their loved ones and to tell them that they were safe, but others rushed for the loo. When the panic was over, DCI Jimmy Mercer and his pretty assistant came back in and told staff to sit in their office or the rest room as he would need to take a statement from everyone.

Outside, the press was already bussing around as many had already been there to cover the plastic protest and the arrival of the Environment Secretary.

DCI Jimmy Mercer came out of the bank and was surprised to see the media already set up and filming. Sky, BBC and ITV were recording, and the reporter from Sky shouted a question at the DCI, '"Do you think that the robbery at the jewellers and the bank were linked, and can you also confirm that there was a bomb also in the bank?' The DCI said that he couldn't comment but they would be informed of a press meeting late in the day.

The DCI had come out to ask whether the soco team had been called in, and his partner confirmed that it had and would be arriving as soon as they can get through the traffic. He told the young constable to guard the entrance to the bank and make sure that no one enters or leaves. He told the constable that the staff had been told not to touch anything and they would all be questioned as soon as he had the officers to do so. He said that he had been called to the Nat West bank further down the street as it looked as if they had also been hit.

DCI Jimmy Mercer called his superior and made him aware of the situation and it would be best to call this a major incident as he was going to need more officers on the ground. His boss said that he had already briefed the chief constable, and that all leave was being cancelled and they were calling in any available officers. The DCI then made a quick call to the duty sergeant at the Greyfriars Police Station and just wanted to get his thoughts on what was happening. The sergeant said that the alarm system had gone off at six large banks in the town, but, as they all went off at the same time, he thought that it was a technical fault. The DCI said that he had just left the Barclays bank and was on his way to the Nat West, but if these were just two of the six banks, they needed to get officers to all of the other four banks to ensure that the crime scene wasn't being contaminated. The sergeant said that he didn't have any available officers, but he had just heard that the chief constable had announced that this was now a major incident and other officers were being made available. The DCI asked him to get someone to call each of the other four banks and speak to the manager and tell him officers were on their way and that his staff were not to touch anything until they arrive. He also asked the duty sergeant if he could set up a roadblock on all the main exits from the town, as if the robbers were trying to escape by car, then they had picked the wrong day and would probably be stuck in traffic somewhere in the town. The sergeant said he would do what he could. The other banks were a copy-cat of the first two banks, and Bedford has come to a standstill as streets were closed until the alleged bomb had been made safe. The bomb disposal unit could only deal with one bank at a time, and it wasn't until 2p.m. that the all clear had been given and the police could take back control.

***

Chapter 59. After the Heist.

Once we had all safely got back to the Kempston Hardwick railway station, we all presented our suitcases to Doug, and he would scan them to see if any of the bundles of notes which had been quickly placed in the suitcases didn't include any GPS tracker microchips. Doug asked all guest if they had placed their gun, gloves and any disguises used in their suitcase. I gave the team leaders their parking ticket for this morning's meeting which should only be shown if asked for by the men in blue.

There were seven cases that showed that they included a tracking device, so these would need to be dealt with quickly. I asked every party guest if they had used the phone, I had provided them with at any time other than calling or texting me. Geoff said that he had called 999 to call for an ambulance for the old lady as he didn't want to leave her without first calling for help. I told him not to worry but to give me the phone so that I could place the SIM card in the microwave and scramble it later. I gave him a new phone so that I could keep up to date. I also asked if anyone else had a problem, and Jacob couldn't wait to tell the others what had happened, and to his shock it was a real gun and had bullets in the chamber ready to be used.

I told the team well done, and thanks for not talking on the train back as walls have ears and you couldn't trust anyone these days. They all laughed out loudly, but it wasn't at my joke, but a release of all the pent-up stress and tension they had kept inside during the morning. I finally said to my guest just before leaving, just one more thing before you go, did anyone get tempted to pocket any cash from the raids or even pocket a nice-looking iPhone? If they had then tell me now as all modern phones could be tracked, and any new bank notes could also be traced. I told them if they come clean now it would be better for everyone as just one mistake could put us all back inside.

I looked at all the men and could see that Steve Marshal wasn't making eye contact, and I asked Doug and James to search him. He protested, but Doug was too strong for him, and he soon found a wad of new £20 notes and an iPhone in his pocket. These were both confiscated, and the iPhone was given to Geoff Laxly to wipe it and place it in any rubbish bin he found at the service station but to make sure he took the battery and the SIM card out first. I told Steve that I was extremely disappointed with him, but he would still get paid, but I would not be inviting him to any other heist. I didn't want him to think that he wouldn't get paid as I didn't want to give him a reason to grass us up.

I didn't want to hold back all of the guests and told everyone apart from my A team and Geoff Laxly's D team to leave and that I would be in contact with them once the money had been cleaned and we knew what everyone would be getting for their morning's work. It took quite a few minutes to find the chips, and when they were I handed them to Geoff Laxly and told him to stop at the first service station on the M1 and slip them into the small magnetic boxes I had supplied and place them under different heavy trucks. It would also be better if one of his team crossed over the bridge and placed some of GPS trackers, so that they would track going north up the M1.

Once Geoff and his team were on their way, the remaining A team and I headed back to the workshop. Doug had set up some trellis tables so that we could break down the notes and split up the various currencies we had also stolen. It would take the rest of the day to sort and count, and in the end we had over £800,000 in sterling and around £90,000 in various currencies. Of the £800,000, around half were used notes so we didn't need to send these to the cleaner. Once finished, we loaded the notes back into four suitcases ready for delivery by me and Doug to our chosen money laundering bloke. If we were prepared to wait two weeks, we could look to get around 45% back in clean notes, but if we wanted it cleaned quickly then we would only get 29% back. We had already spoken about this and had told all guest that we would be going for the 45%, but they would have to wait a few weeks to get their rewards. This wouldn't be a bad thing as if the police didn't accept that they had been in a meeting they would keep a close eye out to see if they were spending above their means.

***

Chapter 60. Post Heist in Bedford.

The national media were having a field day, and eventually a press conference was called to be held at the Greyfriars police station at 4p.m. At the conference, the Chief Constable started to explain what had happened to his beloved town during the day. He explained that the trigger event had been the explosion in Clarence Street at around 10 a.m. There had been an explosion in a derelict house which had set the first house in Clarence Street alight, and the fire soon spread along the street as there wasn't anything to stop it. The fire crews were struggling to get to the street due to traffic congestion it was nearly 50 minutes before they arrived.

What had delayed them was a gridlock of traffic in the town as there were several sets of traffic lights controlling the three main routes in and out of the town centre. The police were investigating why these had been set up without notifying either the police or the town council. One reporter from Sky News asked if there had been any loss of life in the Clarence Street fire, and the Chief Constable said that he believed that there were two lives lost but, as many of the houses were sublet, it would take time to check things out. He continued to explain that at around 9.30 a.m. all the town's CCTV cameras went down, and they were still investigating what had caused the problem.

A reporter from the BBC asked how long the cameras would be down, and he said that he didn't know but hoped that it wouldn't take long to find and fix the problem. The Chief Constable continued to say that at around 10.45a.m. both jewellers in St. Peters Street were raided and valuable watches and jewellery had been stolen. 'Due to underfunding, we were short on officers on the ground and couldn't reach the jewellers until after 11.02 am which by that time robbers had left the area. At 11a.m. six sets of silent alarms at various banks were triggered, but as they all were set off at the same time, the Duty

Sergeant assumed that it was a fault on the system as it had never been known that six banks could be robbed at the same time.'

It wasn't until around noon that they realised that the Nat West bank had been raided. 'Just after 11a.m. my officers decided to evacuate the Environment Secretary George Eustice as we now knew that two bombs had been located and we were unsure if it wasn't a terrorist threat on one of our cabinet ministers, so we arrange for the minister to be escorted on foot to a near-by rugby pitch to a waiting helicopter. I'm glad to say that the minister made it back to parliament safely. The Prime Minister and the Home Secretary had been kept informed of the situation at all stages.'

The Chief Constable went on to state that he was sad to report that the total now dead from this morning's nightmare was at least three, as it looks as if a lady had a heart attack when in the Lloyds Bank, and, although we assume that it was one of the robbers calling for an ambulance due to the traffic grid lock, it didn't arrive on time. We will release further details when known, and once we have contacted relatives. A reporter from *Bedford Independent* asked the Chief Constable if the explosion in Clarence Street, the two jewel robberies and the six bank robberies were part of the same criminal group, and had the police made any progress on the jewellery robbery as we understand that one of the employees felt that she had recognised one of the robbers as being a young male from Bedford.

The Chief replied that an armed response team had been sent to a known address in the town and that the investigation was ongoing. A reporter from *The Daily Mirror* asked if the attack on Bedford was down to the Chief Constable continuing message that he couldn't answer all 999 calls as he didn't have the manpower. The Chief hesitated before answering but couldn't miss this opportunity to get his message over yet again. He said he knew of no town in the UK that isn't short of police officers, and we are all falling right into the criminals' grasp when a major incident takes place.

By the time the Chief Constable ended his press conference, myself and all my men were safely on their way home. What I didn't realise was that after the hectic day in Bedford the CCTV system and the traffic grid log continued. The gangs and anyone who wanted a new TV raided the large stores in the town centre as soon as it got dark. Some stores were set alight, and havoc took over. I hadn't planned for this to happen, but with social media making it easy for the word to get out, criminals from all over the Midlands and the home counties started to loot and the police were powerless to stop them. It was turning out to be a heist to be remembered.

*＊＊

Chapter 61. Spreading the Word.

The Chief Constable had said at his press conference that they would try to find out who was behind today's events. He didn't have to wait long for an answer as all media received an untraceable email during late afternoon which would be on every front page and news bulletin. The email read:

Bedford at war. Today saw a chain of events that were set up by a group of my friends who were sick to their back teeth of having their conditions ignored by the powers that be. Any problem in the free world usually finds its way inside and, due to overcrowding and under-staffing, HMP service is doing little to solve the problems. Our group of highly trained robbers will continue to hit the rich and funnel the money to the poor. The only time we will stop is when these top ten problems have been rectified.

1. **The NHS.**
2. **Booze in Britain**
3. **How gambling is ruining lives.**
4. **Prisons have become dumping grounds for the mentally ill**.
5. **Drugs in Britain**.
6. **Austerity & Non-dom status.**
7. **UK Housing Crisis.**
8. **Get rid of zero-hour contracts.**
9. **From a hero to inmate.**
10. **Children need to know whose boss.**

Until these problems are dealt with my team will continue to bring towns to their knees and in the end the government will have to take matters seriously.

***

Chapter 62. Three years later.

I know three years seems a long time, but my group of merry men haven't been idle. I didn't pay them in one lump sum as I didn't want the police noticing one of them was spending beyond their means. I found some of them jobs and thankfully they are still working and keeping on the straight and narrow. I set up a charity for ex-cons to enable more inmates get a better chance in life, once released from prison. I had also opened an offshore bank account and registered a company overseas so that the police would have a problem if they ever tried to trace the money. I couldn't get all of them jobs and told them that they would work on various projects the charity was running and would be paid by the charity for their work. I used my share of the heist rewards along with my wife's life insurance and persuaded the poor old farmer to sell me the barn that we rented from him. We also purchased the old house that stood alongside it plus twenty acres of mainly woodland. Subject to planning permission I hope to open a special needs holiday camp site with around sixteen static caravans that we would rent out to families with Autistic children as it's difficult to go on holiday when you have an autistic youngster. The site would have an indoor swimming pool, therapy room, sensory room, a bar and clubroom plus a few pinball machines and adapted playground.

I also helped find a good care home for my Autistic brother. He didn't like it at first and his Autism grew worse but the staff at the Sense run home never gave up on him and along with the other five residents he has found new friends and has become more tolerant of changes. He loves swimming, trampolining, and horse riding. He also goes out to various parks during the Spring and Summer for a picnic and walk amongst the trees. My mother is still going strong and visits him every two weeks, but she found it very difficult to cope when he left as he had taken everything out of her during the thirty years he was at home.

I never sent these details as a press release (after the raid) as I didn't want to give them any further clues on what really made me angry, which may have given the police more information, that they could use against me and my merry men. None of the team were ever contacted by the Bedfordshire Police, but we really didn't mind as it just goes to show that we are force to be reckoned with. The problems I mentioned in my first post after the raid haven't changed but have simply got worse. I have listed them below.

If the NHS was a ship, it would be named the Titanic.
With over 7.6 million waiting a long time for operations the problems withing the NHS continue to grow. If the country wants a workable health service, then it needs to start paying its staff better wages and resolve the "Over Management" that has crept into the NHS. It appears that there are more blue-collar staff rather than staff who are hands on. It also needs to solve the bed-blocking problem and Social Care should be separated away from the NHS and run by County Councils. Money should be transferred from the NHS budget to the various providers of social care. To give you an example, the *Northampton Chronical & Echo* reported that in September 2022 nearly a quarter of Northampton General Hospital capacity was taken up by bed-blockers waiting to be discharged. There simply isn't enough being done to find alternative beds or care in the community for these patients. Many would need support of some kind, but they don't need to be taking up hospital beds. Yet in November 2022 the BBC reported that the 51-bed Spinneyfields Specialist Care Centre in Rushden - run by West Northamptonshire Council – will close in early 2023 and will no longer care for people after leaving hospital. A Unison spokesperson said that 'The plans to close a specialist care centre and make 56 staff redundant come at the same time we have ambulances queuing at the local hospitals because of a lack of beds and patients ready for discharge with nowhere to go.'

Community care needs to be supplied outside of the NHS and controlled by the County Councils up and down the country. Central government must supply the funds to do this. What we currently have is disgraceful and unless action is taken as a matter of urgency, the NHS will no longer be "fit for purpose".

Desperate NHS pays up to £2,500 for nursing shifts.
The BBC reported in November 2022 that NHS bosses are increasingly paying premium rates for agency staff to plug holes in rotas. Spending on agency staff rose by 20% last year to hit £3bn in England. For many shifts, bosses have been so short-staffed they have been willing to breach the government pay caps for these agency workers, most of whom are doctors and nurses.

In chapter 15 of The Bedford Heist which covers the sorry saga of Covid-19 the author states in the paragraph on "Couldn't Care Less About Care Homes" it stated, Another worrying tidbit that I heard about some of the current care workers was that they were working two different 8-hour shifts at two separate care homes. This alone could spread the virus from one care home to another. Some care workers from overseas were also living in overcrowded accommodation where several immigrant families share the same Inadequate and cramped facilities. This must have added to the number of deaths in care homes during the pandemic.

What the government must do is to introduce new rules covering the employment of all staff in both our NHS hospitals and care homes within the UK. Anyone working in this sector must be registered with the NHS, along with being checked out and would be paid directly via the various hospital or care home, but the new NHS human resources division would be copied in on who was being paid and the hours they worked. If this were done, then a simple check could be made to see if there were any duplications. All staff would be paid via the PAYE system and only those registered with the NHS-HR could work in the care sector.

Some readers may remember that towards the end of 2021 thousands of care workers refused to take up the Covid-19 vaccination scheme and if they didn't then they could not work in care homes. IMO these workers came via some very cleaver recruitment agencies and as I will explain in my next novel "The Bedford Revenge" due out in 2024, several thousands of care workers were scared to give their true details to the vaccination body as many were undocumented immigrants and couldn't give an NHS number. It had very little to do with fearing needles or other meaningless excuses. It makes you wonder if the Government were aware of this large sector of illegal workers in the care sector and the easy way to get rid of them would be to make vaccinations mandatory. I will show in my next novel how these illegals are forced into labour by ruthless Human Traffickers and how me and my merry men will bring down Europe's largest trafficking gang.

Currently, the NHS and care sector rely on agency staff and end up paying the agency a lot extra for the pleasure. These agencies should be put out of business as anyone wishing to work for the NHS or in a care home must be vetted and then employed via the NHS Human Resources division. This could not be done straight away but it could be introduced to start next April. To bridge the gap the Health secretary should offer a three-month tax-free contract to retired doctors and nurses. I can assure you that this would save the country billions of pounds every year and at least it would stop the double working that currently is going on.

***

Expanding Mental Health.
Having witness the outcome of addiction, I strongly believe that all addictions should fall under the Mental Health Act. People suffering from addictions such as Smoking, Drugs, Alcohol, Gaming and Gambling should be treated as a mental health

problem. If they do not get on top of their addiction, then they could be "sectioned" until they are no longer an addict.

Inmates.
I strongly believe that a prisoner should not be released until they have been clear of their addiction for at least six months. If they are not clean, then they will revert to their old habit as soon as they are released and will once again end back to prison.

The overcrowding and staff shortage is an ever-growing problem. The next Government must correct this problem if they don't want the chance of prisoners escaping to rise.

**

Drugs in Britain. In the UK we spend billions every year trying to fight drugs with little success. We need to seriously look at the way Portugal treats possession of drugs and class use of small quantities of these drugs as a public health issue, not a criminal one. The drugs were still illegal, of course but now getting caught with them meant a small fine and maybe a referral to a drug treatment program — not jail time and a criminal record.

Great Britain needs to look at other ways to stop these drug barons and if an addict could legally buy weed for £2 then the drug pushers would go out of business. The quality of the weed would be better than the current illegal type and it can be grown in the UK. At the same time, you would deprive the drug gangs of easy money and could also reduce knife crime and gang wars. Sooner or later some country will have to take the lead by following Portugal but also make drugs available from a bullet/thief proof vending machine. Purchases could only be paid for via a debit card and limited to two purchases a day. For those that don't have a debit card then they can buy a pre-paid card at several corner shops, supermarkets, or service stations. Once payment has been taken only the cost of purchase will be logged. No names or personal details will be stored. Apart from popular drugs the vending machine could also offer condoms and possibly the morning after pill.

We need to follow the same route we took regarding cigarettes where a warning can be given on the packaging as well as advice on how to stop. A drug user would need to keep the packaging along with its unique purchase number just in case he/she was asked by the police. If this was done, then it would take the money out of the game and should result in less gangs. Owning unlicensed drugs would still be illegal and stiffer penalties would be applied by the courts to any person supplying illegal drugs. If Britain can make this work and build the robber proof vending machine, then sooner or later we could mass produce these machines and export these around the world.

***

Stop the Boats. In the December 2019 Conservative manifesto, it said that the illegal immigration problem would be sorted and promised to sort out this ever-growing problem, once and for all. This never happened yet Labour lost several Red Wall seats as the citizens were sick and tired of seeing an influx of Eastern European's taking over their county.

"Stop the Boats" is still the current Prime Ministers pledge, but it will never happen unless some drastic action is taken. IMO the only way to stop the boats from making the deadly crossing is to allow migrants to register in Calais, France and then be kept in camps until the UK can put the migrants on a coach which will make the safe crossing via a ferry. Whilst in the Calais camp the Uk authorities could run checks on the immigrant to ensure they didn't have a criminal history. Employers in the UK can register their requirements and the border agency could link the two up. If migrants want to enter the UK, then the following rules would apply to all over 18s.

!/. They will have fitted an electronic monitoring (known as 'tagging') for a minimum of two years.

2/. On registration they will be evaluated on their use of the English language. If not to an acceptable level, they will be offered either free training whilst in France or by their employer in Britain.

3/. If they have a verifiable trade, then they will take priority over those that don't. If they don't have a trade but are looking for unskilled work, then their details will be noted and any UK employer looking for staff could be notified. The employer will need to supply accommodation and meals but would be allowed to deduct the cost (A maximum of 50%) from their minimum wage.

4/. The planning rules on temporary accommodation (such as static caravans) would be eased and the local authority would grant planning permission for a period of five years.

5/. Accommodation at the workplace must be single sex and if any migrant worker became pregnant, they would immediately be returned to their birth country or another safe country.

6/. If any migrant breaks any of our UK laws, then they and any family member will be returned to their country of origin. No lengthy appeals will be allowed.

7/. Entry into the UK would be solely for them alone and would not be a fast track into the UK for any of their relatives.

Once in the UK they will be held in Marquees or Yurts based on unused military sites or in ships in dry dock. Costly hotel rooms should not be a choice. I can hear some people saying that being held in a tent is cruel, yet a vast number of migrants would have already spent years in tents in one of the 22 migrant camps in Turkey which has much lower winter temperatures than the UK. The Republic of Turkey hosts over 3.7 million registered refugees and are paid by the EU to do so.

Unaccompanied children should be found foster homes in the UK until they are 18. They will then be offered a free flight to their country of origin or stay in the UK as a full citizen. Any adopted child will not have the right to invite family members to join them.

Any immigrant's still trying to cross the English channel in a small boat would be met en route and be forced to return to France.

***

Green Energy.
If we are ever going to reach Net Zero, then the country must invest more in solar power and wind farms. Firstly, the government must Nationalise the National Grid so that they can build the infrastructure to move power around the British Isles. The privatised power network has given £28 million in dividends since it was sold off in 1990. This money would be better used to upgrade the grid so that it can cope with the extra demand required if we are going to reach Net Zero. Currently when wind farms create more energy than the grid can handle, the National Grid pays them to shut down – at a cost of up to £62m a day.

This will mean that more pylons will cover our countryside but it's a small price to pay to be self-sufficient and not be reliant on countries such as Russia. For those that object to pylons being erected near them then their electricity supply should be turn off. If they ask why, simply tell them that someone ten miles down the supply line didn't want pylons in the field where they lived, so the Nation Grid couldn't get the supply to you. They will soon shut up.

Solar power. I don't like seeing good arable land being covered with solar panels as the world needs these fields being used to provide food. If the Government wants to see more solar panels, then a national scheme should be set up to supply solar panels on nearly every roof in the UK free of charge to the property owner. The homeowner would save money on their electricity cost and the surplus going back to the new national organisation that will finance the installation and servicing cost. The government could also start by insisting all newly built homes should have Solar panels fitted at the time of construction. There are currently companies who charge over the odds to supply private owners with solar panels. Some of them IMO are worse than Timeshare sales staff. Their sales pitch can be quite convincing and the tricks they use are to offer gullible fools a finance deal, but they won't tell you that in many cases the interest charged includes a 2% commission paid back to the installer. These cowboys would be put out of business and the installers could be taken on by the new national (Not-for-Profit) company. The primarily photovoltaic solar panels (solar PV) should be made in the UK along with all the other materials needed to carry out the installation. The Smart Export Guarantee scheme which replaced the old feed-in tariff, should be set at 5.4p/kWh, so that investors can see a quick return on their investment. Once the initial installation cost has been repaid, the homeowner would continue to receive cheaper electricity, but the balance should be paid to their local authority who can continue to service the scheme and they could do a lot of good with the extra cash.

If the current governments target to ban the sale of petrol and diesel cars and vans is to be reached, then the program to set up charging points must be multiplied. There should also be a maximum charge set to car owners who want to charge their vehicle away from home. An answer to people who live in terraced houses (row homes to our American readers), or blocks of flats needs to be addressed. It pointless to own an electric car if you can't charge its batteries. I hope that car and van producers can come up with a portable battery that could be charged at home and then placed in the boot of the vehicle.

***

How gambling is ruining lives.
If you are concerned about the way those suffering from gambling addiction, then please email your MP and ask him/her

to introduce a Private Members' Bill to pass a new law to introduce a betting tax and with the money raised to supply counselling for addicts. State in your email that you have just finished reading a crime and fiction novel entitled The Bedford Heist where in chapter 29 it says that there should be a tax of 20% levied on any betting. This way, the William Hills of this world would have to declare their UK income and pay the 20% to the tax office. Punters would then know that if they were gambling a pound then only 80 pence would be staked, or they could pre-pay the tax when placing their bet. For £1 bet they would need to part with £1.20. Any overseas gambling websites should be blocked or follow the Australian way that requires overseas companies to collect goods and services tax (GST). This GST is different to VAT and will be placed on luxury items such as gambling, booze, cigarettes, etc. The USA introduced the Unlawful Internet Gambling Enforcement Act (UIGEA) in 2006 to give more weight to the Federal Wire Act of 1961. The overarching purpose of the law was to prevent gambling companies from partaking in "restricted transactions," which means they cannot accept payments related to wagers using the internet from overseas players and if they did, they would run afoul of any federal or state laws already extant. The chapter went on to say according to the *Guardian* newspaper the Bet365 boss netted £323 million in a single year. The 2018/2019 year saw Bet365 customers stake £64.49 bn on sports over the 12-month period, a 22.7% improvement on the prior year. Just think what good the government could do with 20% of £64 billion every year.

***

Booze in Britain. Having witnessed the damage drinking is doing to our society, the government must close all pubs and clubs by midnight (last drinks sold at 11:30 pm) and start charging drunks £50 for using a Drunk Tank and £100 if an ambulance is called to take the drunk to A & E. It was very noticeable during the COVID-19 lock down that crime rates dropped by a third and not one person was rushed to A&E drunk after a night out. I know of some youngsters who party at home on cheap supermarket booze and then drive to clubs and continuing the party until 4 am. The prison service should also be given extra funding to enable them to offer better detox services for alcoholics. No prisoner should be released until they had been free of their addiction for at least six months.

***

Prisons have become dumping grounds for the mentally ill. Many prisoners are a danger to themselves but are no danger whatsoever to the public and therefore shouldn't be in prison. With the NHS and local governments being under-funded for the last decade, mental health appears to be bottom of the list, yet if the mental health problem could be controlled or fixed, then it would be in everyone's interest to release these sick patients back in the community, where instead of costing the taxpayer around £47,000.00 every year to keep them locked up, they could start to contribute to society.

***

Austerity & Non-dom status. Austerity could only work if it applies to everyone. Austerity is a political-economic term referring to policies that aim to reduce government budget deficits through spending cuts, tax increases, or a combination of both. Governments needed to raise more in taxes from the people who could afford to pay them most and this was the rich who pay a maximum tax rate of 45% on earnings over £125,140. Anyone earning (if that's the right word) over a million pounds should pay tax at a rate of 80% for the next two years. The governments HMRC should set up a separate police force to ensure that everyone who owns a British passport or works in the country, is paying their correct taxes and a law should be introduced where advisors would also be responsible for their actions if they advise their client on a way to avoid paying taxes. All income should be included, including earnings from overseas, and the non-Dom system scrapped. Anyone holding a

British passport should be taxed at the correct rate and if this were done then austerity could work for the very first time.

***

UK Housing Crisis. The housing shortage is a problem that faces young people in every small village and town throughout Great Britain. If no one is getting on the property ladder then nobody is moving up it and, in the end, when people die, there will be nobody able to buy the vacant property and prices will crash leaving millions of homeowners with a negative mortgage. The government must build starter homes, even if these are for rent only, as many of the current private sector homeowners started their married life in rented accommodation and the low rents made it possible to save up for a deposit on their new home.

Depending on the tenant's financial situation they could be offered an economical rent plus the right to pay double. If the rent is £500 per month, then the tenants could double that with the extra £500 being entered into a tax-free home deposit scheme which could earn interest. This extra scheme could only be used to pay the deposit on a mortgaged home. Any new social housing can be sold to the tenant, or we could see the same disastrous result as in the Housing Act 1980, which was one of the first major reforms introduced by the Thatcher government.

When the current government took over from Labour new social homes built in 2010-11 was 39,570 however in 2016-17 it had dropped to just 5,380. If the country is to ever solve the housing crisis, then it must build more social housing for rent. Recent figures released from the Institute for Fiscal Studies said that "the biggest decline in home ownership in the last 20 years has been among middle-income 25 to 34-year-olds. In 1995-96, 65% of this group owned a home, but just 27% did so in 2015-16. I hear some people saying that no new homes should be built on "Green" land due to dangers of overloading the sewerage system, so I ask them where all our children and grandchildren going to live. Social housing must be a priority for the next government (using brown field land if possible), and it must be done quickly as when the war between Russia and the Ukraine ends all construction and building trades will be tempted to relocate to the Ukraine for considerably higher wages.

***

Get rid of Zero-hour contracts. In the UK there's an ever-growing number of workers who are having to accept a zero-hour contract which is a type of contract between an employer (or its agency) and a worker, where the employer is not obliged to provide any minimum working hours, while the worker is not obliged to accept any work offered. Many companies, who are household names, offer many of their workers a zero-hour contract. It is alleged that Sports Direct has 90% of its workforce on such contracts. J D Wetherspoon has 80% of its workforce. McDonald's has 90% of its workforce in the UK on zero-rate contracts which equates to 82,000 staff. Burger King Franchisees and Domino's Pizza operations in the UK extensively use zero-hour contracts. The Spirit Pub Company has 16,000 staff on zero-hour contracts and even Boots UK have 4,000 staff on zero-hour contracts. Amazon's US founder Jeff Bezos, 53, is the world's second richest man who last year made £1.6million an hour, so perhaps he could afford to pay a decent wage to everyone who is part of the Amazon family.

***

From a hero suffering from PTSD to homelessness and Prison. After leaving the forces sufferers of post-traumatic stress disorder (PTSD) should be treated as a mental health issue and not criminal. Nearly 6,000 people sleep rough every night in the UK and many end up in prison which must seem like paradise to them. A warm bed, three meals a day and security may appear to be great for them but it's costing the taxpayer £47,000 a year to provide them with a room. It would be considerably cheaper to care for these people in the community as the majority are not a danger to society but are a danger only to themselves.

If Jesus came back as a homeless person, would we tell Him that the Inn is full of needy migrants. Would we send Him to the stable? Have we not learnt anything over the past 20,000 years? The UK needs to follow the successful Housing First scheme that has been set up in Finland. To learn more about this solution go to https://www.weforum.org/agenda/2018/02/how-finland-solved-homelessness.

***

Children need to know whose boss. The Government needs to retake control of family life as by taking the Politically Correct (PC) route we are ending up with far too many unruly young adults. Parents should be taught how to control children as many are just being left to run wild. Most of these little porkers will develop diabetes and be on prescription drugs the rest of their lives. Far too many youngsters are playing war games on their x-box well into the night and this is not only affecting their schooling but turning many into dangerous young adults. I don't normally agree with what China does but they have limited under 18s to just 3 hours a week to play games on their computers, More on how Chaina can do this can be seen at https://www.bbc.co.uk/news/technology-58384457

***

UK aid to India.
According to the Daily Telegraph 14 Mar 2023 · Britain had sent £2.3 billion in aid to India since 2016. No wonder they can afford to send a rocket to the south side of the Moon as well as sending another rocket to Sun. What a waste of public money especially when millions are struggling to feed their families. If that wasn't enough, India grows 40% of the worlds rice. They

decided that in 2023 they would not export any rice and would keep it for home consumption. They obviously only care about themselves and sod the rest of the world. Maybe we should do the same.

Overseas aid has always been a tricky subject and I would hope that in future governments that money given in aid should fund a particular project such as birth control or building new hospitals and schools. Any money given for specific projects should be managed by the UK rather than sending millions of pounds of aid that can disappear within the country's budgets.

***

People struggling to pay their Mortgage.
Why doesn't the government make it Law that if the borrower pays the interest on their loan/mortgage they could not be evicted. After all, any lender only makes money on the interest charged. It would save families being evicted and the local authority having to pay out for B&B accommodation.

***

Prison and IPP.
As of November 2019, seven years after IPPs were abolished there were 2,223 people serving IPP sentences who have yet to be released and a further 1,206 serving an IPP sentence who are back in prison having been recalled while on licence. With over 3,000 IPP prisoners still behind bars it not only makes our prisons overcrowded but cost the state over £1.35 billion every year to keep them locked up. If you believe that these IPP inmates deserve a better deal, then please ask your MP to push the Home Secretary to find a solution to end this injustice.

***

Muslim inmates & Halal meat.

If you are concerned about how halal meat is slaughtered then please email your MP and ask him/her to introduce a Private Members' Bill to pass a new law to make this form of cruel slaughter illegal explaining that apparently, most animals are slaughtered humanly in the UK by stunning (electric shock to the brain) the animal first before killing the animal. Halal slaughter means no stunning and the animal throat is slit whilst it is still conscious. According to an inmate who was a butcher he told me that without stunning all the muscles (which is the meat we eat) tighten up due to the shock and you end up with very tough meat. The animal could still be blessed by a priest before being humanely slaughtered. If the government didn't want to ban this cruel method, then an alternative would be to introduce a law that once an animal is slaughtered using the cruel Halal method then the carcass should be stamped 'Halal' on all sections of the carcass such as on the legs, shoulders, loins, etc and any packaging used in the supermarket or butchers shop should clearly state that the meat is halal.

This would prevent many UK shoppers unknowingly buying something that had been cruelly slaughtered which ends up as tough meat. Denmark who produces a large amount of pork that is shipped around the world have banned this cruel method of slaughter since 2014, prompting a furious backlash from Jewish and Muslim community representatives. If you believe that an animal doesn't suffer then try creeping up on your partner or friend and hold a knife to their throats and see whether they relaxed or tensed up.

***

Bullying in schools.
If you believe that bullying is a problem in schools within your area, then please email your MP and ask him/her to introduce a Private Members' Bill to pass a new law on bullying in schools. The new law should be called Julie-Anne's Law to tackle this

problem that is ruining many children's lives with some cases resulting in suicide.

Julie-Annes Law.
Children have always been bullied in schools but a seven-year-old girl who lived in Spalding came up with a way to stop bullies in her school. Julie-Annes mother was a school governor, and this helped her to set up her anti-bullying campaign in her school.

Each school year should be given a form so they could nominate the pupil they want to become that years Anti-Bullying Prefect. The headteacher will then let the pupils know who had gained the most votes.

If any child was being bullied, then they should tell the Anti-Bullying Prefect who would then take it up with the headteacher on a weekly basis.
The pupil(s) who was doing the bullying would be dealt with by the headteacher. A letter would be posted to the bullies' parents informing the parent that if the pupil did not mend their ways, then they would be expelled for 7 days and if the bullying continued then they would be expelled.
The headteacher must make all pupils aware that any bullying of the named Anti-Bullying prefect would be treated very severely and could end up with permanent expulsion of the bully.

***

Buying from far away countries.
Let the people decide. It would help our battle with climate change if the UK government insisted on any product or produce from overseas should clearly show the country of origin. Supermarkets and any listing on websites such as Amazon or other media must also make it clear to customers that they are buying something from overseas. If the customer

can see that something was produced in a country that as a Human Rights record or comes from the other end of the world, then they can make up their own mind if they want to buy an item that has a large Carbon footprint.

***

The BBC.

The good old BBC is in a mess and apart from the World News and Countryfile I watch little else as it isn't worth watching. Government should take stronger control of the corporation and explore the possibility of allowing programs to be sponsored. The BBC should never carry advertising, but allowing something like the news to be sponsored would bring in much needed cash and perhaps we could then start watching better programs along with a reduced License Fee. The word "Our" BBC on their current promotional video should be changed to read "Your" BBC.

***

Get rid of useless Quangos:

Ofgem. In 2016 Ofgem was keen to remove the Daily Standing Charge (DSC) but only a couple of small service provisors did so, with the rest continuing to stick two fingers up to this toothless Quango. This change would have resulted in users with low energy use paying less, while increasing bills for those with high energy use. *Did I hear someone shouting, "the rich get richer, and the poor get poorer".* Ofgem looked at this DSC again in 2022 but after pressure from the BIG service providers they dropped the idea. It does make you wonder if this quango is fit for purpose. Ofgem stated that all high energy use, including people with disabilities who need to run medical equipment or elderly people who are housebound and sensitive to cold temperatures, would be disadvantaged by an increase to the unit price of electricity. I can agree to this but most people with special needs have already turned the thermostat down to reduce cost but there is no way to reduce the DSC. It does annoy me when organisations use the "disability card" to try and justify unjust rate rises. Before Russia invaded Ukraine my DSC for electricity (via EDF) was 23.77p but from October 1, 2023, it will be increased to 50.71p. On the 18th of August 2022 Rocio Concha, Which? Director of Policy and Advocacy said: 'Consumers are caught in a perfect storm of rising wholesale energy costs and picking up the tab for the collapse of energy firms after years of regulatory failure. This decision from Ofgem to take no action may be the right one if changes would have had a negative impact on vulnerable consumers, but the regulator must work with others to urgently look at how bills can be made fairer.' *If Ofgem were honest they would tell you that due to government placing the Energy Price Cap they allowed the increase on the daily standing charges so that the energy suppliers could still, make a profit and sod the millions struggling to make ends meet and are forced to make a choice between heating or eating.*

A more thorough review is needed to support the many low-income consumers who are paying substantial bills because of the high daily standing charge, despite using less energy. As part of this review, it should also address the need for protections for vulnerable customers with unavoidably high usage, such as those who are housebound or who need to run medical equipment.

IMO Ofgem is looking out for the big suppliers, but Ofgem was set up to look after customers, to ensure everyone was treated fairly. Ofgem is not fit for purpose and its overpaid board should be sacked for not doing the job they were employed to do.

Ofwat
The Water Services Regulation Authority, or Ofwat, is the body responsible for economic regulation of the privatised water and sewerage industry in England and Wales. IMO they are as useful as a chocolate teapot. Ofwat was set up to protect users but it's

obvious to see that it's doing a poor job when it comes to enforcing the Law. On the 25 Oct 2021 MPs vote to allow water companies to dump raw sewage into rivers and seas. Only 22 Conservative MPs rebelled by voting for an amendment to the Environment Bill, which sought to place a legal duty on water companies not to dump the risky sewage into rivers. Hugo Tagholm, who runs Surfers Against Sewage, commented: 'In this most important of environmental decades, it is shocking that the Government recommended that MPs reject progressive and ambitious amendments that would protect water, air and nature.'

Thousands of gallons of clean water make the way to the sea around our coast every day. If the water companies cleaned up their act, then they could call on this natural event and store that clean water to cover the dry months which appear (due to climate change) to be getting longer every year.

To me privatisation of essential services should be re-nationalised as the country as gained very little from doing so. Next time you go to do a number two just think about where your waste is going to end up. You might come face to face with it when you take your next swim in a river or the sea.

On the 3rd of October 2023 the BBC reported that 'Customers with 11 water firms are set to see money taken off their bills after fines of almost £150m were handed out by regulator Ofwat. The suppliers did not meet targets in water supply interruptions, pollution incidents and internal sewer flooding. Thames Water and Southern Water performed the worst and will have to return almost £80m. I bet that the CEOs of these companies will still pay themselves millions in bonusses in 2024.'

***

Online reviews.

According to the Competitions & Markets Authority (CMA) it said that more than half of UK adults use online reviews before buying a product or service. Businesses that mislead consumers may be in breach of the Consumer Protection from Unfair Trading Regulations 2008. However, there needs to be a body where customers can make their dissatisfaction known as there are far too many reviews that are rated as 4.5 out of 5 which are simply not true. It's pointless having a Law if there isn't a government department to enforce the Law. I recently sent a review to Feefo regarding a booking made over the phone with Hoseasons. I had booked a static caravan that was wheelchair friendly (WF) but when I arrived the WF Caravan wasn't available. For this reason alone, I gave the review a two-star rating (2.0 out of 5). Feefo came back and said that the review didn't meet their "Content Rules". I did contact the CMA but I'm still awaiting a reply which will probably never come. I contacted ABTA but they came back and said that they were powerless when it came to refunds. Pretty pointless clients relying on the ABTA symbol, if they have no teeth. I contacted Hoseasons but didn't get a reply, so I went online and issued a claim via the small claims court. Within 48 hours Hoseasons came back and offered a £250.00 refund. Never be scared to take a company to court. It really is easy and does get results. IMO there should be a website where you could send your rejected reviews could be sent and the Competitions & Markets Authority (CMA) could check it out.

***

Millionaire Minsters.
In 2024 you will have the chance to vote but not everyone takes up this right. Many people don't vote as they don't understand the system. As a simple answer I can say that there are three sections you should consider. The Right Wing, The Center, and the Left Wing. The Right Wing of the Conservative Party made Liz Truss Prime Minister in 2022 but her ideas and shoddy right-wing cabinet sent shockwaves around the financial world and after just 45 days as PM she had to step down and make way for Rishi Sunak.

The Left Wing is usually associated with the Labour Party and in 2019 it was led by Jeremy Bernard Corbyn and voters made it clear that they didn't want a left-wing government, especially with him as party leader. After a disastrous result Corbyn was replaced by Sir Kier Starmer who claims to be center of left. The vast majority of the Conservative party members are center of Right with last year's debacle by Liz Truss and her right-wing cabinet proved that the Right of any party sends shivers down the spine of the international monetary market and Liz went after only 49 days as Prime Minister. Much of the current Conservative cabinet have never had to worry where their next meal or the rent or mortgage payments were coming from. The sad news is that they never will, nor will they understand how the ordinary citizens of this once great country struggle to get by. The danger with the 2024 General Election will be that in some seats the anti-conservative voter will vote either Labour or Liberal. This could split the anti-conservative vote in two and in doing so let the conservatives back in. To me if you vote Conservative, you should have a joint income of over a £500 k every year. Many who don't have this kind of income suffer from a syndrome known as "Delusions of Grandeur". I hope they will think long and hard before they vote.

A delusion of grandeur is a false or unusual belief about one's power, wealth, talents, and other traits. A person may believe, for instance, that they are famous, can end world wars, or that they are immortal. **In other words, stop believing that Multi-Millionaire Minsters will look after you better.**

***

For the love of Pets.
Owning a pet can be very enlightening and give the owner a reason to get up in the morning. The dog will need a walk, and this is a good way of meeting other people. A pet becomes a true friend who will never judge you and knows when you are down. People should be allowed to own up to two small pets

irrespective of whether they own or rent a property. Keeping the older generation from becoming a couch potato will save the NHS millions.

***

HS2.

The Conservative government had big hopes that the HS2 project would show voters in the North of England that they were serious about "levelling up". With many constituencies changing from Labour to Tory in the 2019 general election the so called "Red Wall" seats will probably revert to Labour as they feel let down by the Tory party. With the cost this white elephant costing billions more than the original forecast of £37 billion, someone needs to investigate the rise to ensure that the taxpayers are not being ripped off.

Due to this disaster and the failure to "Stop the Boats" these northern Red Wall seats can't be relied upon to vote Conservative next time. With many of these seats having a high BAME population the Tory party hope that having a PM and Home Secretary with Indian roots will give then the upper hand come polling day. Time will tell if they got it wrong.

***

Private schools.

Labour has made it clear that private schools will need to charge 20% VAT. This would bring in Millions of pounds which could be spent on state schools. I'm not sure if this is good or bad as my son was dyslexic and I had no choice but to find the money to go private if he was to overcome this problem (which he did). I do hope that some provision would be made for those family's that would struggle to pay this extra tax. Another thing that worries me is that many schools are registered as a charity. As a charity they would pay lower rates and gain several other benefits. Another part that concerns me is that a rich parent could donate to the charity, and they could then set this donation off against their annual tax return. Could the parent then tell the school to not charge a fee for educating his/her child as they had already made a sizable donation. I do hope that either the government or the Charity Commission is keeping an eye on this.

***

Middle East War. *(Added this so you'll know when I updated this book)*
I never like seeing the atrocities of war and it's sad to see so much evil being done to other humans. The current Israel-Hamas war was unexpected, and one must question how Hamas got hold of all these missiles which were aimed at Israel causing a loss of over a thousand lives. Was Putin involved? He and his cronies are evil enough to do such a thing especially now that sanctions against Russia for starting the war in Ukraine, are hitting the pockets of his Communist country. He is getting a lot less revenue for his Gas and Oil supplies so a middle east war would be ideal as it would push the prices up and it would take the media's eyes off Russia for a while.

I remember my wife telling me about one of the stories I brought back from my short time in Jeddah, Saudi Arabia some 36 years ago. Apparently, we used to be given a set amount of money for our expenses and we soon found out that by eating out in Jeddah was a lot cheaper than eating at the hotel and we could keep the difference in our pockets. My wife re-told the storey about one small restaurant that kept open during prayer time, so we could not only save selling time but make money. The food was good, and the owner catered for our Western palate. On our last night in Jeddah, he made us a very English steak pie and we celebrated our time spent with him. He looked sad and I didn't realise at the time that he was a Palestinian and at that time he didn't have a home to return to. We don't appreciate how lucky we are. The world must find a way around this ongoing problem, and everyone should have a place to call home. We found a solution in Northern Ireland and the IRA are now a recognised political party. I pray to God that we can do the same with Gaza and stop this useless killing of innocent woman and children.

***

I have mentioned a few (but not all) of the problems that UK citizens face daily. If you wish to help, put the Great back in Britain then you could send an email to your Member of Parliament (MP) or any Minister. If every reader took a few minutes of their time to send an email, then we may see a solution to these continuing problems.

You can find your MP's contact details at https://www.parliament.uk/get-involved/contact-your-mp/

Until all these problems are dealt with, my team will continue to bring towns to their knees and in the end the government will have to take matters seriously.

I hope you enjoyed your time with me, and my Merry Men in Bedford, and I hope you will join me in early 2024 with the launch of The Bedford Revenge, where we take down one of the world's largest Human Trafficking operations. **PLEASE NOTE THAT THE BEDFORD REVENGE DUE TO IT'S SEXUAL CONTENT WILL BE FOR ADULTS ONLY.**

If you feel strongly about any of the above, then why not start a petition with either https://home.38degrees.org.uk/ or https://www.change.org/ which offer you a free way to start your campaign. I have used both in the past but prefer 38 degrees as Change.org is difficult to contact if you have a problem. In your message and you can copy & paste any part of the book providing you mention The Bedford Heist is available from Amazon Books.

***

Afterword's: Chapter 12. UK Housing Crisis.

I asked James what he felt should be done to try to ease the housing shortage, as if nothing happened there would hundreds of future James knocking at my door. James said that his brother John belonged to the Young Farmers Group, and the problem of rural housing had been raised at one of the annual conferences he had attended. He said that his brother spoke at the conference and pointed out the pioneering work done in the villages of Hawes in Upper Wensleydale and the village of Toller Portcorum, Dorset. In both cases locals had got together and with the help of the community land trust had managed to get several affordable new homes for locals built.

The NFU said that they were aware of the problem, but that nothing was being done to resolve the situation. I listened to what James had to say on the matter, and I suggested that he should write to his MP with his ideas and ask that he pass it on to the Minister of State for Housing and Planning. He could use my laptop and printer, and I would post the letter for him rather than it be checked by the postal room. The letter to James MP read as follows:

Mr Norman Lamb MP for North Norfolk
House of Commons
Palace of Westminster
London SW1A 0AA

Dear Sir,

You may already be aware of my name as my sad situation was in the papers and on regional TV last year. My name is James Pringell, I'm from Wells, and I'm currently serving a three-year sentence passed down by the Norwich Crown Court last year. I'm not writing to you about my case or length of sentence, but rather I'm writing to you on behalf of all the other young adults in the vain hope that something can be done, so that they don't take the silly route I did.

The housing shortage, which was partly to blame for my situation, is a problem that faces young people in all small villages and towns throughout Great Britain. My brother John is a member of the Young Farmers Group, where the problem of housing has been raised several times. He was asked to set up a group that would try to find an answer to the crisis. After a year of digging around and climbing a few brick walls, John came up with the following suggestion, which I believe could work.

Tourist villages such as Wells could set up a system whereas when a property is placed on the market it should have a local price and a non-local price. The local price would only be for people who have been living within five miles of the home for the past three years or have a very close relative already living within five miles, or an outsider who was taking up a key job such as teacher, GP, or any service provider. If, however, the home was to be sold to an outside source, then a local levy of £100,000 would be added to the sale price, and this would then be passed on to a local housing trust whose job was to provide affordable homes for locals.

The above could work well in touristy towns and villages like Wells, but the problem is nationwide, and occurs across the country. If no one is getting on the property ladder then nobody is moving up it, and, in the end, when people die, there will be nobody able to buy the vacant property and prices will crash, leaving millions of homeowners with a negative mortgage. With around half a million people dying each year in the UK, children will be inheriting a house that they don't need and will have to keep dropping the price to force a sale. This drop in price will have a ripple effect and draw prices down across the board.

If there isn't a way to get people onto the property ladder soon, then sometime during the 2020s prices will start to fall and banks and building societies will soon realize that they have been lending out money that can never be repaid.

The answer has never been to build more new cities like Milton Keynes, but to spread the housing build across the land to save many of our dying villages and towns. What we feel would work (though it wouldn't be liked by the farming community) was for a regional housing association to pinpoint certain villages that could do well from gaining an influx of residents. Many villages that have an infant or junior school are screaming out for children, as a school must have a certain number of pupils for it to be workable. The same goes for other village services such as the church, the pub, the village store, post office, etc. I urge the government to build starter homes, even if these are for rent only, as many of the current private sector homeowners started their married life in rented accommodation. The lower rent charged meant that the young couple could save up for a 5 or 10% deposit on a new home while still living and working in their hometown or village.

Recent figures showed that just over 160,000 new homes were started in 2018/2019, but that only a small percentage would be for rent. The government said that its target was 300,000 homes by the mid-2020s, but when this figure was last achieved, half of the new homes built were for rent by either the council or housing associations. When the current government took over from Labour, the number of new social homes built in 2010-11 was 39,570, however in 2016-17 the figure had dropped to just 5,380. If the country is to ever solve the housing crisis, then it must build more social housing for rent. If it doesn't, then one day, there will be such a crash in house sales it would make the 2007-2008 money crisis seem like a picnic. The government must get the current generation moving up the property ladder, but with a vast number of university leavers already having to repay their university tuition fees they stand very little hope of ever saving enough for a deposit.

The housing association should be set up and initially financed by the state to start them off. They alone will select either a low yielding field at the edge of the village or an unused site in the village, which would then be compulsory purchased by the association at agricultural land rate. The association will bring together all the village and regional council bodies and submit plans to the local planning office and contract all the various elements to get the new homes built. The site should have a combination of higher priced homes that have been adapted for people with mobility issues, and starter homes or flats suitable for first time buyers who have either a close relative or have been living in or around the village for the past three years. The starter homes could either be sold outright, as 50/50 homes, or rented out by the housing association. Each village via its parish council should state what type of new homes are needed, and the association could bring all the loose ends together.

Now, to try to put a smile on the poor old farmer's face. Once all the new homes have been sold or rented out, then the monies raised should be split three ways between the housing association, local council, and the poor old farmer/landowner. Because the land was compulsory purchased, the association can fix the selling price of the new homes on the site. The better houses should only be sold at market or near-market levels, but the starter homes for locals can have a price reduction. To stop the hungry home grabbers from getting hold of any resells, the resale the price would be fixed at 5% plus inflation to any new owner that fits the "local" requirement. If there are no buyers, then the property owner can sell it back to the housing association who would then rent it out or sell it on at market rate.

Needless to say, that housing associations should be run as a non-profit making venture (like that of a community land trust) and any senior positions within the association will be paid a salary, set by the government. The project should be for the betterment of the community and should not be a way for any official of the housing association or contractors involved with the build to line their own pockets.

Another possibility would be to source the building site, and then build two dozen homes on the site. Half of these could be sold to outsiders wishing to buy a second holiday home, and the money raised from selling the twelve holiday homes could finance the building of the twelve homes for local folk which could be sold at a reduced rate, sold as a 50/50 deal, or rented out. Any new homes built should also be fitted with solar panels and any other energy saving items so that these would help the government reach its "green" target by 2040.

I do hope that you will pass this letter on to the Minister of State for Housing and Planning and that the government can start to tackle this ever-growing problem. I should make it clear that I'm not doing this for myself as I have been lucky (apart from breaking the law) as my fiancée has stood by me, and because of all the publicity a wonderful lady has offered us a home to rent when we get married, and, to place a cherry on top, another local bookmakers has offered me a job, but I think they may get somebody else to cash up.

Apparently, the local community are treating this as a crime of passion, and I could never thank them enough. So please do what you can to help other young couples the breadth of the country gets a step on the housing ladder as in the long run it would be cheaper to help them than to keep paying out £47,000 every year to keep some of them in prison.

Yours sincerely,
James Pringell

I posted this for James, and did get a standard reply from his MP, who thanked him and his brother for their input and confirmed that he had passed on his letter to the Minister of State for Housing and Planning. He would write again if he made any progress. James is still waiting for a follow up letter from his MP. I really felt sorry for James, but his problem was a massive one and can only end with a price drop for homes that will make the 2007/08 saga seem like a picnic. The Institute for Fiscal Studies recently stated that "the biggest decline in home ownership in the last 20 years has been among middle-income 25 to 34-year-olds. In 1995-96, 65% of this group owned a home, but just 27% do in 2015-16, with the biggest drop in south-east England". If nobody is moving up the property ladder there will be no buyers in a few years' time to buy the homes vacated by people who have died. With housing prices spiralling downwards, even those with a mortgage will end up with a negative mortgage, which is a repeat of 2008. Something must be done quickly, and the current government's promise of 300,000 homes by 2025 will be far too late.

***

Afterword's - Chapter 15. Covid-19.

As the virus spread across China, many western companies who had moved their production to China so that they could benefit from cheap labour and less health and safety measures were now worried about getting their products out of China.

Dr. Martens Boots & Shoes is a brand that my friend in Northamptonshire loved. His father and mother had worked in the company's Rushden factory but in 2004 production was moved to China and Thailand. He said that it was a way of life for the community, and with Max Griggs at the helm they had even built a football stadium for the Rushden and Diamonds team. In 2005, owner Max Griggs sold the Club to the Supporters Trust for a nominal £1. However, without its wealthy backer the football club struggled and eventually went out of business in 2011. In what seemed a rather bizarre move at the time, Kettering Town moved into the ground, but left in 2012, after which the ground became unused.

What went wrong with Dr. Martens?

An article in *The Guardian* on the 30th of November 2019 stated that "it was just a small question in our regular Consumer Champions column. Why, a reader asked, had her £170 Dr Martens boots fallen apart after just six months? The response was huge, with readers accusing the bootmaker of sacrificing quality, offshoring production, and chasing profits. Another reader said that the leather, which was sourced in Asia, was a lot thinner than that used in the UK. Under the new ownership of a London-based private equity company a long way from its roots in Northamptonshire." Wikipedia state that Dr. Martens AirWair International's revenue fell from US $412 million in 1999 to $127 million in 2006. In 2003, the Dr. Martens company came close to bankruptcy. On 1st April that year, under pressure from declining sales, the company ceased making shoes in the United Kingdom, and moved all production to China and Thailand.

I told Lewis that when my wife and I went on holiday to Orlando, my wife wanted to look around the shopping malls, and I noticed that one particular shop was busier than most, so, being nosy, I had to find out why. It was a shoe shop, and in the window was a big stack of trainers, but what caught my eye was the big Union flag on one side of the shoe box. I asked one of the shop staff why they were flying off the shelves, and she said that people liked to buy British as it was always good quality. Pity Dr. Martens and the hundreds of UK companies who moved production to China wasn't there to see this simple example of why satisfied customers are more important than cheap labour.

Joke.
A good neighbour visited her good friend and noticed that she was having a stroke. She dialled 999 and a few minutes later the ambulance arrived, and the paramedic asked her what had gone wrong. She said her friend had a big shock as being disabled she shopped online with Amazon. So, what was so shocking, and the good neighbour said she was shocked to find something on the website that wasn't made in China.
***

Afterword's Chapter 29. How Gambling is Ruining Lives.

In the main pages I wrote about Pete Griffith's becoming addicted to gambling. I also want to mention Henry Mathews, who was a happily married man until he became hooked on 'crack cocaine' slot machines in betting shops. It started in 2015 when he had made his usual bet for the Grand National, which was the only time he placed a bet apart from Derby day, and this was due to his father inviting all the family around for a fish and chip lunch, followed by the greatest steeple chase in the world. He never usually had any luck but this time he had backed Many Clouds the 25 to 1 winner and his wife had an each-way bet on Saint Are who finished second at a starting price of 25 to 1. He told me he was so excited about his win that he had stopped at the betting shop on his way back from his fathers to pick up his winnings. What he didn't realise was that with the race being so popular, hundreds of people had placed a bet on the National and checking all the betting slips by the bookmaker took a long time. While he was waiting to pick up his winnings, he had a go one of the slot machines to see if he could continue his winning run.

The machine with all its flashing lights said that you could win thousands of pounds with stakes from £10 up to £100. He decided to have a punt and put in £50 of his winnings, and he won a few times, but just before he was to go home, he won £320. *Great,* he thought at the time, and he was back the next available Saturday to try his luck again. This time he wasn't so lucky, and, in the end, he had lost £200 on the day. He wasn't put off and decided to try again in the week as the shop was open well into the evening. This time he won a further £300, just missing out on a £30,000 win. He gambled all the money back and some more besides, but he kept just missing out on the big prize. He then went to use his debit card and drew £200 out and gambled the lot without any luck. He went home, and the misses asked where he had been, and he told her that he had a problem with the car, but a chap fixed it at a cost of £200.

He kept going back to try for the big money, but he kept losing. He had a joint bank account with his wife, and she had noticed that he had been withdrawing large sums of money and asked him to explain why the money they were saving for a dream second honeymoon had gone. He couldn't think of any other answer but to come clean and tell her the truth. His relationship had hit a difficult patch, and she had set it in her mind that the second honeymoon would solve any problems and get the candle burning again. After sleeping on the couch for a few nights, she made him promise that he wouldn't ever gamble again, and he agreed. However, he was having a tough time at work, and wasn't reaching his sales target, and he was drawn back to the machine as all he needed was one big win and all would be hunky dory. He couldn't get money from his joint bank account, so he had to keep his stakes low.

When he was nearly down to his last tenner, he noticed some punters approaching a man who sat near the door, and he was giving money out to people who had approached him. 'I asked one of his visitors what the man was up to and he said that he offered what they call pay-day loans. You could borrow money from him, and if you paid him back within a week it would only cost you a few pounds in interest.' However, he and others kept going back and borrowed more, as they all believed that they were going to hit the jackpot and all their problems would be solved.

Henry got into debt with the money lender and obviously couldn't pay him back within seven days, so he borrowed more to cover his debt and to give him money to put into the machine. After a month he was in real debt, and he had to offer some security, and all he had was his home. Well, you've probably guessed the outcome, and when he had to tell his wife how stupid he had been she left him. The interest on the pay-day-loans worked out at 1,472% interest, and in the end, he was forced to sell the home to clear his debt and give the balance to his former wife. Since he had been taught a hard lesson there were rumours that the Government was going to deal with the problem, but the Treasury opposed the drastic cut, warning it could slash tax receipts. These machines alone rake in about £1.8 billion every year, contributing more than £400million to the Exchequer. The Government never considered what damage was being done to families of addicts who put in the £1.8billion. Obviously, the betting shops didn't want to get rid of these as they make £1.4 billion from them every year. There were also more rumours that the Government would bring in a rule to reduce the largest bet to a much lower level of £2 per bet which came into force at the end of March 2019.

I asked him, 'So, you lost your wife and your house, but what brought you to my door?' Henry said that he was very angry and wanted to make the bookmakers pay but he didn't have the courage to rob a betting shop, but he still needed to find a way to make them pay and bring the problem home to the Government once and for all. He said that he had always been a keen flyer of microlight planes, and he had a Quicksilver "e" type 28240 Champrond en Gatine stored at his brother's smallholding in Surrey. The fish and chip lunch were no longer a possibility as his father was shocked at what had happened and he wanted no more to do with horse racing. Since his troubles his brother and sister-in-law had been trying to get me down to visit them and my two adorable nieces, so he took them up on their offer.

'I said that I wanted to test out my microlight on the Saturday afternoon and we set a date for my visit which would be the first weekend in June. I drove down on the Friday and stayed at my brother's place and on Saturday morning checked out the plane. On the Saturday afternoon my sister-in-law had to take her daughters to a birthday party, so I said that I would play around with my plane and would meet up in the evening. Before flying you are supposed to log a flight plan with the CAA, but I didn't want to take a chance and I wanted to surprise everybody in the afternoon with a plan that I had been hatching since my wife left me. The first Saturday in June is always Derby day, and millions would be bet on the race from around the world. The Queen always attends the meeting, so I had to keep clear of the grandstand or the plane would be treated as a terrorist attempt on her Majesty's life and would be shot down by her security team.

He went on, 'My plan involved in stopping the race after the first three furlongs of the one-and-a-half-mile race. The race started out at the far side of the Epsom racecourse and included a four-furlong steady climb by the horses before taking a left-hand turn to start their downhill journey to the winning post. I had my earpiece tuned in to Radio Five Live, who were covering the race, and as the horses were making their way to the start, I started my flight south of the course, rising to a thousand feet. I was making progress and flying next to the racecourse ready to pounce. Through me earpiece I heard the race commentator saying, "And they're off", and I could even hear the Epsom crowd cheer when the race started. I turned my microlight so that the horses would be approaching me and started my decent. As the horses reached the top of the climb, I swooped down, scaring the shit out of the horses and the jockeys. The first two horses reared up, and all the other horses went into the back of them, causing a pile-up that reminded me of the time I had seen cattle being dumped on the fire after the breakout of foot and mouth in 2001.

'The race was stopped and six of the thoroughbreds worth millions of pounds were put down. I then returned to my brother's house and explained what I had done and the reasoning behind it, and we watched the shocking carnage on the BBC News. I could clearly see my microlights number B-625, so I knew that I would be getting a call from the men in blue once I returned to my lodgings. When I got there the police were waiting, along with a host of media vans all signalling my return home, and the media would show my arrest to the rest of the world. I was sorry that horses were destroyed as this was never my intention, but all actions have consequences and mine was a long prison sentence at her Majesty's pleasure, hopefully at the Bedford jail.'

In a further session, Henry went on to state that he had recently seen an article about 'Skin Betting'. I asked him why someone would bet their skin, and he laughed at me. He said that he thought the same when he first heard of it, but he soon realized the massive problem facing children and teenagers around the world. A report recently showed that around 370,000 11-16-year-olds spent their own money on gambling in the past week. I asked Pete to explain in simple terms what skin betting was all about as I had never heard of it before. He said that 'Skins are collectable, virtual items in video games that change the appearance of a weapons - for example, turning a pistol into a golden gun. Sometimes skins can be earned within a game, but they can also be bought with real money. Some games also let players trade and sell skins, with rarer examples attracting high prices. Several websites let players gamble with their skins for the chance to win more valuable ones. Since skins won on such a website could theoretically be sold and turned back into real-world money, critics say betting with skins is unlicensed gambling.'

The BBC showed that Bangor University student Ryan Archer's love of gaming spiralled into gambling when he was 15 and he became involved in skin betting. Four years later he has lost more than £2,000. He told the BBC that when he got his student loan, some students spend it on expensive clothes, but he spent it on gambling virtual items. 'There have been points where I could struggle to buy food because gambling took priority.' Ryan wanted to build an inventory of skins, but when he could not afford the price tag attached to some of them, he began gambling on unlicensed websites to try to raise money. He said: 'It's hard to ask your parents for £1,000 to buy a knife on CSGO (the multiplayer first-person shooter game *Counter Strike:*

Global Offensive), it's a lot easier to ask for a tenner and then try to turn that into £1,000.' In *CSGO*, players can exchange real money for the chance to obtain a modified weapon known as a skin, and several gambling websites have been built around the game. 'You wouldn't see an 11-year-old go into a betting shop, but you can with this, there's nothing to stop you,' Ryan said. He went on to quote that he had read that 'It is estimated that half of the UK online population - more than 30 million people - play video games.'

The Gambling Commission said it had identified third party websites that enabled players to gamble their skins on casino or slot machine type games, and then these could later be sold and turned into real-world money. Henry was another victim of the gambling epidemic facing Britain and the world today and, as he would be inside for many years to come, he wouldn't be getting an invite to my heist in Bedford but I did want to share Henry's story with you as I'm deeply concerned about the number of lives being ruined every week by the Government not having the balls to tackle the problem.

***

Afterword's - Chapter 33 – Autism.

This was Glen Toogood's third time in prison, but the first time he came under my wing, and he had been caught again for dealing in drugs. During the sessions I tried to get a breakdown on the inmates' childhood, and Glen said that 'one of the worse childhood experiences was to do with his brother Tom who suffered from Autism.' I told him that 'I also had an autistic brother and could understand how hard his childhood had been.' Glen went on to say that 'his brother was born with a bent spine and had surgery in his first year of life to try to correct the problem, but with little success. Apart from this he seemed like a normal infant, but that ended when he was around 20 months of age when we were told that he had autism.'

Glen told me, 'My mother's only knowledge of autism was from seeing the film *Rain Man (1988)* where Dustin Hoffman played the lead role as an autistic savant. My brother Tom was always in and out of hospital for either treatment or more test, but the autistic label came as a shock. Up until then he made the usual progress, apart from his spinal problem. He had started to say a few words such as *momma*, *papa*, and *Len* (he never could pronounce the G part) and always loved cuddles. This changed once the autism stepped in, he could no longer say a few words, hated being cuddled, stopped eating, and disappeared into a world of his own. My mother tried to find more help and speak to other mothers with an autistic child, but at that time there was little going on and no support groups in our area.'

Glen continued, 'My mother was told by a friend that she had heard of a man in Northamptonshire, the next county to ours, who had been pushing for better provisions for autistic children in his county. She went along with her friend to several of their group evenings to see if she could learn anything that would help. Up until my brother's birth, she was a reporter for our local paper, and she had been taught shorthand at college. This skill was a blessing as my mother could keep notes and then type them up later. She then kept them in a lever file, which was handy as it meant that I could refer to them when needed. My mum came back extremely late at night, but she was so happy, I thought she was drunk. She sat us all down and reading from her notes explained what she could remember about the meeting.'

'She told us that there was around a dozen parents at the meeting, all of whom had an autistic child, and people from various care providers. The Chairman was the main speaker and had given a brief history of what the county's autistic group had managed to achieve in the past eight years. He said that his daughter, born in 1985, was born two months early due to his wife's illness, and it had been touch-and-go whether she would survive. When his daughter was about nine months old, the Northampton General hospital came up with a list of her medical problems. She had cerebral palsy, brain damage, and her sight and hearing were extremely poor, and her paediatrician said that she probably wouldn't see her second birthday (she's now 38). He went on to state that both he and his wife were in shock, and he asked the paediatrician, "Where do we go from here?" The paediatrician said that it would be best to just leave her there and walk away. He and his wife were so shocked by the comment that he nearly hit him. Well, he didn't hit him but told him that they never would walk away, even though it would be tough.'

If that wasn't enough, he went on to state that 'when his daughter was around 18 months of age things really got bad. Up until then his daughter would say a few baby words and crawl about the room and would love cuddles, but overnight everything changed. Like most caring parents he and his wife wanted answers, and he had read somewhere a story of a child in America who had similar problems to his daughter. The word autism was mentioned, and so he started to do some digging around to see if his daughter could be a sufferer. They had contacted the hospital, but they knew nothing about autism in those days, very few did, and the consultant said that they didn't think she was a sufferer.'

Glen went on to say that 'according to his mother's notes, the man had by chance heard of a specialist, Doctor John Richer who was based in the John Radcliffe hospital in Oxford and was one of the country's leading specialists on autism. However, he only took on private patients, and the fee would be £400 (£1,219.98 in today's money). The man went on to say that although money was tight, as his wife was now a full-time career, they went along for the assessment. After several screaming hours, the specialist reported back that his daughter was the most severe case of autism he had seen in the UK. It was then that he decided to see what if anything was available in Northamptonshire. There was extraordinarily little, but he did find a support group which had been set up by a lady who had a son who suffered from a form of autism known as Asperger's Syndrome. After a few monthly meetings, the lady wanted to step down as chairperson and he was elected to the position to continue the fight for better provision in the county.'

Glen said that his mother went to further meetings, and managed to learn a lot more about autism and what if any help there was. After the brief formal part of the meeting, they had tea and biscuits, and she asked the chairman more about his time as chairman of the county autistic group, and how things had improved during his time at the helm. He was always honest and said that after only a few months in the unpaid role as chairman he received a call from a member who had a severely autistic son aged 14. Sadly, the boy's father had taken his son for a drive, so that his wife and daughter could have a break but had not returned. She was worried when her husband and son hadn't returned by lunch time and called the police and the local hospitals. A few hours later she received a visit from two police officers, who had said that they had been found but were both dead. He went on, 'I was called in by a friend of the family a few days later, as the mother was worried that her husband would be classed as being insane when he took his own life and that of their son and asked me if I could state that he was far from insane at the forthcoming inquest.'

He said that he would, but before doing so he needed to know much more, so he could make a case when he attended the coroners court. The wife was upset but pleased to hear that someone was willing to help, and she told him the sad facts that led up to their deaths. She said her son had been severely autistic from 18 months and, although things were hard for them, they managed to cope until he reached the age of ten. Her son then became more agitated and started continually banging his head. They were told to put a padded helmet on his head so that he wouldn't do so much damage. This really didn't help as he continued to bang his head, but now banged it even harder. This resulted in effecting his eyesight, and by the age of 14 they were told that he was going blind and there was nothing they could do. He enquired whether they received any respite care but, although they lived on the same street as an old hospital which had a ward used for respite, they were told that their son was too difficult to handle, and they never received any help whatsoever. He asked about her husband and was told that he was a professor at a local college, and tried his best to help where he could.

The mother said that he wasn't insane, far from it, as what he did was for her and her daughter, so that they could have a 'normal' life. He had left letters of apologies for the person who found them and the police and other rescue services who had to attend the sad scene. He had known what he was doing and had planned it right down to the last detail. He left letters for his daughter and me which clearly explained the reason he decided to take two lives. At the inquest he said that he had given the facts as they were and had explained to the Coroner just what autism was and the effect it had on family members. The Coroner returned a verdict of suicide and unlawful killing and ruled out insanity. From this sad event he manged to bully the Oxfordshire Health Authority (which was also responsible for Northamptonshire) into pulling down the Victorian hospital which housed the Carlton respite ward and replace it with two modern respite care hospitals in Rushden. One was for children, and the other unit was for older sufferers.

Updated August 2023.

At that time, he didn't connect the family name of "King" to a childhood incident that happened when the author was 7 (in 1954) and lived in Wolverton which is now part of the City of Milton Keynes. It wasn't until he spoke to his sister Sally (who was 54 weeks older) and due to the authors memory loss in 2000 his beloved sister was trying to rebuild his lost childhood memory. Sally reminded him of the time when he was seven years old and came home and reported that they had a black kid in his class. That was the first time they ever saw a black person in the town. She said that I had become friends with the boy who lived with his family in Victoria Road and the boy had taught me to do my shoelaces up. Being the BIG sister, she was always playing jokes on me, and she reminded me of when I asked her where Black babies came from? She told me that women have two holes, one at the front and one at the rear. She explained that white babies came from the front hole and Black babies came from the rear hole. Being older than me I believed her, and it wasn't until a few years later that I knew that I had been had. My sister who had suffered from MS for over 25 years sadly died in 2004 and I still miss her and always will. Anyway, getting back to my main point and that at the time I didn't put two and two together and realised that Professor King would be the same age as the child who taught me to do my shoelaces up. I do hope that I was able to return the good deed.

Glen went on to state that his mother and a friend continued to go to the monthly meetings, and kept asking questions, and continued to learn about autism. Again, the chairman tried to answer my mother's questions as best he could. My mother asked what he thought caused autism and was it anything to do with the triple vaccination given. In answer to her question, he gave this answer. To the best of his knowledge, an infant's brain develops in stages during the first 18 months of life. With each of these stages the brain develops the key to walking, talking and other common stages. However, when the final stage tries to activate itself there is a wiring fault within the brain. He said that the easy way to try to explain the brain was to compare it to a very old computer disc. When you have typed something into your computer, you press the save button, and the computer stores that text in a new section of the computer's brain (hard drive). When you want to open the saved work later, it goes back and opens the file so you can read or edit it. The workings of the 'normal' human brain isn't that different. We hear or read something, and the brain sends an electrical signal to a part of the brain to store that information. If we want to retrieve that information the brain again sends an electrical signal to search and open the stored content, so you can reach it again and use it. However, this stage of opening and closing boxes within the brain doesn't for some unknown reason kick in, and when it doesn't, the start of autism is the result. Hopefully, one day scientist will be able to find the fault and offer a cure.

He went on to state that many mothers thought that it was the triple MMR vaccination that was causing the problem, but he didn't think that this was true as his daughter didn't have the triple vaccination due to her week lungs. Many groups said that the increase in autism was down to the MMR as since its introduction those having autism had increased tenfold. He said that this in his opinion that wasn't the case as the figures could not be trusted for two reasons. Firstly, up until a few years after he had taken over as chairman, doctors were not diagnosing the condition, but once the template of what had happened in Northamptonshire had been rolled out across the country, more and more paediatricians were aware of the condition and were now diagnosing the problem. The second reason was that the old data couldn't be trusted as prior to the late 1980s autism wasn't being diagnosed, and sufferers were treated as being brain damaged with many severely autistic sufferers ending up in mental institutions or even prison.

He said that he had only two concerns about the MMR vaccine. The first concern was the time it was given, which was usually around 18 months. If it could be given a few months later, then it may not have the same effect as the child would have passed the final infantile brain development stage. His second concern was with the vaccine itself, as it wasn't a live vaccine and the preservative used in the vaccine was mercury. Mercury is a poison and large amounts can kill, and that's why he always said to worried parents that if they can afford the cost, they should have the vaccine given privately in three separate doses. However, pressure put on the Government by organisations such as his forced the Government to stop using Thimerosal, mercury, in 2002.

At a later meeting my mother asked him what else he and his team had done to make the county one of the leaders in provision for autistic children in the country. He replied in one word, 'Education', although he said that he couldn't take full credit for this as another group in the county started the ball rolling with the introduction of the Teacch method (Teacch is spelt correctly), which was used in some states in America. Education is important in any child's life, but with autism it brings extra challenges as few autistic children can cope with crowded classrooms and noise. He went on to explain that his daughter was very happy at a special school in the county, but that someone in Maggie Thatcher's government came up with the bright idea that there shouldn't be any special schools as all kids were equal and should attend mainstream schools. This looks like a great idea on paper, and if we lived in an ideal world, it would be great, but we don't. As usual with the Thatcher era, everything was down to money. The Government could save money by closing these special schools and the Education (Schools) act 1992 was introduced. Many of the older generation remember Maggie for the disastrous poll tax, but I will always remember her for the woman who ripped my family apart. There wasn't a state school in the county that could cope with his daughter's severe autism and other disabilities, so she ended up in a residential school elsewhere in the country. This was devastating for his wife and family, but they were powerless to do anything about it. As a result, the family had to make a three-hour trip to visit her for an hour every fortnight. Thankfully, the school she had been sent to wasn't prepared to install all the special equipment she needed as she got older, and after four very long years, she was found a place at a RNIB Rushton Hall school in the county.

But again after a few years the RNIB sold the school building she was happy in and again shifted her out of county and ended up in another residential RNIB school in Coventry. The meaning of the phrase "sent to Coventry" had a disastrous new meaning to his family. He warned that my mother's task would be far from easy, but in his experience those parents that shouted the loudest usually get the best out of the system. You will continue to battle education, social services, and health, and just when you think you know all the answers the Government will change the questions. In his opinion it would be best for one public body to take charge of all the child's special needs and the main body could buy services from the other bodies. This would mean that parents only had one body to deal with, and the Government could save a lot of money by duplication of key service providers.

My mother's friend who drove her to and from these meetings became ill and couldn't take her anymore. My mother or father couldn't drive, so this valued source of information stopped. I did however hear that the chairman had pushed the county's social services department to provide residential care for autistic adults, and a care home which was managed by the National Autistic Society had opened in Wellingborough. I also heard that the man had also helped open another home in Kettering (in which his daughter is now a resident) and that this was run by the charity Sense. He also heard that Linden had stepped down as he felt that he had done all he could, but before leaving he had managed to obtain a grant from The National Lottery for over £113,000 which would enable the local society to employ a full-time manager to continue the great work the Linden and his team had started.

Glen said that his brother was now in a special school for autistic children, and his parents were now looking for suitable adult care for him. More about the Teacch method can be seen at http://www.autism.org.uk/teacch.

Note from the author.
My thanks go to my lovely wife Julie and my son Stephen for helping me write this section as I was the man referred to as Linden above. My thanks also go out Sir John Lowther, who died on April 11, 2011, aged 87, who proved to be an exceptional Lord Lieutenant for Northamptonshire from 1984 to 1998. Sir John was always willing to help, as was his friend Cecil Pettit MBE, who set up Ability Northants, which was founded under the name Northampton & District Council for the Disabled in 1978. At a time where no disability legislation existed and equality was almost unheard of, they were dedicated to enriching the lives of people living with disabilities. Cecil sadly died in August 2000 aged 79, but his legacy lives on as he set up the Cecil Pettit Fund which now helps fund projects for people with disabilities within Northamptonshire. Finally, is my dear friend Eric Mather-Franks who ran several care homes and respite care centres in Northamptonshire with his lovely wife Marie who was an excellent nurse. He also helped me set up and run the East Northants Council for All Disabilities which enabled us to open a swimming club for disabled people in Rushden, Northants. Sadly, Eric passed in 1996 but will always be in our hearts.

Special thanks also go to Dr Beverley Samways who was one of my daughter's teachers whilst at Coventry. I'm please to say that Beverley continued to visit my daughter when she returned to Northamptonshire and has become a valued friend to my daughter. Many people say that severely Autistic children/adults can't make friends, but I'm pleased to say they are wrong.

***

About the author.

Frederick Linden-Wyatt is a happily married man with a son and daughter plus a son and grandson by an earlier marriage and now lives in Lincolnshire, England. In 2000 he went into a private hospital in Kettering for a well overdue hip replacement after paying into BUPA for many years. Before his operation he had risen the ranks in the newspaper printing industry and in the 1990's he was made a sales director of a leading PLC. He left the security of a "proper job" to venture on his own as a newspaper print consultant and helped fill the new press at the eastern newspapers plant at Norwich. Several of his contracts were for some of the UK's top weekly newspapers such as Motorcycle News which was one of the first newspapers to be printed in full colour on all its 128 pages. He also managed the print side for groups such as Home Counties Newspaper which owned popular weekly tiles such has the Ham & High. At the same time his family owned a large kennels and cattery in Northamptonshire.

However, on the 7th of April 2000 Frederick's hip replacement went pear-shaped and he went into a coma. Frederick was in and out of his coma and when awake didn't recognise his wife Julie or his son Stephen. He had become violent and had to be sedated on several occasions before leaving the private hospital 10 days after his operation. He later found that BUPA had charged him for a private ambulance to take him to Northampton GH so he could have an MRI scan to see if they could see what had gone wrong. They also charged him £450 to see a psychiatrist so they could see if anything had caused the problem. Everything came back as normal, but he was concerned that he doesn't remember visiting the psychiatrist. So bad was his memory that he had to close both of his business and take early retirement. It was years later he learnt that he had suffered from a fat embolism which got into his blood stream. The surgeons now ensure they "washout" the opening preventing this problem from happening. The coma did a lot of damage to the memory part of his brain, and he had to rely on input from his family to try and rebuild his memory bank. He still suffers from the memory problems after 23 years and his mobility is worse than when he went into hospital.

***

Epilogue

This book is a work of fiction. Except for politicians' names, characters, businesses, organisations, places and events are either the product of the author's imagination or are used fictitiously. Any resemblance to actual persons, living or dead, events or locales is entirely coincidental. The prison mentioned in this novel does not exist. Nor do its staff or inmates.

The spelling is British English, except where fidelity to the author's rendering of accent or dialect supersedes this. Although this novel is "fiction" the story line in each chapter has been fully researched.

Please bear in mind that most chapters were penned in 2019 and 2020. Where possible, updates have been added based on 2021 to 2023.

Thanks also go to James Anders Banks of Reedsy who assisted with editing this novel.

The right of Frederick Linden-Wyatt to be identified as the author of the work has been asserted in accordance with the UK Copyright, Designs and Patents Act 1988.

First published June 2020
Updated September 2023

© Frederick Linden-Wyatt

***

Printed in Great Britain
by Amazon

36562283R00172